handwritten: *savers RO*

"JULIE KRAMER IS A MINNESO̶̶̶̶̶"
—*Post Bulletin* (Rochester, MN)

"KRAMER'S BOOKS ARE COMPULSIVELY READABLE."
—WCCO-TV Minnesota

The news is out . . . critics and authors adore
Julie Kramer and her Riley Spartz mysteries!

SILENCING SAM

"Julie Kramer combines real-life experience with just the right amount of humor layered on a great plot."
—*Crimespree* Magazine

"Another delightful read. . . . I'd kill to have Riley on my case!"
—Linda Fairstein, *New York Times* bestselling author of *Hell Gate*

"Her finest Spartz novel to date."
—*Library Journal* (starred review)

"[A] brisk mystery, in which homicide is leavened with deadpan humor. . . . [A] winning series."
—*Booklist*

"Very relevant . . . with [an] insider view of the media."
—*Deadly Pleasures*

"Kramer's richly developed characters and spot-on delivery make *Silencing Sam* a sit back, put your feet up, laughing good time!"
—*Suspense* Magazine

This title is also available as an eBook

"[A] media-savvy thriller. . . . Sharp observations regarding the changes rocking the journalism industry."

—*Publishers Weekly*

"The plot zips along . . . the dialogue is right on."

—*Pioneer Press* (St. Paul, MN)

"A perfect summer vacation read."

—*Romantic Times Book Reviews* (★★★★)

"Readers will relish this adventure with their favorite intrepid reporter."

—Blogcritics

"At its foundation, the book is a journalism procedural, a choice that distinguishes it from the bulk of mysteries published so far in the twenty-first century."

—StarTribune.com

"The latest super-fun beach read from our favorite local mystery writer."

—*METRO* Magazine

MISSING MARK

"A crowd-pleaser. . . . Smart dialogue and a fleet pace."

—*People*

"A fast pace, a smart heroine, and a fresh voice. Julie Kramer has what it takes to keep readers turning pages."

—Tami Hoag, #1 *New York Times* bestselling author of *Secrets to the Grave*

"A surprising final twist and a neatly satisfying ending."

—*Booklist*

"Riley Spartz is fun, spunky, and completely loveable."

—Book Bitch

ALSO BY JULIE KRAMER

Missing Mark
Stalking Susan

JULIE KRAMER

SILENCING SAM

A NOVEL

Pocket Books

New York   London   Toronto   Sydney

Pocket Books
A Division of Simon & Schuster, Inc.
1230 Avenue of the Americas
New York, NY 10020

This book is a work of fiction. Names, characters, places, and incidents either are products of the author's imagination or are used fictitiously. Any resemblance to actual events or locales or persons, living or dead, is entirely coincidental.

First Pocket Books paperback edition June 2011

POCKET and colophon are registered trademarks of Simon & Schuster, Inc.

For information about special discounts for bulk purchases, please contact Simon & Schuster Special Sales at 1-866-506-1949 or business@simonandschuster.com.

The Simon & Schuster Speakers Bureau can bring authors to your live event. For more information or to book an event contact the Simon & Schuster Speakers Bureau at 1-866-248-3049 or visit our website at www.simonspeakers.com.

Designed by Meghan Day Healey
Cover design by John Vairo, Jr., woman wearing red coat © Lauren Ulm / Getty Images

Manufactured in the United States of America

10 9 8 7 6 5 4 3 2 1

ISBN: 978-1-4391-7800-3
ISBN: 978-1-4391-7803-4 (ebook)

To my agent Elaine Koster,
who's helped me navigate from news to novels

SILENCING
SAM

CHAPTER 1

It felt satisfying to leave a funeral with dry eyes.

I wasn't mourning a young life taken too soon. I wasn't mourning a tragic loss to senseless violence.

He died old. In his sleep. In his own bed. Just the way we'd all like to go.

For the last decade, he'd been a reliable source of scoops around city hall, so I'd paid my respects. I didn't stay for the ham-sandwich-and-potato-salad lunch in the church basement; I needed to get back to the station before my boss realized I was gone.

As I reached the parking lot, I heard my name. I'm Riley Spartz, an investigative reporter for Channel 3 in Minneapolis. People recognize me frequently. Sometimes that's good. But not this time.

I turned and saw a short man with perfect hair and stylish clothes, waving at me from behind the hearse.

"We have nothing to talk about," I said, continuing to walk—but faster—to my car.

"How can you be so sure?" He ran to catch up to me, his cologne getting stronger as he got closer.

As a policy I didn't speak to Sam Pierce, the local newspaper gossip writer, but I shouldn't have been surprised to see him lurking outside the church. He liked sneaking into funerals and later listing in his column who cried and who didn't. Who wore black and who didn't.

"Let's talk about what's going on in your newsroom," he said. "I hear that new reporter from Texas started today."

Sam liked to hit fresh TV blood with some cruel observation in print soon after they arrived. Maybe something mortifying they did at their old company Christmas party—like sitting on a supervisor's lap. Maybe something embarrassing that happened the first day on their new job—like mispronouncing a local suburb, perhaps Edina—during a live shot. Sam adored branding newcomers as outsiders.

"I heard some interesting things about his marriage," he continued.

I ignored him. Sam Pierce was a verbal terrorist.

A lot of what he wrote simply wasn't true. When pressed, he'd admit it, justifying publication with the explanation that, unlike me, he was *not* a reporter and didn't *have* to prove anything was true. He just had to prove people were gossiping about it.

Often he purposely refrained from calling the subject for confirmation or reaction. Otherwise, he might officially learn the morsel was false and have to kill the item. That would create more work, hunting down last-minute trash to fill his gossip column, "Piercing Eyes."

Sam's newspaper photo was cropped tight around a pair of intense eyes. The design achieved a striking graphic look for his column, plus it gave him the anonymity that allowed him to show up in places he'd normally have been unwelcome if recognized.

Sam had adopted a media technique used by the newspaper food critic to help keep her face incognito while dining. He appeared as a frequent radio talk-show guest but avoided television interviews like birds avoid cats.

Because I was part of the local press corps, I could pick Sam Pierce out of a crowd but was always surprised how few public figures recognized him. Until it was too late.

"It might be in your best interest to cooperate," Sam hinted to me. "Think of it as buying goodwill to keep your *own* transgressions out of the newspaper."

"You've got nothing on me." I climbed into my car.

"Don't be too sure. I have my sources."

"Not only do you have nothing on me," I said, "you have no sources."

Then I slammed my car door, drove away, and hoped it was true.

CHAPTER 2

The new reporter Sam was planning to blind-side was staring at a giant map of the Twin Cities hanging over the newsroom assignment desk. Tomorrow, he'd be thrown on the street to bring back a story. But today, he was getting to know the anchors, producers, and other behind-the-scenes players at Channel 3.

He'd apparently offered to listen to the police scanner and that pleased the bosses, because for most of us, the constant cop chatter was just more newsroom white noise.

Clay Burrel had been working at a TV station in Corpus Christi along the Gulf of Mexico when our news director, Noreen Banks, saw something special in his résumé tape and brought him north. A nice career move for him. Market size 129 to market size 15. I figured Noreen got him cheap.

He walked like a man who's good-looking and knows it, not unusual in television newsrooms.

More unusual was his footwear, cowboy boots of an exotic gray and white reptile skin.

"Glad to be working together, Clay," I said, trying to live up to our Minnesota Nice reputation. "I just want to give you a little heads-up . . ." I started to warn him about the gossip writer when he suddenly went, "Hush, little lady."

"There it goes again," he said. "Most definitely 10-89. Homicide." He pointed to the 10-codes taped on the wall next to the scanner box.

And because his ears heard news gold in a homicide call, within minutes he was on his way to get crime scene video with a station photographer and was soon leading the evening newscast with the EXCLUSIVE story of a decapitated woman—her nude body dumped in Theodore Wirth Park, about ten minutes from the station.

Wirth Park has a bird sanctuary, a wildflower garden, and a woodsy lake and creek framed by lush fall colors this time of year. But it also has a reputation for danger that's stuck with it for the last decade or so after two prostitutes were found murdered there. In all fairness, their bodies were dumped. So they could have been killed anywhere, even the suburbs. And frankly, unless you count unleashed dogs and occasional complaints about sodomy in the bushes, the crime there isn't any worse than in any other Minneapolis park.

Yet, when the news hit that another dead body

had been found in Wirth, all across town, folks nodded knowingly.

Minneapolis Park Police had been waiting for this day to come and had installed a surveillance camera in the parking lot to record any future criminal suspect's vehicle. But there was apparently a problem that night and the machine malfunctioned. So authorities had no video leads in the grisly slaying.

I was impressed—okay, I'll admit it, jealous—as Clay Burrel broke one scoop after another regarding the homicide, starting with the fact that the woman's head was missing.

> ((CLAY, LIVE))
> WITHOUT THE VICTIM'S
> HEAD . . . IDENTIFICATION IS
> DIFFICULT UNLESS HER DNA
> OR FINGERPRINTS ARE ON
> FILE . . . AND SO FAR,
> AUTHORITIES ARE COMING UP
> EMPTY ON THAT END.

Besides making it problematic for the police, I've often found that without the victim's name, face, or history, it's difficult to get viewers to care about a specific murder amid so much crime.

So at first, it didn't bother me that I was missing out on the missing-head case. The way news assignments generally work, if you claim a story, it's yours. You eat what you kill. Clay found the story; Clay owned it.

But interest in the murder continued to escalate as our new reporter explained that the victim had a nice manicure and pedicure, thus eliminating homeless women and making the deceased seem a whole lot like all the other women sitting home watching the news, doing their nails.

Or maybe it was simply curiosity about Clay Burrel that made them click their remotes in our direction.

With his Texas background, he was a little more flamboyant than the rest of the Channel 3 news team. Though he didn't wear a cliché ten-gallon hat, he had several pairs of distinctive cowboy boots. (I suspected he wore them to appear taller. With the six-foot-five-inch exception of NBC's David Gregory, many TV news guys, like Clay, tend to be on the short side—and self-conscious about it.) But viewers seemed instantly enamored with Burrel's faint drawl and Texas colloquialisms as he chatted with the anchors about the status of the mystery.

((CLAY/ANCHOR/SPLIT BOX))
SERIOUSLY, SOPHIE, WITHOUT
THE WOMAN'S HEAD, POLICE
STAND ABOUT AS MUCH
CHANCE OF SOLVING THIS
MURDER AS A GNAT IN A
HAILSTORM.

I could see him becoming as popular as Dan Rather once was on election nights.

Noreen was thrilled with her young and hungry new hire because for the first time since she had taken over the newsroom four years ago, her job was on the line.

Channel 3's market share was tanking after Nielsen installed a new ratings-measuring system in the Twin Cities—electronic people meters. The media-monitoring company claimed the devices were more accurate than the former handwritten diary system and could reveal ratings year-round instead of just in designated sweeps months.

This was supposed to take the drama out of February, May, and November, when television stations artificially stacked their newscasts with sensational stories of sin and scandal. In reality, newsrooms were now finding every month becoming a sweeps month.

"When it's done, it airs," Noreen had told us in a recent news meeting. Which introduced, in my opinion, an unhealthy—even desperate—speed-up factor to news investigations.

"I'm not interested in philosophy," she responded when I tried to discuss the matter. "I'm interested in results."

Not these results. How *many* people are watching the news isn't as important as *which* people are watching. And women viewers ages twenty-five to fifty-four are the prize demographic.

Under the new ratings system, Channel 3 had fallen from a normally close second in that coveted tier to a distant third. That audience drop made our newscasts less attractive to advertisers and meant our sales staff couldn't charge as much for the ads they did land. Barely six hundred people meters are used in the Minneapolis–St. Paul market to gauge the television habits of three million viewers. The station's owners cried foul over how the new Nielsen households were selected. But Nielsen didn't care.

Then Clay Burrel came along with tantalizing tidbits of murder and mayhem, and overnight, the numbers started shifting.

I was in the station green room, pulling a ceramic hot iron and styling brush out of my cubby for a quick touch-up before leaving to shoot a standup about identity theft. As I gazed in the mirror while I flipped my hair under, I appreciated the decades of history the green walls reflected.

Besides news talent, famous guests—presidents, athletes, even a rock star fond of the color purple—signed their names on these walls. I noticed a fresh addition, larger than the rest, as conspicuous as John Hancock's on the Declaration of Independence. The sweeping signature read "Clay Burrel." I actually wasn't surprised, as I'd heard more than once over the last couple of days that everything was bigger in Texas.

As if on cue, Clay walked in to powder his nose and share with me the news that he was about to go on the air and inform viewers that "sources now tell" him the victim in the missing-head case was a natural blonde.

I congratulated him on his legwork. Then he started grumbling about how, when he accepted this job, he thought he was joining one of the top news teams in the market. Instead, by the look of things, *he* was the top.

"I guess what they say about Texans and bragging is true," I replied, a little miffed he was acting like a star right out of the gate.

"If you've done it, it ain't bragging, little lady."

"Stop calling me that." The moniker was as condescending as a pat on the head.

"Sure don't mean anything by it," he said. "Just keep hearing what a hotshot investigator you are and so far I haven't seen much investigating. Makes me wonder if you're all hat and no cattle."

I threw him a much-practiced If Looks Could Kill glare but instead of shutting up, he told me I was about as "cute as a possum."

That was when I vowed to steal the headless murder story from him and make it mine.

CHAPTER 3

The next morning I got a news tip of my own and was on my way in the station helicopter to the Minnesota-Iowa border with Malik Rahman, my favorite cameraman. I'm not crazy about flying, but for this story, aerials were a big bonus.

An hour later, we were over an unusual crime scene.

The corn in the farm field below us was flattened into an odd shape, but unlike crop circles (the first of which discovered in the United States was actually found in Minnesota thirty years ago), there was nothing graceful or mysterious about what had caused this crop damage.

A giant wind turbine, part of a recently developed wind farm, lay flat on the ground, its trio of propellers spread wide. Dozens of other turbines stood in straight rows, spinning with no concern for their deceased comrade.

Minnesota ranks fourth in wind power production, following Texas, Iowa, and California. As the national debate over energy becomes more urgent, wind has become a valuable and controversial crop.

Malik zoomed the camera lens to the base of the turbine. Charred and mangled, it appeared to have been blasted from its cement foundation.

The chopper landed on a gravel road where a group of local farmers, including my father (who had called me when he heard the breaking news), stood around, uncharacteristically unsettled by the sabotage. A young boy in bib overalls clutched the hand of one of the men.

While wind turbines have attracted organized opposition in other parts of the country, for the most part, folks living here have taken to the idea of "farming the wind" and leased chunks of their land to energy companies. This part of the state hasn't seen so much economic growth since Hormel invented Spam. And the money is welcome insurance against cyclical catastrophes familiar to rural America such as floods or locusts. Besides, the lofty turbines don't seem that big a leap from their own agricultural ancestors, the windmills that not too long ago ground corn and pumped water.

"Someone's making some kind of statement," I said to Malik after we interviewed people at the scene. "But what does it mean?"

I gazed at the symmetrical rows of turbines, appearing smaller as they got nearer the horizon.

Was some modern Don Quixote on a melodramatic quest to bring down these giants? Perhaps from a misguided sense of chivalry? While the entire world wants to boo bad guys, it's important to remember that every villain is the hero of his own story.

Some resistance to the wind industry has come from environmentalists who claim turbines harm birds. But so do airplanes, cars, and even patio windows, and no one's protesting them.

And there are plenty of complaints from people who claim wind turbines ruin their view. But at a time when America is challenged for energy, Not In My Backyard is not a particularly patriotic argument.

The only other time there'd ever been an explosion in this county was some twenty years earlier, when a grain elevator accidentally blew. This was different. And the rural crowd wasn't sure what to make of the toppled turbine. I tried to get some reaction on camera, but Minnesotans are generally not an excitable bunch and are more comfortable expressing pessimism than optimism.

"It could be worse," one farmer said.

"You betcha," another responded.

And because things can always be worse, the rest all nodded in agreement and didn't have much else to say about the situation, except for "Whatever."

Malik, an outsider to this manner of conversa-

tion, gave a little growl of exasperation, because
he knew we had little usable audio and even less
chance of getting any.

"You can figure out what it means later," he
said. "Let's shoot your standup and head back."

I noticed a monarch butterfly paused on a
milkweed plant. Most monarchs are almost in
Mexico by now. A late bloomer, apparently. I
closed my eyes and imagined the magnificent migration of orange and black wings against green
jungle.

"Come on, Riley, let's roll."

The monarch still sat there. "You better head
south," I advised it, snapping my fingers. The butterfly scattered.

Malik positioned me about forty feet to the left
with the broken turbine in the background centered between a row of spinning blades while I
practiced my scribbled standup.

> ((RILEY, STANDUP))
> AUTHORITIES HAVE NO
> MOTIVE IN THE DESTRUCTION
> OF THIS WIND TURBINE IN
> RURAL MINNESOTA . . . BUT THE
> INVESTIGATION CONTINUES.

With a thumbs-up, Malik signaled he was rolling.

((RILEY STANDUP))
AUTHORITIES HAVE NO
MOTIVE IN THE
DESTRUCTION—

Suddenly a blast shook the ground, almost knocking me over. I turned in time to see another wind turbine crash behind me. I wondered whether this was the way an earthquake felt.

"Malik?" I was glad he was shooting with a tripod and not off the shoulder.

"Yeah," he answered, "we got it."

Of course, when Noreen heard we had dramatic-explosion video, she sent the satellite truck so I could go live from the scene. Malik also got video of a crying child in the arms of his father, which helped visually emphasize the danger at stake.

The old bachelor farmer who owned the land where the blast had just happened was not crazy about being on TV, but I assured him it would only last a couple of minutes, and my dad, arguably one of the most popular men in the county, helped talk him into it.

Gil Halvorson was a bit of a rural survivalist, but in an adorable sort of way. He had a shy smile, a power generator, a propane tank, a private well, and a stash of ammo in the root cellar for when the end came near. No kids of his own, but lots of nieces and nephews.

Back at the station, Sophie Paulson sat at the anchor desk, reading a narrow column of print off the teleprompter. It's typed about two inches wide, so anchors can read it without their eyes darting back and forth. Producers like it because it times out to about a second a line, making it easy to estimate story length.

((SOPHIE CU LIVE))
RILEY SPARTZ GOT CAUGHT IN
THE MIDDLE OF SOME
BREAKING NEWS TODAY
DOWN IN SOUTHERN
MINNESOTA. TAKE A LOOK AT
WHAT HAPPENS NEXT.

News control rolled the video for viewers to watch the smash.

((RILEY REPLAY))
AUTHORITIES HAVE NO
MOTIVE IN THE
DESTRUCTION—
((BOOM, CRASH, SCREAMS))
((ANCHOR DOUBLE BOX))
RILEY JOINS US NOW FROM
THE SCENE WITH THE
LATEST.

Then news control went full-screen with Malik's close-up shot of me as I recapped what little information had been released about the explosions. Because of the immediacy of the situation, neither law enforcement nor Wide Open Spaces, the energy company that owned the wind farm, had given an official statement.

On my cue, as I introduced Gil Halvorson as the landowner, my cameraman pulled wide to include him for a live interview.

> ((RILEY/GUEST/TWOSHOT))
> WHAT DID YOU THINK WHEN
> YOU HEARD THE BLAST, GIL?
> ((GIL/LIVE))
> SOUNDED LIKE A FREIGHT
> TRAIN.

Those first words out of his mouth are the ultimate cliché in broadcast interviews: *It sounded like a freight train*. The sound tech back at the station marked the audio booth wall with a check each time the "freight train" phrase aired. The tradition dated back years and the marks covered an entire wall.

> ((RILEY/GUEST/TWOSHOT))
> THEN WHAT, GIL?

Though I expected him to give me the inevitable *It could have been worse*, I pressed him for something a little more original and he sure gave it to me.

((GIL/LIVE))
THEN I SAW IT CRASH AND
THOUGHT, FUCK, THERE GOES
THE NEIGHBORHOOD.

Suddenly news control voices were screaming in my ear as I tried to wrap my guest.

"Fuck" is a word stations aren't allowed to broadcast because the airwaves are owned by the public. Radio has a seven-second delay, but not local TV news. The Federal Communications Commission is prone to levying big fines for such indecent utterances. And in the current economic turmoil facing the news business, Channel 3 can't afford potty-mouth talk.

Because I was reporting live from the field, I couldn't see the ensuing chaos in the news control booth. Later I learned the station had gone black. That's one of the worst things that can happen during a television newscast. Someone, maybe a producer, maybe a director, decides they can't risk staying live and utters the command, "Go black." That sends the station off the air and into a commercial break. Or even worse, puts a slate on the air that reads "Technical Difficulties." The fear is that viewers are immediately switching channels, especially when this transpires during the first minute of a newscast.

"Do you have any idea how much the station might have to pay?" Noreen yelled at me when I got back to the newsroom. "And even if we challenge the FCC and win, the attorney costs could be staggering." Noreen hollered some more; the rest of the staff could hear as well as see the fireworks through her glass-walled office. What she sacrificed in privacy she made up for in sending a message to the rest of the troops.

"This wasn't my fault, Noreen," I insisted. "The guy never said the F-word once during our pre-interview."

"Well, Riley, we need stories that will get ratings but won't get us in trouble with the FCC. Sure, the explosion video was cool, but who really cares about windmills anyway? What else have you got?"

I remembered the monarch butterfly and suggested going to Mexico and covering the migration. As cold weather approaches, our audience enjoys warm-weather tales.

"Minnesotans love nature news," I said. "And the video is guaranteed to be spectacular."

Noreen was especially fond of stories about animals—even fish. But that affection apparently didn't apply to bugs. She nixed the butterfly idea in about two seconds flat.

Too much money.

"Not in today's economy." She shook her head. "We need more close-to-home scoops like that headless murder." She pointed through her glass office at Clay Burrel, typing away at his desk. "That's what people are talking about. The police chief even called up screaming about our cover-age."

I smiled, imagining the chief's fury—having lived through it during a story or two myself. "But, Noreen, I thought our station image was warm and fuzzy. Channel 7 is the blood-and-guts station."

A look of regret passed over Noreen's normally Corporate America face. "Riley, we can't afford warm and fuzzy."

CHAPTER 4

I saw an unattractive close-up photo of myself with my mouth open when I paged through the newspaper early the next morning.

Sam Pierce had frozen a shot of me from yesterday's wind story for his gossip column, apparently just as I'd realized that my guest had uttered the F-word. No surprise, Sam made a big deal out of how much trouble I was in for the gaffe.

Then he took a cheap shot and wrote how some local TV reporters had made a better transition to high-definition TV than others, while I was starting to look my age. After our confrontation the other day, I expected some kind of dig like that.

But the next line made me almost stop breathing: *"Sources also tell me Riley Spartz appears to have recovered from her husband's hero death quite nicely and is finding comfort in the arms of a former cop—which raises the question of just when this relationship started and how good a wife she was when she was a wife."*

I wanted to heave just then, but my stomach had twisted into a tight, uncomfortable knot.

When my husband, Hugh Boyer, died in the line of duty nearly three years ago . . . well, I nearly fell apart with grief. Only a handful of people know how close I came to killing myself. If Sam ever found out, he'd probably attribute it to guilt, not grief, and lead with it.

The journalist part of me noticed that the gossip writer didn't name my companion, Nick Garnett, probably because he didn't meet the standard of a public figure. But as a TV reporter, I was considered fair game.

I dialed Garnett. He'd left a cushy security-director job at the Mall of America and moved to Washington to work for the Department of Homeland Security. The phone rang four times before he picked up. I stumbled a couple of times before I could explain the problem.

"I'll get a flight back right away," he said. "I'll hold you tight and pound that gossip guy hard."

"No. You'll just make things worse."

As much as I craved his consolation, I also dreaded the finger-wagging of others. And I hoped no one showed the "Piercing Eyes" gossip column to my parents. While they knew I was "seeing someone," the timing had never seemed right to introduce them to Garnett.

"Maybe it's best we cool things a bit." He couldn't see it, but my eyes were damp as I said the words. "Us in tandem simply gives credence to that article."

"We've done nothing wrong." He reminded me our romance had not started until recently, nearly two years after Hugh's death.

"I know. But I still want you to stay in DC. I think this chatter might die down faster if we aren't seen together for a while."

He didn't agree with my decision but had no choice.

When I got to work, Noreen came over to my office to tell me the article was definitely unfair.

"Except for that part about your appearance," she said. "I've been thinking maybe you should take a look at airbrush makeup now that we've gone digital."

Colleagues tried to cheer me with examples of their own victimization by the gossip writer.

We all knew Sam was not above blackmailing local personalities into inviting him to their weddings or giving up dirt about friends and colleagues for amnesty themselves.

Because Minneapolis has fewer and lower-level celebrities than places like New York or Los Angeles, fairly minor indiscretions by fairly unimportant people that otherwise would be shrugged off get blown into headlines.

Anybody who complained to Sam's editors about the coverage went on his shit list and got bombed harder the next time. And there *always* was a next time.

The newspaper knew he was trouble (they'd quietly paid out some settlements) but the editors didn't want to fire him because his "Piercing Eyes" column generated more web hits than even Minnesota's most beloved sportswriter. And these days, hits are money.

I needed reassurance, maybe even forgiveness, so over lunch, I drove to church in downtown St. Paul to visit Father Mountain, my childhood priest, who'd long since been promoted from rural pastor to urban clergy.

He agreed with Garnett's take on our relationship.

"You can't let bullies determine the path you take in life," he said.

Then he pulled out a Bible and quoted various verses about the harm of gossip, including Romans 1:29: *"They have become filled with every kind of wickedness, evil, greed and depravity. They are full of envy, murder, strife, deceit, and malice. They are gossips . . ."*

Father Mountain assured me God would punish gossips and slanderers.

"I might not want to wait for God," I said.

"We all must wait for Judgment Day," he replied. "Patience is a virtue."

He handed me the Bible, reassured me the

Lord was on my side, and offered to take my confession if I had any real sins.

None that I wanted to share with him.

After work, I headed to an old bar where the newspaper people hang out and ordered a glass of wine. While I waited for a word with Sam, I spent the next twenty minutes or so marking with sticky notes Bible passages condemning gossip.

All my attention was focused on my own grievance, so I didn't notice Rolf Hedberg until he pulled out a chair and sat down across from me. He was the kind of guy who looked fifty when he was twenty-five, and now that he was fifty he looked older than Larry King.

He had his own reason to hold a grudge against the newspaper. Until six months ago, he had been their political columnist. In the latest round of budget cuts they'd shoved a buyout down his throat—not caring that losing him meant losing much of the newsroom's institutional memory.

The bosses told him news was more important than opinion, so they were getting out of the political commentary business. For him it was either take the money or take the overnight shift.

He publicly groused to any radio station that would put him on the air that he was canned because of his liberal slant. And there might have been some truth to that, except a conservative columnist was also cut.

Rolf's bitterness wasn't reaping a lot of requests for repeat appearances—much less his own radio show—so now he'd lost his platform as well as his paycheck.

"Let me buy you a beer, Rolf." I waved over a waitress and she brought him whatever was on tap.

He raised the glass in a toast in my direction and told me he was surprised to see me.

"Especially here, Riley. Especially after that 'Piercing Eyes' column. You know this place is newspaper stomping ground. Sam walks in, there's just going to be trouble."

"Maybe he deserves trouble," I answered. "Maybe he deserves the wrath of God."

I showed Rolf my list of biblical gossip quotes and he rolled his eyes like I was some kind of religious fanatic. I tried to explain, but he cut me off before I could tell him that today was the first time I'd held a Bible since last year, when I'd used one as a weapon to slow down a serial killer.

"Just walk away," he advised me. "Can't you see Sam's rolling in clout right now? Don't you think every morning when I open the paper I ask myself why they kept a dirtbag like him and axed me? Don't you think if there was anything I could do to change that I would?"

"Well, Rolf, I still want a word with him."

"Don't bother," he insisted. "Sam always gets the last word."

He slugged down the rest of his beer and waved good-bye as I pondered the inevitable truth of what he'd said—the downside of picking a fight with people who buy ink by the gallon.

His wisdom sank in and I was about to abandon my reprisal mission when in walked Sam Pierce himself. I smelled him before I saw him, his cologne so potent, I glanced around the bar to locate the source. Sam spotted me at the same time, and the next minutes unfolded like they came off a movie script.

He sauntered over and sat down in the same chair Rolf had occupied minutes earlier. But instead of the look of a broken newsman across the table, Sam had a proud "gotcha" look on his face.

"Come to trade some secrets for future clemency?" he asked.

I didn't offer to buy him a beer and any thought I had of shrugging away the whole encounter disappeared when he flashed a smug smile.

"No, Sam, I came to rub this in your face." And I opened the Bible and quoted Psalm 34:13: *"Keep your tongue from evil and your lips from speaking lies."*

He laughed. "What does the Bible have to say about adultery?"

I should have thrown the book at him; instead I threw my drink.

Unfortunately, it was red wine and stained an expensive peach-colored sweater he turned out to be particularly fond of. And unfortunately, because most of that day's news copy was already filed, there were plenty of witnesses in the bar.

Apparently, under Minnesota law, throwing a drink falls into the category of battery, so even though I never actually touched Sam, I was charged with misdemeanor assault.

CHAPTER 5

I had to get a criminal lawyer because there was no way for Miles Lewis, the station attorney, to argue that the First Amendment guaranteed me the right to fling alcohol in public.

So in a gesture of extreme overkill, I hired Benny Walsh, the top criminal attorney in town. Usually he defended big-name murderers, embezzlers, bank robbers—more interesting cases than mine.

"So you're saying I should just plead guilty?" I asked my lawyer. "What about what he wrote about me?"

"Well, you could sue him civilly, but, to be honest, you might lose. And it would cost you plenty because no one will take it on contingency. I sure won't. My advice is to end this and end it fast."

Benny convinced me that because it was a lousy misdemeanor, if I committed no other crimes in the next year, it would be erased.

The deal was I'd get community service.

"You can give disadvantaged kids a tour of the TV station and be done with it," he said.

Begrudgingly, I agreed.

"So what are you going to wear to court?" he asked.

"Don't worry, Benny, I'll pick out something suitably appropriate for a court of law."

"Pink," he said. "I want you to wear pink. And not an aggressive pink, either. A delicate, harmless pink."

So on the advice of my attorney, I bought a pale pink, feminine-cut blazer that the salesperson guaranteed made me look "pretty." I figured I could always wear the soothing shade when I had to interview crime victims or their families.

But when I got to court, and the clerk called my name, Benny's cushy deal didn't exactly fall together.

Apparently Judge Tregobov harbored some rancor against the media. And she wasn't fooled by the color pink, either.

"Since you journalists enjoy garbage so much, your community service will be picking up garbage somewhere in the county, location to be determined later."

My attorney tried to argue, but the judge cut him off.

"You heard me; trash for the trash. Keep quiet or I'll find you in contempt."

But when the prosecutor wanted to talk, the judge allowed him to request a protective order keeping me a thousand feet away from Sam Pierce. I was given no opportunity to point out that anyone who compared our body of work would easily see who regularly wrote trash and who wrote award-winning public-service investigations.

But with a bang of her gavel, the judge consented to this last piece of humiliation. And that's the way it was. Whether Walter Cronkite would have agreed or not.

"What just happened?" I asked Benny. He gathered up his papers and mumbled something about the unpredictability of the legal system.

Sam was snickering in the back, waiting to goad me as we walked out.

"I thought you wanted me to stay away from you," I said. "Get lost." I wanted to give him a little shove, but if throwing booze got me hauled into court, pushing and shoving would probably land me in jail.

Benny stepped between us and told me the order for protection didn't actually start until after we left the courtroom.

Figuring I wouldn't get another chance, I decided to throw one last verbal barb at Sam. "Staying away from you will be a relief, you rumormonger. Have I told you how much your cologne reeks?"

Sam smiled with the confidence of a man used to getting the final word. "I just want to assure you Channel 3 will get plenty of column space in tomorrow's newspaper."

I told him it just better all be true and quoted another Bible verse about men giving an account on the day of judgment for every careless word they have spoken.

"God doesn't scare me," he replied.

"Maybe he will," I answered.

Something about the tone of our voices, our body language, or maybe just how we were staring at each other made the court bailiff come between us and make sure we rode down on separate elevators.

Instead of going back to work, I went home sick. By the time I got there, Sam's "Piercing Eyes" gossip column already had the story posted online with a splashing headline: "Let the Punishment Fit the Criminal." Unfortunately, I couldn't complain. For once, his report was all accurate.

The only email I had was a message from Rolf Hedberg, commiserating with me and telling me he'd like to throw a six-pack in Sam's face himself.

Just when I thought it couldn't get worse, I learned the wire service had picked up the main points, sending the story to radio stations all over the Midwest. My parents, huge fans of AM radio, were sure to be listening.

I let my clothes fall to the floor and didn't even bother hanging up my new pink jacket. Then I curled up in bed in a fetal position with a pillow over my head. The phone rang a couple times, but I didn't answer.

Probably just the damn media.

CHAPTER 6

I dragged myself into the newsroom the next morning. Noreen hauled me into her office to wave a copy of my contract in my face and quoted certain sections involving "moral turpitude" and "public disrepute."

No one else knew what to say to me; I tried pretending their pity didn't bother me, but while I'm a good reporter, I'm not a good actress. Different tools, except for the voice.

But then Clay stood up, addressed the whole newsroom, and said I ought to be proud I took a stand against that "gossip rascal."

"I've only been here a few days, and he hasn't written anything nasty about me, but from what I can tell, that man is wolverine mean."

Everyone applauded, more for Clay than me. But I started feeling better about myself and the new hire.

"You're right," I shouted. "Sam Pierce got what he deserved!"

• • •

My voice mail light was flashing on my desk. Various messages from other news organizations wanting to know how I felt being compared to garbage. A message from the front desk telling me I had a package. And a message from my parents wanting to know what they could do to help.

That last one was tough; my folks didn't seem to understand that I'd outgrown the kind of help they could provide. I looked at my watch and figured they were at daily Mass, like clockwork, praying for my salvation. So, knowing I wouldn't have to be drawn into complicated explanations, I called the farm and left word telling them I was fine and not to worry.

I ignored the media messages. No way was anyone getting quotes from me.

Then I went to the front desk, where a spectacular wildflower bouquet was waiting, and I found myself thinking of Nick Garnett . . . and how a bouquet might be a reasonable substitute for a beau. But when I opened the card accompanying the flowers, it contained no professions of love. The handwriting was feminine, the message anonymous.

I couldn't be sure whether it was congratulatory or caustic. *"Thanks Alot, Riley, Give Everyone The Disturbing Information Regarding That Bad Ass Gossip."*

I crumpled the note, dropped it in the garbage, and headed back to the front desk to ask where the flowers had come from. A woman, was all the receptionist remembered. No real details.

Heading to the back door, I got the security guard to pull up the lobby surveillance camera. Channel 3 hadn't upgraded the system since it was first installed more than a decade ago. The only money spent on cameras these days was for on-air cameras. Even convenience stores had better-quality security technology than the station. The black-and-white image of a woman carrying a child and my bouquet resembled those grainy shots of bank-robbery suspects that seldom get identified.

So the mystery woman remained a mystery.

I wasn't even sure if she was the actual author of my note or merely handling the delivery duties. She appeared to be in her midtwenties, had a dark pageboy haircut, and was dressed in an upscale sweater and jeans. She carried the flowers in one arm, a toddler in another. I couldn't be sure whether the child was a boy or girl.

I made three copies of the image, leaving one at each station entrance, with instructions to call me if she returned. I pinned the last one on the bulletin board over my desk. I supposed it was possible we'd met. But she seemed a stranger, with no obvious reason to want to creep me out.

Though she certainly appeared to bear a grudge against Sam.

Retrieving the note from my wastebasket, I smoothed the paper and pinned it next to her photo. *"Thanks Alot, Riley, Give Everyone The Disturbing Information Regarding That Bad Ass Gossip."* Clearly, she wanted to send me a message—not an overt threat, but not best wishes, either. I was certainly curious about what "disturbing information" she was referring to. She must have calculated the note would be more likely, or perhaps faster, to reach me via flowers than the post office. Or maybe she just liked creating a scene.

I inhaled the blooms, but the fragrance was not overwhelming. Seasonal, they might have come from the remains of a home garden or backyard. Dried milkweed pods teased me with dreams of orange and black butterflies traveling south.

I carried the vase toward Noreen's office. My motive? Twofold: I no longer wanted to look at them, as the sender's intention seemed dubious; and regifting fresh flowers appeared a prime boss suck-up move for a reporter with a suddenly shaky platform.

"They're beautiful." Noreen stretched her hand to fondle a red-colored berry on a twig. "But I can't imagine what either of us is celebrating. Especially not you."

My news director seemed to have settled down; at least the morals clause of my contract wasn't dribbling from her lips. So while Noreen was in a semisympathetic mood, I started whining about how Sam's order for protection was going to interfere with my life—professionally as well as socially.

"Just stay away from the guy," Noreen said. "Then you won't have any problems."

"Look at it from my point of view," I said. "Our newsrooms are less than a mile apart. How am I supposed to know where the jerk is going to show up? I'm going to have to give up the turkey special at Peter's Grill. I'm not going to be able to check criminal records at the cop shop."

Then I thought of the worst scenario of all. "What if we both show up at the same news event? Am I supposed to leave?"

That possibility got Noreen's attention. I could tell by the suddenly stern management look in her eyes I'd have been better off keeping the rumination to myself.

"Don't worry," I reassured her. "Benny's going to fix this. A thousand feet is unreasonable; maybe he can change it to a hundred feet."

I flashed my news leader an optimistic thumbs-up and raced back to my office to call my attorney and plead for results. Benny didn't pick up, so I left him an urgent message saying, "We need to talk."

"I hate 'Piercing Eyes,'" I muttered to myself, slamming down the phone.

I tried thinking of an out-of-town story that would take my mind off the gossip columnist and take my body away from any chance of violating the order for protection. But all that came to mind was Mexico.

CHAPTER 7

Soon after, word hit the newsroom that the royal family of Saudi Arabia, including the king himself, was visiting the Mayo Clinic for medical checkups and spending money around Rochester like it was oil. Giant tips at restaurants. Women in veils buying out boutiques. A caravan of Lincolns with dark windows.

I surprised Noreen by volunteering to cover the city's economic boon. My phone message light was flashing with voice mails from even more news organizations wanting to interview me about my day in court. I was anxious for an excuse to leave town, even temporarily.

On my way out the door, I stopped in the green room. Clay was staring at the mirror like he owned it. More than a decade in this business had taught me to be wary of men prettier than me. Too many could look smart on air for the necessary minute and a half, but after that, there wasn't much there.

The green room closet contained clothing stashed away for emergencies and props. Spill coffee on your jacket just before the newscast starts? Run to the green room for a replacement. Way in the back I found a black burka another reporter had bought last year for a story on discrimination against Islamic women.

I held the head-to-toe covering in front of me, wondering whether it might come in handy tracking the Saudi royal family or if it would be seen as an enormous international insult.

"Little early for Halloween, isn't it?" Clay asked.

"I'm considering an undercover look." I explained the significance of hijab—dressing modestly—in Muslim culture. But I put the burka back on the hanger, deciding I couldn't risk more trouble.

Malik and I drove south and an hour or so later, when we reached Rochester, the Mayo Clinic wouldn't confirm or deny the royal visit because of medical privacy rules. City officials were also mum for security reasons. But keeping the visit hush-hush was impossible because a 747 with the Saudi crest dwarfed all other aircraft at the city's small airport.

Malik shot some video through the fence. With only six gates, Rochester just might be the smallest international airport in the country. It speaks to the clout of Mayo that the airport has a runway long enough to land a 747, as well as its own customs office.

We staked out Chester's, where we heard some of the royal party were dining in a private room. I hoped to get an interview, or even ten seconds of video, with anybody in a turban or flowing robe.

Malik waited in the van across the street, his camera by his side. I sat inside the restaurant, eating lunch very slowly, so I could call him with a heads-up when it was time to start rolling.

But one phone call changed that plan.

I almost didn't answer because my parents' number came up on the screen, and I figured they wanted to talk about my court hearing. Then I decided it was better to get it over with now rather than later with Malik listening.

"There's been another bombing on the wind farm," my dad said. "A big team of investigators just got here."

I called the station with the news and was told to forget chasing royals and head south to the blast.

Down at Wide Open Spaces, the scene was much the same as before. A toppled giant lay across a field of straw. But nobody was blaming a big bad wolf for huffing and puffing.

In the distance, a K-9 unit seemed to be inspecting turbines. A chocolate Labrador and his human partner worked the fields, but I couldn't tell if they'd found anything newsworthy.

I tried to call the station and report the latest in the mysterious crime, but neither my cell phone nor Malik's worked. That seemed odd because a cell tower was just up the road, and ten yards away, a sheriff's deputy had his phone to his ear.

"You getting cell service?" I called over to the deputy, waving my phone after he'd hung up his.

"Yeah, but you won't." I couldn't tell if he was laughing at my question or his answer.

"What's going on?" I walked over since he wasn't behind any crime-scene tape.

He shrugged. "Check with the boss. I'm not authorized to talk to newsies."

He pointed to where a team in uniform had gathered. As I got closer, I smiled when I saw one of them wore a sheriff's badge. Because sheriffs are elected to office, they often like to appear on television, showing their constituents how hard they're working.

"Good day, Sheriff," I said. "What's up with my cell phone?"

"It's complicated," he replied.

"It's none of your business," a man wearing a dark suit said, interrupting us.

He looked familiar to me. Then I recognized him as the FBI guy who'd investigated the theft of Minnesota's record largemouth bass this past spring. He'd suspected an animal-rights group of freeing the fish.

"Nice seeing you again," I said. I could never seem to remember his name. "Funny how news brings us together."

"The bureau is aiding local law enforcement in the wind turbine bombings. That's all the information we're prepared to release about Operation Aeolus."

"Operation Aeolus? What does that mean?"

"It's the Latin name for the god of wind," he answered.

I recalled he had a fondness for using Latin to sound important, but I refrained from making any remarks about windbags, no matter how appropriate. I could tell the sheriff wasn't pleased to be cast aside and figured there was a chance he and I could do business together.

"I think we owe it to the residents in the area to keep them updated on the status of our investigation," the sheriff said. "I think the media, as well as the FBI, can be of some help in avoiding public panic."

"Does that mean you'll do a camera interview?" I asked.

"I think that's reasonable under the circumstances," he replied.

"Just a minute." The FBI guy motioned for the sheriff to follow him out of earshot. From the waving of his federal arms, I got the message that he wanted the media frozen out. Then when the sheriff poked a finger in his federal chest, I got the message that he was telling Mr. FBI just whose turf he was on.

Sheriff Taber explained that the bomber had used cell phones to detonate the explosives in the turbine blasts. The FBI had brought in a device that blocked all cell calls in the area unless the phone number was part of a preapproved law enforcement list, or obviously 911.

"That's why I can't call out," I said.

He nodded. "Have to keep our team safe from any more bombs while we're in the post-blast investigation."

Currently, the K-9 team was moving from turbine to turbine, hoping to find clues to the culprit's identity. Parts of the explosives, or perhaps even an undetonated cell phone bomb, could have been critical in developing leads. But so far they'd sniffed out nothing but a few far-flung pieces from the blast. They were collected, bagged, and their locations marked on a map.

"Does this mean terrorists?" I hated to be the first to bring up that word, but I wanted to gauge his reaction in person.

"No one knows what it means," the sheriff said. "We're asking folks to report any suspicious characters. Strangers or not. Could even be a disgruntled neighbor."

"Could I meet the dog and get some close-up shots?" I knew those shots would please Noreen and elevate my story in her mind.

"Make it quick." Sheriff Taber radioed the K-9 unit to come over. "Her name's Scout. She's down from the Twin Cities and is one of the best explosives-detection dogs in the country."

I felt a pang of loneliness for Shep, a German shepherd who'd come to my rescue more than once. He'd joined the K-9 ranks and was now a top drug-sniffing dog. I understood how drug and cadaver dogs operated, but I'd never seen a bomb-sniffing dog up close. Scout was all muscle, covered with sleek fur.

Like a pro, she ignored me.

The sheriff introduced me to her trainer, Larry Moore, who explained that Scout could detect nineteen thousand explosive combinations.

"It would take fifteen people to cover what she can in ten minutes," he said. Then, along the side of his pants, he showed me a pocket full of dog food. "She eats by finding explosives. Pavlov's theory. Every time she makes an alert, she gets food."

He agreed to let Malik shoot some video of her in action. "Seek," he commanded.

Scout went to work, sweeping through a soybean field. After a couple minutes with her nose to the ground, she sat down. Larry bent over and put a small charred item in a plastic bag.

"Notice how she's starting to drool?" He reached into his pocket and pulled out a piece of dog food. "Good dog." He praised her and gave her the treat.

"Can she also find drugs?" I asked.

"No cross-training," he said. "Those are separate skills. For example, let's say we're called for a school bomb threat, and she alerts at a student's locker. Does she smell pot or explosives? How would we know?"

I was about to comment on the perfect sense of that when the FBI guy interrupted with an "Enough for now." Scout and her partner resumed their sweeps. Malik grabbed the gear. I thanked the sheriff and told him I'd be in touch.

I loved my story. I loved the video, the sound, and that it was unfolding far away from Minneapolis. Selling my boss on follow-ups would make my bumping into Sam Pierce and accidentally violating any restraining order less of a threat.

A small band of local farmers had gathered to sing the terrorist tune. Now that a bombing pattern seemed to be forming, they needed outsiders to blame. And they were much more vocal than before. A comparable thing happened when the I-35 bridge in Minneapolis had collapsed a couple years earlier. The first reaction was that terrorists—rather than design errors and an overloaded structure—must be responsible. A similar reflex could be observed across the country in other situations of calamity.

"Must be Islamic fundamentalists," one man said.

"They want America dependent on foreign oil," another theorized.

A third nodded his support of the hunch. "They're threatened by our wind power."

It was a much worldlier conversation than I expected, so I joined the chatter. "But why here?" I asked. "There're wind farms throughout the United States."

"Lots of Muslims live up in the Twin Cities. They might be organizing it from there. Some probably have al-Qaeda connections."

Nearly a decade later, American Muslim communities were still feeling the backlash from the September 11 attacks. While I listened politely to the locals' speculation, there was no way I was putting any of it on TV without definitive evidence.

The idea that al-Qaeda might be behind the wind turbine blasts was unlikely but not implausible. Law enforcement officials consider Minnesota a center for terrorist training. Zacarias Moussaoui, considered by some the twentieth hijacker, was arrested after raising suspicions at a local flight school just before September 11. More recently, twenty young Somalian men left Minnesota, recruited by a terrorist group with ties to al-Qaeda to fight in their homeland. At least one ended up a suicide bomber.

I could tell Malik was uncomfortable with the

entire conversation. He was getting suspicious stares because of his Middle Eastern heritage.

We left just as one hothead was suggesting armed shifts to watch for intruders. The trouble was, Wide Open Spaces Wind Farm had nearly two hundred turbines, spread over fifty miles, and I would bet that less than a handful of area farmers could shoot well enough in the dark to play sniper without hitting each other. It would be like hunting deer drunk.

I waved at my dad, who was standing with an old schoolteacher of mine who wanted to say hi. They were both curious about the latest happenings.

"What do you think, Dad?" I whispered as we walked along the ditch while Malik shot more video of the investigators. Dad had bad knees, so it was slow going. "What's with these explosions? Who around here hates the wind farm?"

He hesitated. I pressed him.

"Come on, Dad, you're the ultimate insider."

My family had farmed our land—some of the finest dirt in the world—going back more than 130 years. I long suspected my father was the custodian of numerous small-town secrets. I figured most would go with him to the grave but thought maybe, if I remained patient and he grew slightly delusional, he'd spill some real whammies on his deathbed.

"You must have some idea, Dad. I'm not going to air it, I just want to get a feel for what I should be watching for."

So he coughed up two names—one I recognized, the other I didn't—but assured me neither man would ever resort to this kind of violence.

We started with the name I knew: Billy Mueller. He'd graduated two years ahead of me in school, but I still remembered his temper on the playground. Billy the Bully.

"Billy's plenty mad about not getting any wind money," Dad said. "He kept after them to include his land in the project, but the engineers drew the line a quarter-mile from his property. He feels he got cheated."

My parents also missed out on the wind deal, by about a mile. Being Minnesota stoic, they'd never mentioned any anger about the five grand a year per turbine some of their neighbors received, but I'd never asked.

So I did now. "You and Mom ever feel any resentment about that?"

"Can't complain," he said, utilizing another regional colloquialism. It means you could complain, but you're too well mannered.

"Come on, Dad, it's me. Let's be honest with each other."

"Whatever."

"Whatever is not a full-fledged answer."

"All right," he said. "Disappointment yes, resentment no. I can't begrudge my friends their windfall." He smiled when he said "windfall."

Money can be a powerful motive for crime.

So can jealousy. I didn't agree with Dad that Billy wouldn't mix with violence, but the Billy Mueller I knew didn't seem smart enough to stage something like this. Of course, that was back when we were kids. Maybe he'd gotten himself an education since then.

"Think Billy could build a bomb?" I asked Dad.

He shook his head. "We guess Billy to be the one who egged the turbines while they were lying on the ground."

"He threw eggs at the wind turbines?"

"Just the propellers. They're huge up close."

I'd heard enough about Billy and moved on to the other name my father had thrown out. "How about Charlie Perkins?"

His was the name I didn't recognize, and I was familiar with most of the surnames for miles around. Kloeckner, Jax, Schaefer, Miller, Merten, Koenigs. There weren't all that many.

"What's his problem with the windmills?"

"Charlie moved here maybe five years ago from up in the Cities. He bought the Meyer place and fixed it up. Sank a lot of money. Guess you'd call it a hobby farm."

He snorted at the idea of farming as a hobby. Farming was work. He ought to know; he'd done it all his life, even before tractors got air-conditioning. Anyone who wanted a hobby should play cards or go fishing.

"Charlie came down here to get away from skyscrapers and other eyesores. That's what he calls the turbines. He was supposed to be part of the wind farm. Turned them down, even though his land is right smack-dab in the middle." Dad motioned south of where we were standing. "Now he's mad at everyone who signed up. Says he doesn't like looking at the wind machines. But he doesn't have much choice; they have him surrounded."

Didn't seem like enough of a motive to me. But I'd never met the guy. And I didn't have any wind turbines across the street from my house, ruining my view. Of course, I didn't even have a view these days, unless you counted the bus lane.

I was back renting a house in Minneapolis, having opted for convenience to work. After a perilously close brush with crime under my own roof, I'd tried retreating to the safety of the suburbs but found that battle cry to be just another urban myth. Danger lurked everywhere, from big cities to small towns to rural countryside. Personal experience lately made me wary of most strangers. Mentally, it might not have been the healthiest approach to life, but physically, it seemed the most pragmatic.

"Know anything about Charlie's background? What he used to do for a living?" I asked.

"Something for Honeywell."

Best known as a manufacturer of thermostats, Honeywell International used to be based in Minneapolis, when it was a controversial weapons manufacturer.

I glanced at my watch, wishing there was time to meet Charlie Perkins.

Even without a firm suspect or motive, I was still confident I had a decent lead story that included all the elements Noreen normally relished: action, fear, and dogs.

> ((RILEY, CU))
> AUTHORITIES SAY CELL
> PHONE BOMBS HAVE BEEN
> USED TO BLAST WIND
> TURBINES IN SOUTHERN
> MINNESOTA. WHILE THEY
> HAVE NO SUSPECTS, THEY
> CONTINUE TO INVESTIGATE
> THE BAFFLING CRIMES WITH
> EXPLOSIVES-SNIFFING DOGS.

But when Malik and I arrived back at the station, we found it surrounded by police cars, and no one gave a hoot about wind turbines.

My story had been killed.

And so had Sam Pierce.

CHAPTER 8

The gossip columnist had been found murdered outside his garage.

Noreen had tried to phone me as soon as she got word, but the call didn't go through because of the cell signal block. Later the cops arrived and asked that the station not inform me about the homicide.

Since everyone knew about my confrontation with Sam, homicide investigators were waiting to question me. When they got to the part about me having a right to have an attorney present, I called Benny Walsh. This time he answered his line, and this time me bringing in the state's top homicide defense attorney didn't feel so much like overkill.

He told the police he wanted to speak to his client—me—alone first. Then he and I went into my office and shut the door. My desk was a mess, but at the moment, it matched my life.

"What have you got to tell me?" Benny grabbed a chair and motioned for me to also sit.

"Nothing. I haven't a clue what's going on."

"Yet you left a message for me midmorning, saying we needed to talk. And you sounded a bit agitated."

Benny looked as serious as I'd ever seen him.

"You don't think *I* killed him, do you?" I asked.

"I don't *care* whether or not you killed him. All I care about is what you're going to say when the cops question you. But it did cross my mind on the way over here that maybe your earlier message had something to do with seeking the advice of counsel in regard to this homicide."

"I didn't kill him. I had questions about the fairness of the protective order, Benny. That's why I called you."

"Well, the order for protection is irrelevant now," he said. "And if you violated that in the course of killing Mr. Pierce, that's the least of your troubles."

"I didn't kill him."

"Our immediate decision is whether to allow police to question you." Benny's face tensed, like he was weighing the pros and cons of that predicament.

"I have nothing to hide."

"Maybe. Maybe not. Where were you last night? Unless you can assure me you were at a party with lots of people and went home with one of them, and stayed until daybreak, I'm not sure we want you talking to the authorities."

"I was home alone."

He sighed deeply, stared at the floor, then back at me.

"Did you talk to anyone?"

"No."

"Did anyone come to the door? A salesperson perhaps?"

"No."

"Can you see now why I'm reluctant to have you interviewed by the detectives? You tell them you've got no alibi, and you're going to make my job harder."

"Benny, after that fiasco in court, I just wanted to be alone last night. And I'm not afraid to say that, because I know I didn't do it. Sam had a lot of enemies. I need to talk to the cops, so they can eliminate me as a suspect."

"It doesn't always work that way," he insisted.

"This won't be the first time cops have looked at me funny in a murder investigation. I just want to get it done with."

Even though his legal advice was that I stick with my right to remain silent, I told police I was happy to answer any questions they might have. They asked us to follow them back to the cop shop, where I suspected they wanted to have a videotape rolling during my interview.

"How was he killed?" I asked the detectives once we were all seated in a tiny interrogation room.

"We're asking the questions here, Ms. Spartz," Detective Delmonico said.

"Sorry, I forgot my role. I'm used to asking questions. You know, reporter's curiosity."

"Well, we're not prepared to release any details to you about this homicide just now," he said.

"Well, unless the murder weapon was a glass of wine," Benny interrupted, "I don't think you have anything on my client."

"We'll see," the other detective said. "Let's hope you're right."

The tone of the actual interview was softer than with Benny back at the station. They wanted to hear firsthand about my altercation with Sam at the bar and seemed to accept that it was one of those regrettable, out-of-character incidents that sometimes happen when we're unfairly provoked. They didn't act much at all like they thought I was guilty. Mostly, they did a lot of nodding. Never once reaching for the handcuffs. Or their guns.

I felt okay afterward.

Sure, I didn't have an alibi. But I also knew they didn't have any evidence. And there had to be other suspects with better motives. After all, the murder victim was Sam Pierce.

"See, Benny, that wasn't so bad."

He didn't answer.

But when we walked down the stairs outside city hall, cameras swarmed. And not just television crews. Print reporters and photographers pushed and pressed, much more aggressively than normal. The broadcasters were definitely more objective, yelling, "*Did* you do it?" While the print journalists yelled, "*Why* did you do it?"

Understandably, the newspaper staff were angry. Their hero with the highest web hits was dead.

They wanted justice.

But all they got was a brisk "no comment" from my attorney.

CHAPTER 9

A couple hours later, Nick Garnett stood on my doorstep, a carry-on bag in one hand, a bouquet of black-eyed Susans in another. The flowers were a little joke between us stemming back to a serial-killer story we'd worked on together.

"Surprise, Riley. I rented a car at the airport."

Frantically, I pulled him inside. He figured it was because I missed him terribly and wanted to hold him close. Really, it was because I didn't want the neighbors to see him.

Once I got him past the threshold and slammed the door, I felt torn. I wanted him to kiss me long and hard because we hadn't seen each other in a month. But it was a few minutes before ten and I also wanted to watch the news.

I compromised by pushing him onto the couch, kissing him quickly, and fumbling for the remote. I found Channel 3 in time for us to hear Clay Burrel leading the newscast with the gossip murder and word that he'd just learned—exclusively—that the killer had shot Sam Pierce to death.

"At least I don't own a gun," I said.

"Hard to prove a negative," Garnett replied. "And just as easy for a woman to pull a trigger as a man. Now if your pal had been fatally beaten, size and strength might be a factor."

He put his fingers around my upper arm like he was measuring my muscle. I shrugged him away, clicking the remote off when the newscast shifted from violence to politics.

Clay had also latched on to this homicide. And to be honest, I was impressed that he, being new to Minneapolis, had gleaned another hot lead early in the investigation, even though the cause of death can come from numerous sources.

I know journalists are supposed to have tough skins, but in the early days in my news vocation, I'd thought that feature only applied to our professional work, not our personal lives. Being on TV, I'd learned otherwise—nothing was off-limits to the public. Over the years, I'd built a successful career pointing the finger at wrongdoers and now was discovering that I didn't like having the finger pointed at me—as either an adulterer or a murderer.

So I reminded Garnett I still didn't want us to be seen together in public. Forget holding hands. I didn't even want to walk down the street with him.

"Well, then it's a good thing we've got the blinds pulled."

As he unbuttoned my shirt, he pointed out that Minnesota prisons don't allow inmates to have conjugal visits, so I better rendezvous while I could.

I whacked him over the head with the yellow and black bouquet he'd brought, leaving a dusting of sticky powder in his barely gray hair, but I was happy he'd flown back to Minneapolis and glad not to be alone that night. And not just so I'd have an alibi if anyone else I knew was murdered.

CHAPTER 10

The next morning, I grabbed the Minneapolis newspaper off the porch and read in a banner headline that a copy of the "Piercing Eyes" gossip column about me, the one that started the whole drink-in-the-face fiasco, had been found stuffed in Sam's dead mouth.

The newspaper attributed that damning detail to "an anonymous source."

Garnett set down his coffee and wrapped his arms around my shoulders. "Well, darling, someone seems to be going to a whole lot of trouble to make the police think you're the killer."

"So you believe me, right, Nick, that I didn't do it?"

"Absolutely, we just have to figure out who hates you as much as they hated Sam."

My cell phone rang just as I was pondering that idea; it was Benny Walsh ordering me to keep my mouth shut and nixing any media interviews. I promised to keep quiet, figuring Garnett didn't count.

At least Clay would see what it felt like to be beat on a big story, though I could certainly understand how a homicide investigator might be more up-front with the employer of the victim than a competitor. Not all crime reporters are perceived the same in all cases.

Garnett, however, was disgusted that the cops would leak such a sensitive clue—no matter which media outlet was involved. "As a practical matter, they need to hold back some facts only the killer would know so they can weed out false confessions."

False confessions. Facts only the killer would know. "I love it when you talk cop talk," I said.

Over breakfast, he'd raised the idea of me moving to Washington for a fresh start. I'd lived in Minnesota my whole life and had been offered plenty of opportunities to relocate, but the timing had never seemed right. Not then. Not now. Not even with the Sam Pierce mess looming.

Moving a thousand miles for Garnett was a commitment I wasn't ready to make. If he wanted us to be together, I thought he should move back. I could tell my answer didn't thrill him. So I sent him out the door with a lingering kiss, a playful pat on his rear, and the desire that he not overthink our tête-à-tête. As our lips touched, our bodies wanted to follow, but we both had jobs.

To justify his visit as work, he'd agreed to handle some security business at the airport involving changes in passenger screening by using new technology to detect weapons and explosives. Trouble was, privacy complaints were raised because the equipment made it appear passengers were naked. Effectively an electronic strip search. A new, improved piece of X-ray equipment made it look like they were wearing underwear. A small improvement, but still offensive to many. It would probably take an international incident, like a terrorist with a bomb in his pants, before the public welcomed such scrutiny.

I'd given Garnett a house key, and we made plans to meet up that night for dinner. He vowed to call over to the cop shop later and try to find out where all the inside info was leaking from. Knowledge is power, so that promise cheered me.

As journalists, we like to think of ourselves as professional observers, recording what we see, hear, smell, even touch. But in reality, much of what we report is what people tell us. Secondhand information.

That's why sourcing is so important. And why we guard our sources jealously.

In the newsroom, I dodged Clay as he tried to cajole a camera interview about how I felt being the prime suspect in Sam's murder.

"Nothing to say," I insisted, walking to my office and shutting the door before he could "little lady" me again.

I had more than ratings riding on this story. I sat at my desk for maybe ten minutes, ignoring phone calls, weighing the personal and professional implications I faced from the gossip homicide.

Besides a front-page story with screaming headlines, the newspaper had run an editorial that morning criticizing police for not arresting me and prosecutors for not charging me in Sam's death. Normally the paper didn't name suspects unless they'd been officially accused of a crime, or were considered to be a danger to the public, or were fleeing the jurisdiction.

Until Sam's death, I'd have bet that most of the paper's newsroom employees felt more camaraderie toward me than him. Over the years, they'd been impressed by some of my work, ashamed of some of his. But in the last twenty-four hours, he'd gone from being a journalistic embarrassment to his news colleagues to being a martyr of sorts. Or maybe they were just realizing that the popularity of his column had provided insurance for their own jobs. And that his murder made their employment futures even more uncertain.

Noreen chose that very moment to page me overhead to her office. Pronto. There she greeted me with questions that made my own future sound iffy. "Riley, do you realize what all this talk about you is doing to the station's image?"

"Innocent people have nothing to worry about," I replied.

"Aren't you always telling me the jails are full of innocent people?"

"No, I'm always telling you the jails are full of people who *say* they're innocent." I was thinking back to Dusty Foster, an inmate who claimed to be falsely imprisoned for the murder of a girlfriend named Susan.

"Well, if you end up joining them," Noreen continued, "make sure we get some exclusives."

"I'll get you an exclusive," I promised. "I'll dig deep and break something open on this story. If you ask me, there's more going on here than just a dead gossip."

"Well, if there is, you're the last person we'd let cover it. Every time you turned around, your motives would be suspicious. So stay away from the Sam Pierce case. I've already assigned it to Clay."

"But being so new to the market, there're things he'd miss. Clues that would go right over his head. I'm an insider, I'll recognize local connections."

"But being an outsider, he'll have objectivity. Something we highly value in this profession."

Noreen was right about that, and I couldn't argue her point. But that didn't mean I was going to stay away from the gossip investigation. I would just stay under my boss's radar.

"Well, how about if I dig around in the headless homicide?" Given a little time, I was certain I'd come up with an irresistible lead that would show that Texas windbag just who was high in the saddle.

"Riley, I know you enjoy covering crime, but I think it's best you stay away from any homicide investigations until the 'Piercing Eyes' case is solved. Your involvement puts the station in a thorny situation. And frankly, I'm pleased with the job Clay's done. He hasn't broken every scoop, but he's done fine."

I couldn't really bicker about either conclusion without Noreen accusing me of professional jealousy, and honestly, I was jealous. A little competitive zeal can be both a help and a hindrance.

Viewers expect reporters to compete head-to-head, pushing and shoving with their counterparts across town. What they don't realize is reporters compete against colleagues in their own newsroom. For interviews. For awards. For resources. For the most time. For the best play.

And we're judged by ratings. Constantly.

I'd mentored plenty of rookie reporters over the years, but the difference between them and Clay was spelled R-E-S-P-E-C-T. He didn't respect me. He walked into Channel 3 and acted like I was all washed up just because the only thing breaking a 40 share in this market these days was Brett Favre and the Minnesota Vikings.

Clashing with Noreen wouldn't bode well. So I nodded silently, promised myself I'd show him a thing or two about breaking news, and changed the subject.

"Want me to work something up on the wind farm story?" I asked. "There's good stuff that never made air because of the timing of . . . the murder."

I didn't say Sam's name out loud, lest she suspect I was scheming.

She nixed the wind idea as anything special. "Old news, now."

"I've got some interesting stuff about bomb-sniffing dogs."

She pursed her lips, then, dog lover that she was, told me to package something to hold for the Saturday newscast as long as we'd already shot video. Saturday is about as low a priority as a news story can land. So I almost wished I hadn't brought it up.

Noreen seemed to sense my disappointment and tried to rationalize her decision. "Riley, it's not like there's any dead bodies. Viewers care about danger and money."

So because the economy was tanking, she ordered me to do a quick-turn crime story about the increase in drive-off crooks at gas stations and dine-and-dash thieves at restaurants.

Sam Pierce had moved from Chicago to Minneapolis four years earlier for a reporter position on the newspaper's suburban beat. A couple months later, when the paper posted a gossip columnist job none of the rest of the staff would touch because it wasn't Real Journalism, he raised his hand. To the surprise of everyone but the top editor, Minnesotans quietly ate up the dish.

"Piercing Eyes" was entertainment, not news, though it ran in the news section, creating some periodic confusion and debate.

Sam's newsroom colleagues envied the buzz he began to generate and the job security he seemed to possess in a troubled industry. At a time when award-winning reporters were being cut or their beats were being eliminated, Sam seemed immune to such job angst because of his star status.

So he kept up his routine of making newsmakers cringe. Until his death.

At my desk, I dialed the Minneapolis Police public information officer to set up the shoot on gas and meal bandits. Normally, I'd just have called some street cops directly and hoped I got lucky, but until my name was cleared from the Sam Pierce murder, I wanted to make a show of following the department's media procedures. Also, this particular idea was straightforward and fairly soft as far as crime stories go. So I didn't anticipate trouble.

While I waited for the PIO to get back to me with some leads, I retrieved the computer archives of Sam's gossip columns.

Starting with day one, I listed anyone whose life Sam had ruined. Some he ran out of town, others he drove mad. It was a long, intriguing list of potential grudge holders. By midafternoon, the tally numbered just over a hundred men and women.

I didn't include myself.

Three of the names I recognized as being in prison (because I'd also covered their cases)—first, a repeat drunk driver who caused a child's death; next, a Ponzi scheme engineer who cheated dozens; last, a crooked car dealer who'd been a household name—so I crossed them off.

By then the police flack had located some surveillance photos of cars whose drivers didn't pay at the pump. While he didn't have similar pictures of diners who left for the bathroom and never came back, he had the names of restaurant owners who'd reported such pilferage in the last couple weeks.

I thanked him like a good reporter and asked him to email me the pictures. But he suggested I pick them up in person: there was something else he wanted to discuss. I reminded myself to keep my lips sealed if any questions delved deeper regarding my whereabouts during Sam's murder. Quite possibly, the cops might see this as an opportunity to chat me up away from my lawyer.

Because street parking was difficult to find outside city hall, Malik waited in the van while I ran inside.

The PIO handed me the gas station photos and mentioned that the cops were noticing a pattern in reports concerning one particular grub grabber. "Instead of the kind of bum you'd expect to dine-and-dash, this guy is slick. Well dressed. Suit and tie even."

"Any pictures? Give us a photo, I'm sure we could give you an ID."

"No, that's the problem. But from the description, we're starting to wonder if the same man is walking the check in about a third of our downtown meal-theft cases."

"So he's not just forgetting his wallet?"

He shook his head. "He's hungry, broke, or a jerk. Maybe all three."

We laughed. And just as I was getting up to leave, the PIO got to the other point of our visit. "We're kind of curious about where your buddy's getting all his information."

"Which buddy are you talking about?" I asked.

"Your Texas buddy." He meant Clay. I imagined the cops were annoyed that he had the inside track on the headless homicide.

"Why don't you ask him yourself?" I was curious, as well as envious, about which homicide detective he'd gotten tight with.

"I already did. Your new reporter referred us to your station lawyer, who referred me to the state shield law."

I smiled. Minnesota's shield law protecting reporter sources is among the best in the nation. I'd hidden sources behind it myself more than once.

After decades of debate, a federal shield law was still unresolved.

"Sorry, I can't help you," I replied. "No idea who he's talking to. I'm just as interested." I sure was, because Clay doing good made me look mediocre.

The PIO didn't respond, like he was trying to decide whether or not to believe me.

"Maybe you should warn your investigators about the perils of releasing unauthorized information to the media," I said, smirking a little.

Such an admonition would be pointless. Sources have their own reasons for leaking stuff. Sometimes it's to curry favor with a reporter. Sometimes it's to screw a boss. Occasionally their rationale is more noble; they believe it's for the public good. I've broken stories with insider information for all those reasons and more. The best physical features for a source are keen eyes and a sharp tongue. If the chief caught this latest leak, somebody's career in law enforcement would be over.

I gave my thanks and left to go find sound and cover for my economy filchers story. Because gas stations have surveillance cameras, their thieves are generally easier to catch, unless they've duct-taped over their license plates. The lunch larceners are the bigger challenge.

My afternoon turned out to include a fun interview with a restaurant owner complaining about dining-and-dashing miscreants who order steak instead of soup and wishing, if they truly were broke, they'd at least have the dignity to offer to do dishes.

I tried to firm up whether, like the cops suspected, one criminal might be responsible for many of the meal thefts, because one big bad guy is always more newsworthy than a bunch of little bad guys. But it was still too fuzzy, though I did get several food managers to promise to call me if Mr. Dine-and-Dash came back for seconds.

I stuck around after the news to run through my gossip suspect list again, loading the names into a spreadsheet. Bad haircuts. Party flirts. Cheating in the carpool lane. Those accusations were probably true. But that didn't mean the victims couldn't still be pissed at being outed by Sam.

I made a subcategory of more-subjective smears. A politician who yelled at her misbehaving toddler while shopping. Another politician who didn't yell at her misbehaving toddler while shopping. A department store Santa who hiccuped instead of ho-hoing.

I grouped others together who'd obviously been treated unfairly by the media, even though I hated to disparage the media by lumping Sam in with the rest of us.

A young actress belittled for leaving a meager tip when it was a case of mistaken identity. A world-renowned transplant surgeon about whom Sam repeated rumors concerning a hospital nurse and a supply closet. A judge whose reputation was hurt after his crazy ex posted doctored photos online. While the columnist didn't actually publish them, he directed readers to the website that did and reported—truthfully, he'd noted as justification—that the judge was embarrassed about his inability to get them yanked off the Internet.

And this list didn't even count folks Sam had publicly teased with "I know what you're up to but I'm not telling." That stunt was a regular feature in his weekend "Piercing Eyes" column.

I finally gave up trying to see through all the clutter. Nobody seemed to have a more compelling reason than anybody else for silencing Sam.

Glancing at my watch, I realized I was late meeting Garnett. Then I remembered what he had said about the killer hating me as much as the gossip writer and trying to frame me for the crime. Then it occurred to me that Sam's killer might not necessarily bear me malice but simply see me as a convenient scapegoat to deflect suspicion. Without even thinking, my eyes found the mystery woman's note, still pinned to my wall.

"Thanks Alot, Riley, Give Everyone The Disturbing Information Regarding That Bad Ass Gossip."

CHAPTER 11

Clay was also working late.

On my way out, I tried to coax the name of his informant by complimenting his coverage—one reporter to another. He just laughed and insisted a good journalist never reveals a source, especially not to a potential suspect.

"You must think I'm dumber than dirt, little lady."

"Oh come on, cowboy," I said, figuring two could play at Texas talk. "You don't really think I shot Sam?"

"Nope." He shook his head. "I don't expect you're capable of hitting the side of a barn. Heck, missy, you probably never even held a gun."

Then he opened his suit jacket and flashed a shiny handgun in a shoulder holster.

"A gun!" I gasped. "Here at the station?" I looked around, but the newsroom was fairly empty and nobody seemed to be paying attention to us.

"Sure thing," he said. "Handy as a pocket on a shirt."

Clay winked and assured me that Texas gun-carry permits are reciprocal in Minnesota. Now I understood how he'd gotten so chummy with the local cops so fast. Waving a weapon likely helped him bond. So would arguing over who had more firepower.

"Go ahead and grip it," he suggested, opening his jacket again and moving closer toward me. "Safety's on."

I didn't tell him about my dead husband's gun. I'd declined to take it back from the police after their investigation because I didn't want to own a weapon that had killed someone—even though that particular victim deserved to die. I'd already regretted that decision once, but not enough to shop for a replacement.

Clay apparently noticed my hesitation. "You northern ladies afraid of guns?"

I ignored his taunt. My hand brushed against his chest as I pulled the Glock from his holster. I experimented with its heft. Favored by cops, it felt familiar. I stretched my arm, purposely holding the barrel even with my eye, before holstering the weapon behind his jacket.

He insisted on walking me out to my car. Maybe because it was dark, because he was armed, or because a crazy lady sent me pretty flowers with a confusing note, I agreed.

• • •

Garnett had his feet on my coffee table and a beer in his hand when I walked in carrying Chinese food and chopsticks. He'd checked with his old homicide buddies, who'd all denied being Clay's leak, as usual blaming the medical examiner.

"Yeah, well, you'd always deny it too if they asked you about me," I said.

"They don't have to ask anymore," he answered. "They can read about it in the paper. Oops, those days are gone."

He raised his beer in a tasteless toast that I ignored as I opened fried rice and a chicken lo mein dish for us to share. Cops can be just as cynical as journalists.

"Don't joke about Sam being dead," I said. "Or they might start speculating you killed him to defend my honor. You're lucky you were in Washington that night."

He shook his head and laughed. "For a guy no one seemed to like, his murder certainly is getting plenty of attention."

From a journalistic standpoint, Sam deserved the play. Newspapers are a dying industry. That's hardly news anymore. But dead newspaper columnists still deserve coverage. I didn't begrudge Sam his postmortem headlines.

"He seemed to relish being feared more than being liked," I said. "I wonder why."

"Well, you know what they say: if you don't

have anything nice to say about anybody, come sit by me." Garnett patted the couch beside him.

"Olympia Dukakis in *Steel Magnolias*, 1989," I said as I sat down. "But she ripped it off from Alice Roosevelt Longworth, Teddy Roosevelt's socialite daughter."

Garnett and I had a tradition of weaving famous movie lines into our conversations and guessing the film, actor, and year. I associated movies with major news events and recalled watching *Steel Magnolias* about the same time Iran's Ayatollah Khomeini was condemning Salman Rushdie to death for blasphemy.

I was used to viewers complaining about my stories—there'd even been occasional advertising boycotts—but at least I'd never been the subject of a fatwa.

A copy of *The Satanic Verses* sat on a bookcase in the other room, grouped with my collection of other controversial fiction like *Harry Potter*, *The Catcher in the Rye*, *Lady Chatterley's Lover*, and *The Da Vinci Code*.

"An odd thing happened at the station today," I said.

I ran my fingers through Garnett's graying hair as I told him about Clay's gun, but Garnett shrugged off the incident. He carried a Glock himself and didn't understand why more people didn't—as long as they weren't convicted felons. He figured Clay to be a show-off for flashing the weapon at me and probably not much of an actual shot.

From his résumé tape, Clay hadn't seemed much of a crime reporter, either. Noreen likely fell for him because he included standups on horseback and a news feature on why armadillos are adorable. He'd clearly researched and exploited her weakness for animal stories.

Noreen probably also jumped at the chance to add a man to the news staff cheap. Women outnumber men three to one when it comes to TV news résumé tapes because we're willing to work for less and put up with more to break into the business.

But when I'd gone to his former station's website and viewed some of his old stories online, I realized Clay wasn't the himbo I'd first thought. He'd broken some news on a school district bribery scandal. And he'd also landed a compelling interview with a death row inmate.

I hated to admit it, but Clay had the makings of a real newsman. I was beginning to suspect his cocky cowboy attitude just might be a ruse to get opponents to underestimate him.

Since both recent homicides—Sam's and the headless woman's—happened in the same jurisdiction, most likely he'd gotten close to one well-placed source.

"I got a couple of leads on his mystery informant," Garnett said. He'd learned one of the Minneapolis Police homicide investigators grew up in Texas. Between the gun and that good-ole-boy fact, Channel 3's new reporter could have hit the jackpot in source development and murder timing.

"But there's an even stronger possibility," Garnett said. "Your pal was in a closed-door meeting with the police chief the other day."

"Chief Capacasa? He was probably screaming at Clay about the whole mess. He hates reporters."

"Maybe not all reporters. Maybe just you."

Minneapolis police chief Vince Capacasa and I had a history of creative skirmishes, so he was always snarly around me. But I could envision a scenario of him throwing some choice news morsels to a rookie, like Clay, to make him indebted down the line, and maybe to make a veteran, like me, look like I was losing my touch.

"It's all making sense." Understanding his source made his scoops less galling and my misses less vexing. I appreciated Garnett's input on his old career cronies.

These days, he wasn't sharing many juicy details about his new job at Homeland Security. Most of the time, he said, it wouldn't be stuff that interested me. But once he hinted that the folks running the operation weren't the brightest bulbs. And I wondered if he regretted his vocation change. Especially after two flashy party crashers infiltrated a White House state dinner and ridiculed the very idea of security on the federal level. Sometimes, I even got the impression the high-tech toys the feds had access to didn't interest Garnett as much as playing old-fashioned cops and robbers.

I wondered what he knew about cell phone bombs, so I brought up the wind turbine blasts.

"Do you think a terrorist ring might be behind them?" I asked. "Domestic? International?"

He shrugged. "Cell phone bombs sound sophisticated, but they're not all that difficult. Ingredients are easy to come by. Detonation is as simple as making a phone call."

I filled him in on the tension between the sheriff and the FBI guy. Nothing new to him. Feds and locals often clash on the direction of investigations.

"One thing that sticks out," he said, "is that nobody's been hurt. It's almost like your bomber is taking pains not to harm actual people. That's unusual in committed terror circles. Normally you'd see a body count."

Since I knew some of the folks living within the wind farm acreage, that appeared to be a good thing. I'd have hated to see any of them as either victims or perpetrators. Like the rest of the rural neighbors down there, I was betting on an outsider. But Garnett's observation of only property damage supported the theory that a peeved local might be behind it all.

"Can you see what you can find out?" I asked.

"No promises," he said. Which was better than a firm no. Since our relationship had turned per-

sonal, there was less exchanging of professional information. Maybe it was because he had a new job.
Or maybe it was because any scoop I broke might
reflect back on him.

So I changed the subject back to his favorite
topic. Murder. He had once been a top homicide
investigator, and this seemed a good time to get his
take on the headless body.

"Do you think they'll ever find her head?" I
asked.

He shrugged. "No way of knowing. Sometimes
killers dump a body in one state and a head in another. If both are discovered, the different jurisdictions slow down any investigation."

"Quite a road trip," I said. "Driving a human
head across state lines." Not the kind of cargo anyone would want to get caught hauling. "I guess the
murderer got lucky that no one noticed anything
that night in the park."

"No surprise," Garnett said. "The body was
dumped on a Sunday night. That's the dog watch.
When the fewest number of cops are on patrol. If
I was going to dump a body, that's when I'd do it."

Dog watch. Cop talk. I love it.

Amid tangled sheets, Garnett slept.

My mind kept returning to Sam. As a journalist, I pondered questions like how much he bled
and whether the bullets hurt for long.

Even though I hadn't liked him as a person, I

didn't like being haunted by thoughts of him lying dead. Probably because, if I was being honest, I knew that in the mind of the general public, not much separated my work from his. So it wasn't outlandish to visualize an angry viewer coming after me for something I reported. Telling myself that Sam deserved death more would be of little consolation if I joined him on a morgue slab.

To keep my mind off such unpleasantness, I forced myself to concentrate on the headless homicide. That was an even worse mistake. Now I couldn't shake the sight and smell of crime-scene gore. The blood from the victim's head must have sprayed the killer and his surroundings like a brand of death. That image made the bloody elevator in the movie *The Shining* seem tame. And when I closed my eyes, instead of the black comfort of darkness, I saw the color red.

CHAPTER 12

I must have slept because I woke with a start. Afraid. I might have made a strangled cry, but I wasn't sure. It took a few seconds for me to realize I was safe. In bed. A man by my side. A man who loved me. And whom I loved back.

"Are you okay? Riley?" By then Garnett had reached for a lamp switch.

Light brought reassurance that the warmth I felt came from blankets, not blood.

My nightmare stemmed from a childhood memory I hadn't thought about for decades: the day the chickens got butchered. We kids were supposed to take turns holding the comb of the bird's head across a wooden stump while my mother held the feet. I remember the chicken's eye blinking as its neck stretched uncomfortably. Then my father swung the ax.

I tried blocking out the red hue as I rushed to the bathroom to puke. Vomit vapor hit my arms, reminding me of the warm mist of chicken blood on my skin long ago. Then I threw up again.

"Can I get you anything?" Garnett handed me my bathrobe.

I shook my head, rinsed my mouth, and climbed back in bed. He held me close, urging me to go back to sleep. I cried as I told him about the dream. He called it my "Clarice moment."

That made me smile. Instead of screaming lambs, I was tormented by the sound of a whack, followed by frantic, flapping wings.

"Well, Clarice, have the lambs stopped screaming?" Garnett whispered in my ear as our heads lay on a pillow.

I recalled the mesmerizing final telephone scene he quoted. "Anthony Hopkins, *Silence of the Lambs*, 1991."

The film opened just as the first Gulf War was getting under way. To take the eerie emotion out of my bedroom, Garnett and I started comparing Saddam Hussein to Hannibal Lecter. It wasn't the most outlandish stretch. Two psychopaths wielding power. One factual, the other fictional. In each scenario, the government needed to do business with them. Talking politics made the dream seem distant.

But later, in the shower, I found myself envying Jodi Foster for a couple of reasons. Lambs evoke more sympathy than chickens. And Jodi's terror was make-believe.

CHAPTER 13

Neither Garnett nor I mentioned the chicken dream the next morning. While toasting English muffins, I noticed the vase of black-eyed Susans and realized I'd forgotten to tell him about the mysterious bouquet I'd received at the station.

"Not this again," he said.

I had a history of strangers, who ended up being genuinely strange, sending me flowers. No good ever came of it.

"I gave them to Noreen," I said. "Maybe the curse will cling to her."

"More likely it'll slide right off her back, she's so slick."

In a brief domestic moment, we laughed, exchanged a quick kiss, and both left for work.

Clay's gun had given me an idea.

Because of the clout of the Second Amendment, no state keeps a list of gun owners, but Minnesota residents are prohibited from carrying concealed weapons around without a special permit. This allows law enforcement to weed out the mentally ill and dangerous felons, and to require applicants to take special firearms training.

So I sidled up to Lee Xiong, the station's computer geek, for a favor. He'd made himself irreplaceable at Channel 3 for breaking news by matching government databases to obscure story premises, like whether drunks who weren't allowed to drive cars drove speedboats, menacing any of Minnesota's ten thousand lakes.

Xiong had a large library of computer records on voting, vehicles, property ownership, and criminal histories. He was Channel 3's version of Big Brother and probably sat on some good blackmail material, but as far as I could tell, he only flexed his cyber muscles for work-related projects.

I figured the names of people with gun-carry permits were probably collected by one state agency or another. That didn't mean that Sam's killer was on the list, but it was a place to start. And a place Clay wouldn't think of checking.

"We do not own this precise database," Xiong said. "I will have to get a copy from the state."

He was curious as to which local politicians or celebrities might be packing heat. But then I had to tell him why *I* was interested and why I needed him to keep my interest from Noreen.

I gave him my spreadsheet of Sam's gossip victims and asked him to match it against the gun-carry permits. Since motives were too numerous and subjective, perhaps suspects known to actually own weapons might illuminate something.

"I do not like it when you put me in the middle of work politics," he said. But we'd been through enough news scrapes together that Xiong agreed to do it on the sly.

I tried disregarding Clay on my way to my office, but he waved me over to his desk, which was covered with a mess of notes and photos.

"Look at what I have here, little lady."

Rather than argue about the nickname, I ignored it.

Clay showed me how he was comparing the headless woman's physical description with that of recently reported missing women in the Midwest.

"I reckon the cops are probably doing the same," he said.

"Smart move." I had to respect that. But that didn't stop me from wishing the story were mine. "Any leads?"

"I'm sorting the blondes. So far, four possibles."

Since I wasn't able to (at least not officially) cover the gossip columnist's murder, it was starting to feel even more important to me that I make something happen in the headless homicide case. But wrestling it away from Clay seemed less likely now than it had a few days ago when he appeared just a small-market rookie. Clearly, I'd underrated him.

I was just throwing my shoulder bag on the floor of my office when my desk phone started ringing.

"We have a problem." Xiong was on the other end. "The conceal-and-carry permit names are not public."

"What do you mean, not public?"

"Not public record."

"How can that be?" In Minnesota all government data is presumed public unless a specific exemption is made in the law.

Apparently, for the right to bear arms, one was. Gun lovers lobbied under the theory that burglars might target them and steal their weapons if such information should ever be released. The flip side to the argument, that robbers would be less likely to break into armed households, didn't fly. Neither did the idea that Minnesotans should know which of our neighbors are walking around armed and potentially dangerous.

By my pause, Xiong could tell I was disappointed.

"I will think, but I do not see alternatives," he said.

"I know, Xiong. Thanks anyway." I hung up and stared at my office wall.

We didn't have much in the way of options. We could launch a legal challenge, but that would take time and cost money, something Noreen was unlikely to approve, especially once she knew the reason.

Unless I gave her a different reason.

Quickly, some online research told me more than fifty thousand Minnesotans had conceal-and-carry permits. Out of that bunch, I'd gamble there were some newsworthy names. Maybe pro athletes. Maybe religious leaders. Maybe politicians who'd voted for the measure to keep the permit records private.

I imagined confronting some of them on the street, camera rolling, asking to see their guns. And asking why they needed one.

Interesting approach, unless they shot me. Or my photographer.

I decided to do some more research. An hour later I was confident that I could make a compelling argument that without oversight on the conceal-and-carry gun process, abuse could occur.

"What kind of abuse?" Noreen asked when I pitched the story.

"Oh, the usual," I said. "Felons carrying guns. Crazy people carrying guns. Maybe the police chief's ne'er-do-well brother-in-law."

I explained that, across the country, state laws were inconsistent on privacy and concealed weapons. While in most cases Minnesota was known for open records, when it came to conceal-and-carry permits, we were on the conservative side. Probably because of our strong hunting tradition.

Businesses had the option to post signs saying they banned guns on their premises. And many did. From the Mall of America to my neighborhood diner.

Noreen seemed to buy into the news value.

"I wouldn't want you guys carrying guns around the newsroom," Noreen said. "This is such a hothead environment, what if one of you went postal?"

I thought it best not to answer.

"I'd probably be the first one shot," she continued.

I really thought it best not to answer that. But I felt like I ought to speak up about Clay. And it wasn't like he'd made me promise to keep his gun secret. He seemed to enjoy showing it off.

"The way the law's written," I said, "we could be armed, and you wouldn't know. Clay is."

Noreen's eyes narrowed, and she leaned forward over her desk. "What did you say, Riley?"

Okay, so I ratted him out.

"Clay carries a gun. He showed me. He says everyone in Texas does."

"Not in my newsroom he doesn't."

She told me to talk to Miles about what legal steps it would take to access the gun permit information. Then she picked up her phone and paged, "Clay Burrel to the newsroom."

Clay was plenty mad. He probably knew some folksy Texas saying, like being "as mad as a wet cat," except he wasn't speaking to me.

I tried to apologize. After all, I was more fascinated by his Glock than fearful. But he wasn't buying my regret. He turned his back and stomped away, so loudly my eyes were drawn to his tan snakeskin cowboy boots.

I figured that would be our last newsroom encounter for a while. But later that night, I heard the same stomping noise, looked up from my desk, and saw him standing in my doorway.

"Happy now?" He pulled open both sides of his suit jacket. No gun. "You're just jealous," he said. "That's why you're trying to get me into trouble."

He was right about the jealous but wrong about the trouble.

"I'm sorry, Clay."

"You're mad because I'm leading the newscasts and all you've been able to come up with is that stupid windmill story."

Ouch. "I'm not jealous." I said it with a straight face even.

"Texas outranks Minnesota in wind anyway."

He was right about that, too. While most of us think of Texas as an oil and natural gas state, it leads the nation in wind power.

His voice pitch was leveling off and he was starting to seem more confused than angry about my betrayal.

"Maybe you're just one of those crazy gun haters," he said. "You like the First Amendment; well, I like the second."

So that's when I denied hating guns and told him about how my dead cop husband always wanted to teach me to shoot, but it was one of those things we never got around to.

That's when Clay shaped his hand like a gun and offered to take me to the firing range sometime.

For the first time, I noticed his wedding ring and asked how his wife liked him working so many hours.

"My wife left me. So I have no personal life."

Once again, I was apologizing for putting my big foot in my big mouth. This time I meant it. I tried to change the subject, but Clay apparently wanted to talk about his struggling marriage. And I knew what it was like to have personal demons and how hard it is to remove a wedding ring.

He explained that he wanted to accept the Minneapolis TV job and his wife wanted to stay in Texas.

"I told her this was a better news market and would really help my career." I nodded. Quite true. For numerous reporters and producers, Minneapolis–St. Paul is a network farm camp. "She told me Texas was a better weather market and would help her tan."

Also true, I thought, but still, Minnesota has tanning booths.

"I asked her, don't you love me?" he continued. "But she said, 'I love the sun more.'"

Clay's Texas swagger seemed gone, and he appeared almost humble. I told him to pull up a chair and sit for a minute. And he did. Neither of us said anything right away. But resting there together felt sort of comfortable in an unexpected way. It made me grateful my spouse had been able to stomach the desperate world of TV news without going all crazy on me. If I'd had a glass in hand, I'd have raised it to heaven and Hugh.

"So I'm here and she's there." Clay continued the rundown of his marriage. "Want to know something? She thinks I'm the one who left her. That's what she's been telling all our friends."

I tried to reassure him. "From the sound of things, maybe she's not such a loss."

"I hope you're right," he answered. "I'm plumb worn out throwing myself into this job, trying not to get all worked up over her. I need to prove this move was the right one. That's why I'm working so hard. Then maybe she'll come north."

I sympathized with Clay, yet was still determined to show him my street moxie for breaking news by finding a scoop in the headless murder case that had slipped by him.

"I'm leaving now," I said. "You should, too. Don't sit in the newsroom forever."

So for the second night in a row, we walked out of the station together.

Garnett seemed irked, maybe even envious, that for two nights now I seemed preoccupied with

Clay Burrel and guns. Especially since my beau was flying back to Washington late that night. He was printing out his boarding pass at my computer while I whined about how difficult it was going to be getting the handgun carry-permit data.

Earlier, Garnett had finished up some security consulting at the Mall of America, the state's most high-value terrorism target. He'd recommended they add a couple of explosives-sniffing dogs to their protection team.

"You want to go to a shooting range, Riley," he said, "I'll take you shooting. You don't need that Texas twerp. In fact, let's go now."

I was in my frizzy bathrobe, so I quickly slipped on a pair of jeans and opened the closet, debating whether black or pink was sexier in connection with bullets. Black seemed too obvious, so I picked the pink to get my money's worth out of that new jacket.

When I was a kid, my dad let us shoot cans from a fence with an old shotgun a few times. But usually, he'd send us into dried rows of corn to flush out pheasants while he pulled the trigger overhead.

The gun range looked like a bowling alley, except instead of pins at the far end, a paper silhouette of a man hung from a movable chain. We put ear protectors over our heads. Garnett had plenty of bullets and patience.

"This is a Glock nine-millimeter. Full size." He loaded the magazine into the weapon and spoke impersonally, like a shooting instructor to a student. "Fires seventeen rounds." The headphones made it difficult to hear him.

Garnett demonstrated how to grip the pistol with both hands to steady the shot. Then he showed me how he positioned his feet and body. And he pulled the trigger. Six times. I smelled sulfur.

He yanked the paper cutout forward, and I counted the bullet holes in the imaginary attacker. Two in the head. Three in the chest. One in the shoulder.

"Just like in the movies," I said. "You're probably hoping I'll ask you if that's a gun in your pocket or if you're just glad to see me." I made my voice sound sultry, like Mae West's.

"Go ahead. Make my day." He sounded raspy, like Clint Eastwood.

We both laughed. Him—Dirty Harry; me—a bawdy starlet. He handed me his Glock.

"Stop stalling," he said. "Your turn."

In the last couple years, I'd been on the wrong end of a gun twice. This was definitely better.

Garnett positioned the target closer, explaining that I probably wouldn't ever have to shoot anyone farther than twelve feet away. And if I did, I'd probably miss anyway.

I fired six shots. While he pulled the target forward, I nursed a gash on one knuckle where the gun had recoiled.

Four of my shots had missed the paper completely. One hit the paper but missed the human outline. The other hit my pretend assailant squarely in the leg.

"That'll slow him down some," Garnett said.

"I'm willing to practice," I answered.

"Good. 'Cause you need it."

On the way out I noticed the range also included a small gun shop. Garnett tried to nudge me past.

"I just want to browse," I insisted, walking to the counter.

A guy named Mack seemed surprised by my interest but calmly showed me a selection of firearms.

Even though a smaller Sig model fit a little more comfortably in my hand, I was still partial to the Glock for sentimental and practical reasons. Sentimental, because that's what my husband had used before he died in the line of duty; practical, because that's what I'd just fired and it felt familiar.

Garnett reminded me of my lackluster performance minutes earlier behind the trigger of a Glock and discouraged me from locking in on one particular handgun too soon.

"Someday, when you're ready to buy, I'll help you pick out a good model."

"Maybe I'm ready right now," I answered.

"I think it's best to wait," he said, countering.

Even though nobody asked his opinion, Mack the gun guy sided with Garnett. "I definitely think you should take your time."

Remembering the murdered gossip, I felt otherwise and slammed a credit card on the counter. My hunch was that one of Sam Pierce's last regrets was not being armed.

"Ring me up," I said. "And throw in some bullets while you're at it."

Mack and Garnett looked at each other. Like they were each waiting for the other to speak.

Mack finally said, "You know there's a waiting period and background check on handguns, Ms. Spartz."

Clearly he recognized me from television. "That's fine," I told him. "I can wait a few days. Let's do the paperwork."

"It's the background check," Garnett said. "Not a chance you're going to get approved right now."

Mack nodded in agreement. Even embarrassment. "I'm sorry."

And suddenly I realized that they were alluding to the fact that a cloud of suspicion hung over me in a murder case. "Homicide by gunshot" was probably what Sam's death certificate read.

So I left empty-handed and humiliated.

Garnett swung by my place to drop me off on his way to the airport. Our lips lingered. His hand reached for my arm as I opened the car door.

"I might be out of touch for a couple of days," he said.

He had my interest, but one thing I've learned from years of news interviews is to never interrupt a subject who seems in a mood to confide. The same could be said for lovers.

Since ours was a long-distance liaison, and since we were both grown-ups, we hadn't defined our relationship verbally, just physically. Garnett was starting to hint for more of a future, and I suspected what we felt for each other could eventually turn into undying love, but that wasn't where this conversation was headed.

"Where are you going?" I finally asked.

"I'd rather not say."

"Do you need your passport?"

He didn't answer. So I didn't know whether he was staying in the Midwest or heading for the Middle East. I was curious. National security opened a wide range of possibilities. Many of them newsworthy.

It even had a sexy ring to it. So I kissed him again, enthusiastically, in a manner he wouldn't forget.

Later, alone in bed, I thought about my husband, Hugh Boyer. We kept plenty of secrets from each other, too. I routinely left him in the dark on my TV investigations because I didn't want him caught in the middle if I closed in on a crony of his. And as bodyguard to the governor, Hugh kept quiet about the location of certain political skeletons. Maybe that kind of mystery intensified our brief time together before he was killed on the job.

Then I realized I hadn't thought about the actual cause of his death for a long time. He died from an improvised bomb. A pickup truck with a full tank of gas and a load of chemical fertilizer, driven by a malcontent with a grudge. These days, he'd be called a domestic terrorist. Back then, he was simply called deranged.

And my man? Hugh was one of thirteen in the wrong place at the wrong time.

CHAPTER 14

I slept poorly that night. It was like I didn't know where to put my arms. They seemed to be getting in the way of the rest of my body.

Because I couldn't get comfortable, my mind started racing. I did everything I could not to think about bloody chickens. Instead I speculated about Garnett's quest. Might it be dangerous? Whose phone number did he give them in case of an emergency?

A friend of mine who knew us as a recent item had broached concern about him being a good decade older than me. I never thought about the age issue when we were together, only when we were apart. And we were often apart in those days.

Life being such a compromise, I tried to clear my head by mentally debating whether it was better to land a man with nerves of steel or abs of steel.

That was no way to drift off to sleep, so I tried concentrating on work. Not fascinating things like

murder and mayhem, but tedious tasks like tran-
scribing interviews or carrying tripods up stairs.

I thought back on my conversation with Miles
about our legal recourse to get the gun-carry permit data. He'd been discouraging.

This wasn't a case of a government agency
stonewalling by withholding clearly public information—they often do that in hopes newsies will
move on in search of an easier story. In this case,
the data was plainly deemed private by law. To get
formal access, we'd have to get the law changed or
get a judge to strike it down.

"That's not going to happen," Miles said. "The
NRA will lobby and appeal this issue forever. We
wouldn't stand a chance."

So I needed to find a back door to the gun permit information. But right now, I needed to think
of something hypnotic, or I'd never reach REM
sleep before morning.

Unbidden, the image of spinning wind turbines came to mind. Behind the sedative motion
I started hearing songs with wind in the lyrics, almost like lullabies.

The music started with the sweeping prairie
melody "They Call the Wind Mariah" from the mu-
sical *Paint Your Wagon.* Then I found myself wondering if Elton John's observation on living your
life like a candle in the wind might be an apt sound
track for my own memoir. Before I could come
to any conclusion, Bette Midler was advising me

to find a hero who could be the wind beneath my wings.

The last thing I remember is Bob Dylan telling me the answer was blowin' in the wind.

But if it was, I fell asleep before I could hear it.

The next morning, windmills still on my mind, I went into my home library and pulled Miguel de Cervantes's *Don Quixote* from the shelf. Written more than four hundred years ago during Spain's golden age, it's widely considered one of the most influential novels of all time. I kept a special collection of dusty books—best-sellers of yesteryear—because I believed there to be no truly new themes in literature, and I liked to line up breakout books from today next to their kindred noted predecessors.

By chronicling the chivalric adventures of his man of La Mancha, Cervantes expressed his belief that we all have a mission to try to right the wrongs of our world. Though endearing in his exploits, Don Quixote failed more often than he succeeded.

While knights have been out of style for centuries, when it comes to fighting injustice (and this is not something I go around telling people, because it sounds pompous), I regard investigative journalists as modern-day white knights. Idealists in a decadent society. Or I used to feel such zeal. Now cost and time have taken titanic hits as news audiences decline and a panic sweeps the industry like the black plague once swept Europe.

Okay, maybe that comparison is a bit of an exaggeration. Journalists aren't perishing, they're merely being laid off. But there's no doubt the once chivalrous goal of newsrooms—comfort the afflicted and afflict the comfortable—has changed for those newsies left behind.

Nowadays, it's feed the beast.

I put Cervantes's classic on a stack by my bed to page through later. I brushed my teeth, primped in the mirror, and left to face an increasingly hungry monster.

CHAPTER 15

On my way to the station, I drove by Sam Pierce's house. I'd never visited him socially—he was more likely to crash a party than host one. And if I had been invited, I'd have suspected a trap and declined.

I knew where Sam lived from reading the newspaper story about his murder. I wondered how his killer knew.

The neighborhood was upscale—between Hennepin Avenue and Lake of the Isles—his street a desirable address. More so than my current rental on the other side of the freeway near Lake Nokomis.

A two-story with stucco and stone, Sam had done better on a newspaper salary than I'd have expected. The garage was detached, as were most in Minneapolis, including mine. That meant he was open to attack during the time it took him to park his car and walk to his house. In his case, twenty yards of vulnerability that proved fatal.

I parked across the street to take in the general atmosphere. Fog hung in the air. The crime-scene tape was down. A few newspapers lay, unclaimed, by the front door. Besides losing a high-profile columnist, the Minneapolis newspaper had also lost a subscriber.

Sam hadn't shown up for work. Hadn't called in sick. His editor had shrugged off his absence because he wasn't held to the same nine-to-six shift during which most of the news staff toiled. Gossip happened anytime. Anywhere. Sam set his own hours.

Police said a friend had found his body in the backyard. That put it out of view of the street.

I jumped when a hand reached over and tapped on my car window. A woman tapped again. I lowered the window a few inches to see what she wanted. She wanted to know what I wanted.

"We don't need gawkers."

I waited at a downtown coffee shop, shrouding my face behind a newspaper that seemed thinner each day.

About a half hour later, Della Sax walked in, ordered her daily cappuccino, and, sipping it, headed across the street to the Hennepin County medical examiner's office. I'd worked homicides with Della before. She wore ordinary street clothes now, but in the lab, she wore pink scrubs and rhinestone earrings.

She liked to look nice, even though her clients were dead.

"Hey, Della." I wanted to chat with her in person because I feared she might not return my phone calls under the circumstances. "The cops are blaming your office for all the leaks on the last two murders."

She paused on the sidewalk, shaking her head.

"Not us, Riley. So don't think you're going to get anything either. Especially not in the Pierce case. And the second you mention his name, I'm walking inside and not looking back."

I gave her a much-practiced puzzled look. But she wasn't buying it.

"I mean it, Riley. Nothing about his autopsy. This is your only warning."

"Della, I get where you're at, but I'm so tired of telling people that I know nothing about his death. I wish the cops would just arrest his killer so my life could go back to normal."

I held the door open for her since both her hands were full, and she thanked me. I used the good deed as a means of following her into the building.

"How about if we talk about the decapitated woman instead?" I asked. "The cops say her body was dumped. I imagine if they ever find the actual crime scene, it's bound to be bloody."

"Not necessarily," Della said. "Bodies don't really bleed after death. You see, bleeding requires a beating heart. If a victim's head is sawed off while they're alive, like Islamic terrorists with American captives, well, that would result in considerable blood."

Another image to block from my mind—I had enough nightmares—yet I admired how Della could talk so clinically about the horrible. Must have come from years on the job of looking death in the eye.

"But if the victim was killed before she was beheaded?" I asked. "What then?"

"The more time that passes the more the blood congeals," she explained. "If a head was not amputated until eight hours or so after death, you'd be surprised how little blood might flow."

"Really?" Perhaps my chicken dream was out of place in this particular investigation.

"Well, the carotid and jugular would still empty, but the crime scene would not necessarily be the gruesome mess you're envisioning."

"Not even with Luminol and blue light?" I'd seen plenty of TV forensics shows and knew my jargon.

She was not impressed and accused me of watching too much *CSI*. Since crime scenes had gone prime time, viewers were always trying to tell her how to do her job, and juries were always expecting forensic miracles.

"So the headless woman in Wirth Park," I asked, "what happened to her?"

"I don't have many actual details to share. Not only can't we identify the victim, we can't identify a cause of death beyond 'homicidal violence.'"

"Why not? Was it some sort of exotic poison?"

"No, she died from the neck up."

"Huh?"

"She might have been strangled, smothered, beaten, shot, or had her throat slit. Unless we find her head, we're stumped."

This was a new twist. One Clay hadn't reported. I decided this nugget would make the story mine.

I smiled. "Thanks, Della."

"Hey, it's nothing special, Riley. I would have told anyone who asked. You just asked first."

In this business, first is all that counts.

The morning news meeting was under way when I walked in with word that the murder of the headless woman was even more mysterious than first thought.

"Hey, that story's mine," Clay said as I was reciting all the possible, undetermined causes of death.

"Sorry, Clay, but I stumbled across it while I was checking sources on something else. There's plenty of room on this story for both of us."

"How'd you like it if I honed in on your windmill story?" he said.

"Give it a shot," I said encouragingly.

Certain that I had a lock on the locals, I predicted Clay would fumble in the farm field.

"Some neighbors have reason to despise the wind farm," I said. "Maybe you can get them to talk."

He seemed surprised I called his bluff, but from the look on his face, he had no interest in taking me up on it. He may have been from Texas, but he didn't seem the tumbleweed type.

"You could ride the chopper." I knew his old station didn't have a helicopter and new hires are sometimes as eager to get in the air as on the air.

"No, the ceiling's too low," another reporter pointed out. "Can't see the top of the IDS Center."

The rule for flying the chopper was that unless Minneapolis's tallest building was fog free, it was grounded.

"And unless it's breaking news, we can't justify the expense," Noreen added.

"Well, Riley, I say there's plenty of stories to go around," Clay said, "and I think you should go round up your own and leave the headless case to me."

"Sometimes it helps to get a different perspective on a story," I said. "I might ferret out things on this murder that slip by you; same with the wind bombings. Let's trade for a day."

We turned toward Noreen to arbitrate this familiar newsroom friction. She sided with Clay.

"I think mixing up the stories complicates things." She told me to take Malik and head back to the wind farm for some sleuthing. "Talk to these discontented farmers and see what you can shake loose."

I explained there was a chance the authorities might be blocking cell calls again if they were on the scene and that I wouldn't be able to contact the newsroom until I was on my way back.

She said I didn't necessarily need to turn in a story for that night unless something broke. And to make me feel I was getting a special plum, she said, "You can call this a research day." But then she ruined things by telling Clay that he could have extra time for his headless homicide report.

CHAPTER 16

Usually, on long-distance stories, I would drive the van while Malik slept. He had learned to nap on demand during his army days. But I wanted to spend the road time multitasking on my cell phone by grousing to any source who would listen to me about wanting the gun-carry permit data.

Unhappy with this division of labor, Malik wasn't speaking to me, but that just made my job easier.

"I have no way of knowing where envelopes without return addresses come from."

I made the same subtle hint in phone conversations with several computer-literate sources in the state law enforcement world. Occasionally the trolling technique would work, and someone would take pity and drop something in the mail to me. More than one had confided during our discussion that they agreed the conceal-and-carry list should be public.

"I think we have a reasonable chance of scoring." I gave Malik a little punch in the arm but his attention seemed focused on driving and not me.

Then I called my dad to get a little more background on Charlie Perkins and Billy Mueller.

"Take the next left, Malik." I pointed to a gravel road. "We're getting close to Charlie's place."

Entrenched deep in the sensibility of farmers who have lived next to the same families for generations is the idea that you can't tell folks what to do with their land. Whether they want to plant sunflowers when everybody else is planting corn or raise elk when everybody else is raising cattle . . . that's their right.

Same if they want to farm the wind.

Charlie didn't have roots to the land going back more than a century like the others. He'd moved in maybe five years earlier, buying the homestead after old man Meyer died. On one level, Charlie had more in common with his neighbors' ancestors than with them—he picked where he wanted to settle, as opposed to living there because his parents, grandparents, and great-grandparents had.

Those family trees had developed a model of Minding Your Own Business that helped them all get along year after year after year. To them, Charlie complaining that he didn't want to look at wind turbines was about as silly as whining about having to look at sunflowers or elk.

I understood the locals' take on things; I'd been raised with that same philosophy. But Malik and I were there to hear Charlie's logic. He was sitting at a picnic table brushing a collie when we drove in the yard. The dog stood up to bark at us.

"About time someone gave a damn what I think," Charlie said when we told him why we'd come.

We sat and talked, the wind farm about half a mile away in both directions. I would have liked Malik to frame his head shot with a wind turbine in the background, except Charlie refused to let us record his interview. So the camera sat by our feet.

"Bad enough I have to look at the things, now I'm living in a war zone."

I found it surprising Charlie used that term and again wondered if he'd been part of Honeywell's long-abandoned cluster-bomb division. I decided to throw a few softball questions.

"What made you decide to retire here?"

"Wanted to get away from the city," he said. "Thought this would be God's country. Instead it's the devil's playground."

Charlie was full of colorful sound bites. Certainly his reluctance to appear on camera didn't come from being bashful. I figured he just wanted to make me beg him to change his mind. I tried to coax him by telling him what a good talker he was . . . what a critical viewpoint he held . . . and my favorite, that this wasn't live TV and he could always start over if he stumbled.

"We can even put your dog in the shot," I offered.

"I'm a professional," Malik added. "I'll make you look good."

"Not interested in all that glamour," Charlie said, "just want a simple life."

He replied with such ease I wondered if perhaps he had worked in Honeywell's media relations department.

"I hear you worked for Honeywell, Charlie. So what did you do during your career?"

"Sales."

His answer seemed rehearsed.

"So what did you sell?"

"Thermostats."

"Sounds like an interesting job."

He nodded rather than elaborate.

I didn't believe Charlie for one minute. He felt like a man with a secret. But I didn't want to dig too deep without a camera rolling.

"Were you always based in Minneapolis?" I asked.

"Traveled around the world. Met lots of interesting people." Then he asked Malik what part of the Middle East he was from. And my photographer explained that while his father was from Pakistan, he had been born and raised in the United States.

"What do you think about the wind turbine bombings?" I wanted to get to the point of our visit.

"Too late now. The time to send a message was before the spinning started, not after."

"Any idea who might be mad enough to go boom?"

"You must be here because you wonder if it's me." He said it nonplussed, as a statement, not a question.

This time I didn't answer.

"I'm an old man. Blowing up wind farms is a young person's project."

Charlie looked like an early retiree to me. Yes, his hair was white, but planting a bomb is not the kind of crime that requires brute strength.

"I'm following every lead I get," I said. "That's why I was hoping you might have some ideas, sitting here in the middle of the action."

He shook his head. "I'm as puzzled as the rest of the inhabitants."

Then he bent over, pulled the hem of his pants up to his knee, and showed us an artificial leg.

"What's your story?" I asked.

"Don't like to talk about it. But this way you don't have to waste time with me. As you can see, I'm in no shape to bomb anything."

Then he pulled himself out of the chair and told us he had stuff to do. I thanked him, gave him a business card, and asked him to call me if he heard anything.

Charlie didn't have to walk far to get inside, but I noticed he moved with less difficulty than my father.

On the walk to the car, Malik scolded me. "He's probably a highly decorated war vet, and you practically accused him of being a terrorist."

I disputed his interpretation of our encounter and insisted I wasn't crossing Charlie Perkins off the suspect list just because he was missing a leg. An arm maybe, not a leg. Because as far as I could see, he wasn't missing a beat.

I recognized my schoolyard nemesis, Billy Mueller, even though he'd added some weight and lost some hair, but he didn't seem to remember me at all.

He told his wife to run get the yearbook. They apparently kept it handy on the coffee table to relive his football glory days, because she was, literally, back in a minute.

"Oh yeah, you wore the funny glasses," Billy said.

Those and the braces on my teeth reminded me why my yearbook is buried in a box in the back of some closet or another.

"So you're on TV?" Billy asked. "Can you put me on TV?"

I hate it when people ask me that. So does Malik. But he grabbed the camera so he could at least get a shot of Billy in case he ended up being important.

"I can't make any promises, Billy. I'm doing a story on the turbine bombings and talking to people in the area. If you're the one who did the blasting, I can for sure put you on TV."

I smiled like I'd be doing him a favor; he wasn't dumb enough to fall for that one.

"Least I don't have to worry about explosions in *my* farm fields," he laughed.

"So you're okay without the wind farm?" I asked.

"No, I'm good and mad. Just doesn't seem fair everybody else is getting a wind check but me."

"I know what you mean; my folks lost out, too." I played my you-and-me-against-the-world act.

"Then you can understand how I'm not feeling too sorry if that wind farm gets blown to pieces."

I nodded like Billy and I were both on the same page, then said my good-byes to him and his missus. I didn't leave a business card because I really didn't want either of them calling me. And he seemed so eager to appear on the news, I could see that being a continuing problem.

Just then a young girl came out of the henhouse, carrying a basket of eggs and handing it to her mother. I wondered if they were for eats or ammunition.

Her father's final instructions to me: "If you put me on TV, be sure and call me Bill, not Billy." I guaranteed it with a thumbs-up, and Malik and I climbed into the van.

"Where to now?" he asked.

Neither stop had netted a reportable development. "I'm not sure, Malik. While we're here, let's shoot a generic standup to plug in a future story."

He parked at a spot where three turbines were lined up artistically over my shoulder.

((RILEY, STANDUP))
WIND IS BECOMING
THE STATE'S FASTEST-
GROWING CASH CROP AND
CHANGING THE LANDSCAPE
OF RURAL MINNESOTA.

I figured that line should fit in almost any wind farm news story, whether it centered on the ecology or the economy. As we did a couple of takes, a pickup truck with two men stopped to watch. One of them owned the land where we were standing, the other worked at the gas station in town.

"Anything new happening with the bomber?" the farmer said.

"You tell me," I answered. "What do you hear?"

I expected more ranting about Islamic extremists but only got shrugs.

"Any strangers in the area?" I asked.

They both shook their heads, but then the farmer paused and said, "Just those environmentalists."

"What do you mean?" I asked.

"We've started catching them collecting dead bats around the turbines."

"Dead bats?" I asked. "Sure you don't mean birds?"

"Come take a look."

Malik and I climbed in the back of the truck and sat on a pile of rocks covered with fresh dirt, just picked out of a cultivated field. A routine farm chore. The man drove through harvested soybean rows toward a turbine a mile away, then stopped.

"Follow us," he said.

The other man kicked at the mangled plants and upturned soil, telling me, "Keep your eyes open."

I wasn't sure what we were looking for, but Malik followed behind, getting video of the casual search, until the man called out, "Here's one."

I looked where he was pointing and saw a furry brown body. I turned it over with my foot. It reminded me of a worn leather glove. Because I grew up on a farm, I'm less queasy around dead animals than most women, so I picked it up in order for Malik to capture the scale on camera.

About the size of the palm of my hand, the creature definitely had the wings of a bat. Its eyes were open and glassy, but it didn't seem to have any external injuries—mysterious if it had flown into the turbine blades.

"You find dead bats often?" I asked.

"Not 'til the turbines started up," he answered. "If there's one there's usually more."

In the next few minutes, we found two more.

"Did you tell this to the investigators?" I asked.

"They weren't interested," he answered.

Holding up the dead bat, I recorded a short standup—this one not generic. Insurance in case the bat angle developed into a news element. Malik started the shot tight on the frizzy corpse, then pulled wide to me with a turbine spinning in the background.

> ((RILEY STANDUP))
> FARMERS TELL US IT'S
> NOT UNUSUAL TO FIND DEAD
> BATS ON THE GROUND
> AROUND THE TURBINES . . . BUT
> THE REAL MYSTERY IS . . . WHY
> DON'T THEY HAVE ANY
> VISIBLE INJURIES?

I would have liked to wrap the bat in some notebook paper or something, but I'd left my shoulder bag in the truck. So I simply stuffed the bat in my coat pocket to show to Noreen, figuring the animal-in-jeopardy angle would certainly make her more enthusiastic about the wind story.

"So you've seen people collecting the dead bats?" I asked the men.

"They say it's for a study," one said.

"As long as they don't cause trouble we don't care," the other added. "Do you think they might have something to do with the explosions?"

I didn't know, but I thanked them for the bat tour and promised to let them know if I learned anything. Then Malik and I headed for my parents' place.

"Come in and have something to eat," my mom said.

"Sit awhile," Dad suggested.

I lied and said we were on deadline and could only stay long enough to ice the bat, but Malik accepted a sloppy joe sandwich. So we were stuck there for as long as it took him to chew and swallow.

My generation came of age when the bottom was falling out of the cattle market. When it cost more to feed steers than they sold for. I remember a stretch during my youth when it seemed like beef was all we ate for a year because we had cattle on the hoof but no money in the bank. Whenever I tell that story, my mom always insists I'm exaggerating and that we also had green beans and sweet corn.

In fact, she offered a scoop of corn just then to Malik, who smiled and held up his plate.

None of my siblings became farmers, nor did I. Each time one of us left the homestead made it easier for those left behind. Seems kind of brutal to call it the One Less Mouth to Feed philosophy of raising children, but it was no exaggeration to call it a hard-knock life.

A shrink friend once speculated that's why I put in so many hours at work: I'm afraid if this TV thing doesn't work out, I'll have to go back to the farm.

Now my parents rent out the land and feed-lot, watching other people sweat. Not a bad way to spend retirement while they wait to die in their sleep on the home farm. They have their funerals planned, all the way down to buying plots in the same country cemetery where their forefathers and foremothers were buried. They even have a head-stone mounted on their gravesite with the dates of death left blank.

"We know how busy you get," they had re-sponded to my earlier questions about whether it was creepy to scheme so much about one's own passing, "especially during ratings months." So to make me feel involved in their pending demise, they handed me a list of their favorite hymns.

While Malik cleaned his plate of the last ker-nel of corn, I looked for a small cooler for the dead bat, settling for a shoe box with ice cubes. I asked my parents if they'd heard anything about either the bats or the environmentalists.

News to them. "Quite the puzzle," Dad said without too much interest. Dead animals in rural Minnesota don't attract much attention unless a trophy buck is poached.

But since we were on the subject of death, Mom started quizzing me about the gossip homi-cide. And I regretted stopping in to see them.

"Riley, we hear all sorts of things in the news that have us worried about you."

"Very worried," Dad interjected.

They were the kind of couple who finished each other's sentences. Since he was a baritone and she a soprano, their conversations often had a melodic tune.

I didn't care for the topic at hand: Sam's murder. Times like this made me sorry I helped them get satellite TV—just more channels to get them riled up over stuff they can't do anything about.

"Don't worry, either of you," I said. "The media's just going crazy. This will all blow over soon."

Dad tried asking other questions about the gossip columnist homicide, but I told him my lawyer had expressly forbidden me to discuss the case, even with family. My answer seemed to make him even more nervous. And that agitated my mom.

"How can we help you if you won't tell us what's going on?" she asked.

"Listen, Mom, Dad. I don't need your help, and even if I did, there's nothing you can do."

Then I insisted Malik and I really needed to hurry. We didn't do hugs or kisses because we're not a touchy-feely family, but Mom gave Malik a plate of peanut butter bars with chocolate frosting to eat in the car.

On the drive back, Ozzie, from the assignment desk, called to ask us to detour off our route to shoot a jackknifed semi and the ensuing traffic jam. Malik groaned.

I turned on news radio and heard heavy promotion for what was being billed as Clay Burrel's exclusive about how—minus her head—authorities were helpless in determining a cause of death in the Wirth Park homicide.

Of course I was ticked; it should have been my story. "Jerk," I said as I switched channels. Drive-time radio promotion is effective in driving viewers to their TV sets the minute they get home, so I expected Clay's numbers would be high.

When we reached the station, Noreen was busy and brushed me off when I tried to tell her about the dead bat. So rather than press its leathery wings against the glass walls of her office in a vampirish bid for attention, I wrapped it in a piece of newspaper and stuck it in the station's freezer.

CHAPTER 17

I fumbled with the trash when I got home. Garbage day always reminded me I was a widow. Some days I could forget my loss, but never on garbage day. The weekly walk to the curb was the antithesis of my walk down the aisle. Instead of carrying a bridal bouquet, I carried smelly rubbish.

Some papers fell out as I dumped one wastebasket into another. One was Garnett's boarding pass to MSP airport.

How romantic, I thought, pressing it against my heart. The minute Garnett heard Sam Pierce was dead, he sensed my trouble and rushed for a seat on the next plane.

But then I noticed the arrival date was the day *before* Sam was killed. Why would Garnett have lied? And what reason would he have had to come to town without telling me?

I'm ashamed to say the first thought that came to mind was not that he was cheating on me but that he owned a gun and was in the correct geographic region to have killed Sam.

It would have been a relief to laugh together at the zany idea. Him slaying Sam to protect my reputation. A very outdated motive. Something an obsessed Don Quixote might do for his Lady Dulcinea. But Garnett's love for me couldn't have been strong enough to kill in cold blood. Though if it was, would that make me an accomplice?

The truth was, Garnett was one of the good guys in life, so him killing Sam didn't compute. But what was he doing in town that he needed to keep secret?

Some couples are doomed unless they agree on all the big issues in life, like politics, religion, and where to call home.

Garnett and I clashed in all those areas and more. But even though we had our share of squabbles—many of them my fault—I still believed we had a chance at happy-ever-after because we agreed on something pretty specific: that the film *Saving Private Ryan* contains the best movie dialogue ever written.

There are lots of lines that stand out, but we give the prize to the scene where Tom Hanks tells his platoon that, in real life, he's only a small-town English teacher. "I just know that every man I kill, the farther away from home I feel."

Is that enough to build a relationship on?

To prove my confidence in him, I considered crumpling up the boarding pass, throwing it in the trash, and never speaking of it again. Instead, I stuck it in a desk drawer.

The trash can was behind the house, out of view of company. As I went out the back door to wheel it to the front curb, I saw a shadow moving along the side of the garage. I stopped, then heard the crunching of feet on gravel.

Instantly, I remembered that Sam Pierce had been killed in his own backyard. I went back inside, locked the door, and decided to wait until morning to put out the garbage.

I turned on all the lights in the house before finally falling asleep on the couch. In the morning, I didn't wake up until I heard the garbage truck driving past.

CHAPTER 18

Sam Pierce was buried.

I wasn't there, but Clay was. I'd been advised by my boss, my attorney, and my own common sense to stay far away from the service. Because killers sometimes attend their victim's funeral, I figured the cops would use my presence at the ceremony as further evidence of my guilt.

But I remained curious about the service. So I hovered by the edit booth where cameraman Luis Fernandez was loading the funeral scenes into the station server. Videotape is a thing of the past in most newsrooms; now stories are shot on digital cards. Normally photographers screen the best shots and edit out the extraneous. Reporters and producers view the remaining video later on their computers.

"Luis, I'll babysit the booth if you'll let everything load," I said. A shot he considered slop I might consider significant.

"But this isn't even your story," he pointed out.

"But I want to watch it anyway."

He agreed, leaving me and my notebook alone in a room the size of a small closet.

The funeral ceremony took place at a cemetery chapel, not a church, so I figured Sam must not have been the religious type, which probably made it easier for him to commit the sin of gossiping guilt free.

I noted, with some satisfaction, very few flowers and only a dozen or so mourners. None of them seemed teary eyed, either. Then I felt ashamed of myself and wondered if I was really any better than the deceased.

Plenty of folks insist there is only a fine line between news and gossip. Especially since the tanking economy has made all media organizations a bit desperate for audiences. Technically, news is supposed to be the truth, while gossip only contains a grain of truth. No doubt, newsrooms will debate the coverage of pop king Michael Jackson's death for years to come as one of those irresistible overkill situations.

I quickly shifted from philosophical to embarrassed when Clay caught me looking at his funeral video and banged on the edit door window. The video on-screen was a zoom shot of a large photo of a flamboyant Sam on an easel next to a closed casket.

"Hey, you weasel." He opened the edit room door. "I should have guessed you'd be in here."

"Can't we watch together? Please?" I asked. "You got my headless lead."

He weighed my request. "Okay, little lady, but you owe me like banks owe taxpayers. A debt you'll probably never repay."

This time I didn't object to either the moniker or the metaphor, figuring he was probably right.

"Any good sound?" I asked.

"Not really. Afterward, a newspaper editor gave me a short bite about waiting for justice, but no one else wanted to go on camera."

Clay leaned against the wall because squeezing a second chair inside was impossible. Another wide shot came up on-screen, and I reflected that for all his bluster, Sam must have led a lonely life to have such a bleak turnout at a highly publicized funeral.

Was he mean because he was lonely? Or was he lonely because he was mean? The "Piercing Eyes" newspaper logo sat propped against another easel on the other side of the casket but gave no clue to the answer.

A minister gave a generic talk about how unfair life and death can be. He didn't include any personal anecdotes about Sam, probably because they'd never met. But he also didn't quote any Bible verses about gossips being the root of all evil.

Something caught my eye, and if Clay hadn't been watching with me just then, I'd have stopped the video, because one of the floral arrangements

seemed almost identical to the wildflower bouquet
I'd received at the station. Luis had shot a close-
up of the sympathy card but didn't hold still long
enough for me to read it.

Then the camera panned across the audience,
but the angle was mostly the backs of heads; individual mourners were hard to identify. I recognized a homicide detective off in one corner.
Standard procedure.

A good-looking man whom I didn't recognize
sat in the center front row. He wore his suit dark,
his hair slicked, and his expression sober. Perfect
funeral attire.

On one side of him sat the Minneapolis newspaper's top editor. Next to her, another editor
whom I'd met once before, but I couldn't remember his name. They had come to support the soul
of their fallen comrade.

A couple rows behind them, I was surprised to
see Rolf Hedberg sitting beside a couple of other
print reporters. After his inflammatory remarks
about Sam, showing up for his funeral seemed almost hypocritical. But I know from personal experience that it's much easier to badmouth people
when they're alive than dead. This might have been
Rolf's way of making amends.

On the other side of the good-looking man sat
a well-dressed elderly couple. I assumed they were
Sam's parents, until the older gentleman turned
his head.

I gasped in recognition, almost hyperventilating. Clay kept asking me what was going on. But I stayed mum because sitting in the front row of Sam Pierce's funeral were my parents.

"What do you see?" He shook my shoulders. "Tell me."

I shook my head, pretending to be choking; I might not have been able to keep up the ruse much longer, but a shrill scream came from down the hall toward the newsroom.

We both scrambled to open the door and get there first. After all, a scream can mean news.

Clay beat me by about a second and a half. Not bad considering he was a decade younger.

When I got around the corner to the coffee-maker counter, I saw Sophie, our lead news anchor, standing in front of an open refrigerator . . . a dead bat by her feet.

CHAPTER 19

A small crowd had gathered, including Noreen. Frankly, I was relieved all the fuss was just about the bat and nobody was actually going postal with a gun.

"Where did it come from?" A photographer nudged it gingerly with his foot.

"Did it bite you?" a newscast producer asked.

Sophie shuddered as she pointed toward the freezer.

"Calm down, everyone." I stepped forward, picking up the bat. "It's only a bat. I'm using it for a story. No big deal."

Everyone drew back like it was a vampire.

"Where did you get it?" Noreen asked. "How can you be sure it doesn't have rabies?"

Rabies? Visions of Old Yeller's lunging jaws replaced Dracula's fangs.

"I found the bat by one of the wind turbines," I explained. "It was dead. So were a bunch of other bats. I want to investigate what's killing them."

"Sophie, did you touch it with your bare hands?" Noreen asked.

"No," our anchor answered. "I pulled out some frozen leftovers and it fell out and scared me."

"I don't see the problem," I said. "This bat was dead when I found it, and it's still dead."

I waved the frozen bat to emphasize my point. The crowd drew back farther, even the men.

"We had a rabies case down in Texas," Clay said, "where a man contracted the disease from a dead cow's spit."

"Exactly," Noreen said. "Rabies is spread by saliva."

"Victim died a horrible death," Clay continued. "Hallucinations. Thirsty, yet terrified by the sight of water. No cure once you're past the incubation period. I stay as far away from bats as I can."

I'm sure Clay was trying to be helpful, but I didn't appreciate that level of detail just then. Especially when he started speculating about a series of painful injections in the stomach.

"Riley, put the bat in here." Noreen held out a small cardboard box that used to hold copy paper. I dropped the bat inside. She used a paper towel to cover it with ice from the freezer. "Now go wash your hands, Riley. Check them for open sores. Then meet me in my office."

Noreen turned to our assignment editor and said, "Ozzie, call the Minnesota Health Department and tell them we need a bat tested for rabies ASAP."

Then she instructed the station janitor to clean out the refrigerator and freezer and throw out all food. I expected my news colleagues to grumble over that last order, but no one did.

A few minutes later, Noreen was chewing me out in her office as the rest of the newsroom watched in fascination through the glass walls.

"What were you thinking?" She shook her arms wildly. "Bats are almost synonymous with rabies. How could you even take such a chance? This is really the last thing I need to deal with right now."

"I'm sorry, Noreen," I said. "All I thought about was the possibility I might be onto an interesting story about bats and wind turbines. Bats are dying out there, but they don't seem to be damaged by the blades."

My boss glanced into the bat box that sat on her desk, next to a wedding photo of her and a local animal rights activist, whose long face resembled that of a basset hound. Long before he became her husband, Toby Elness was a source of mine, and I had a hunch that if Noreen mentioned this bat mystery to him, he'd push her to cover it.

"I brought the bat back so we could have it autopsied, Noreen. I know how much you value animal stories. Honestly, I thought you'd be pleased."

"You know I care about animals, Riley. But viewers tune in to see likable creatures. Huggable ones that make us smile. I'm not sure they're going to care if bats are dying. Between rabies and vampires, not too many people are fond of bats."

"But they kill mosquitoes. And viewers hate them even more."

Noreen paused as if weighing that fact for promotional value here in mosquito-heavy Minnesota.

Then Ozzie stuck his head in her office. "The health department says they don't need the whole bat for testing. Just the head will do."

"Tell them we're sending the entire bat," Noreen said.

"Then they want us to take it to the University of Minnesota's Veterinary Diagnostic Lab," Ozzie said. "They'll remove the brain and send it to the health department for the rabies test."

Noreen handed me the box and told me to drive it over to the lab.

"Should I take Malik along to shoot the process? If the bat ends up having rabies, maybe we should do a story about it. We could show promo video of me getting rabies shots."

Noreen's eyes got bright and shiny, like they do when she hears a fresh, voyeuristic idea she thinks might draw viewers to our channel.

When we got to the veterinary lab, the receptionist gave me a form to fill out, told me to leave the bat, and said that I'd get a call later that day or early the next regarding the test results.

"Is there someone I could speak with now?" I

asked. "I'm from Channel 3 and we'd like to follow the fate of our bat with our camera." I motioned toward Malik, who was standing off to the side.

After a few minutes, a man in a white lab coat introduced himself as Dr. Howard Stang. I was a little wary of veterinarians after clashing with one in a pet cremation scam a while back.

But I explained the situation, and he led us back through an "Authorized Personnel Only" door, down a long hallway to a room with bright lights and medical equipment.

Malik clipped a wireless microphone on him and Dr. Stang put on rubber gloves and laid the bat on a stainless-steel counter next to a large knife.

"Bats found dead have a higher risk of carrying rabies," he said. "So you're wise to get it tested, at the least to eliminate the possibility of the disease, which I'm sure you know is fatal—if left untreated."

"The bat may have rabies," I conceded. "But I don't think that's what killed it." I told him about the wind turbines and the dead bat bodies below. "Beyond the rabies question, can you find the cause of death for this bat?"

As a veterinarian, he shared my curiosity and assured me he'd see what he could learn. Malik shot some cover of him handling the bat, but we left when it was time to remove its head.

When I got home that night, my parents' pickup truck was parked in my driveway, and they were sitting—overdressed—on the porch of my house. I didn't even know my dad owned a black suit, one reason I didn't recognize him right away on the funeral tape.

"Surprise!" My mom held up a loaf of rhubarb bread covered in plastic wrap that looked like it had been in the backseat too long.

"We came to cheer you up and show family support," Dad said.

"Well, you two sure look nice for the occasion." I plopped down across from them on a lawn chair. "I hope you didn't get gussied up just for me."

They glanced at each other a bit nervously. Dad, in a wicker chair, started rocking back and forth.

"We thought while we were in the Twin Cities, we should go shopping," Mom said.

Dad nodded proudly. "How do you like my new tie?"

"Can it." Clearly, they had each other's back. "I know you crashed Sam's funeral. Just promise me you didn't kill him."

"Why would we kill him?" Mom asked.

"I don't know," I answered. "Perhaps some crazy notion of protecting your daughter's reputation? Why would you go to his funeral?"

"We came to help find his killer," Dad said.

"Dad, leave it to the cops to do their job. You and Mom are just going to make things worse."

"But you're always saying if the cops don't catch the killer in the first days, forget it," Mom said.

"And you're always saying the cops sometimes get tunnel vision on one particular suspect and don't cast a wide enough net," Dad added.

So much for my thinking all these years that my parents never heard a word I said. "Yeah, but I'm also always saying investigating is no job for amateurs."

Then I remembered that small-town folks are keen observers . . . of their neighbors as well as strangers. Maybe my parents could be sources.

"So did you two learn anything useful at the funeral today?" After all, they did have a front-row seat on the action.

Dad shook his head. "It didn't really go like we expected."

"People kept telling us how sorry they were," Mom said.

"Yeah, Riley, everyone thought we were Sam's parents."

For about ten seconds, I couldn't breathe again.

It could be worse, I thought, consoling myself with the Minnesota all-purpose reaction to trouble. "Please don't tell me you told them you were *my* parents."

"Of course not," Dad said. "We were under-cover."

"Yeah," said Mom. "We just played along."

Now I pictured an even worse scenario, because the way I was raised, things can always be worse. "Please don't tell me you told them you *were* Sam's parents."

"No, certainly not. We let them think whatever they wanted to think," Mom said.

"One man said he wished we could have reconciled with Sam before his death," Dad said.

"What did he mean?" I asked.

"We figured he must have been estranged from his family," Mom said.

Interesting. That could explain the low turnout for his burial.

"He gave me his business card," Dad said, "and told me to call him if I ever wanted to know what my son was really like."

I took the card and noted a downtown Minneapolis business address. I put it in my pocket.

"Is it okay if we stay the night?" Mom asked.

"We don't want to drive back so far in the dark," Dad added.

I shook my head and unlocked the front door. "Oh, get in the house, you two."

Dad picked up an old suitcase and stumbled inside, bad knees and all.

I didn't tell them I was a little uneasy about the dark myself these days and actually welcomed some overnight company. And I sure didn't mention the word "rabies."

CHAPTER 20

The bat didn't have rabies.

A merely dead bat isn't as newsworthy as a rabid bat, particularly if a television reporter isn't having a long needle waved at her on camera. But Malik and I still went back to the lab to interview Dr. Stang about the animal's cause of death.

"It's puzzling," the veterinarian explained. "Your bat died of internal injuries consistent with barotrauma."

"What's that?" I asked.

"It's when a sudden drop in air pressure causes a mammal's lungs to expand rapidly to the point of rupturing. It leads to fatal internal hemorrhaging."

"In English, you mean its lungs exploded?" I asked.

"Yes. I've never actually seen anything like it before; it's similar to divers getting the bends. You say there were others?"

"A couple more. The farmer seemed to think dead bats were fairly common."

Dr. Stang seemed puzzled by their mysterious cause of death. "I'd like to study this further," he said. He explained that bats and birds have very different respiratory systems, thus bats might be more susceptible to barotrauma. Bat lungs are softer, while bird lungs are more rigid and better able to withstand rapid decreases in air pressure.

"Well, if you find any more bodies," he said, "bring them in."

The combination of exploding wind turbines and dead bats made me reach out to a name from the past. Toby Elness was quite interested in the bat enigma. And outraged.

"If wind power is killing bats, this needs to stop."

When I called him, I knew there was a chance my boss might consider it going behind her back. My defense would be that he'd been my source longer than he'd been her husband. I figured that ought to count for something.

Noreen and Toby were brought together by their love of animals and their proximity to me.

After their wedding, they'd honeymooned at a wildlife sanctuary in the rain forests of Thailand, helping care for injured gibbons in hopes they could be released into the wild.

Later they'd invited me to their home for a vegan dinner and shown me photos of them nurturing the wide-eyed jungle primates.

I'd oohed and aahed like it was a baby album while one of Toby's various dogs, a husky named Husky, curled up on the couch beside me. But that was the only socializing I'd done with them.

Toby's life mission was the Animal Liberation Front, whose priority was freeing creatures from research labs or fur farms. Their followers weren't above planting homemade bombs to accomplish their goals and draw attention to their cause. I hoped Toby hadn't gone that far himself.

The FBI considered the ALF among the country's most dangerous domestic terrorists, and I wondered if the FBI guy was pursuing that angle in the bombing investigation. But Toby had seemed genuinely unaware of the tiny bodies of dead bats until I told him.

"Bats are misunderstood," he said. "People worry about them getting caught in their hair or sucking their blood. But they are quite useful creatures."

He professed innocence of the wind turbine explosions, though he hinted that if the bombings were done in the name of protecting animals, that might be justifiable.

He promised to do some checking.

I also had made a note to look into the background of Charlie Perkins, the hobby farmer who didn't like looking at wind turbines.

According to his rap sheet, Charlie had led a fairly clean life. His only arrests came in the late seventies for vandalism and trespassing in Stearns County. Minor stuff until I realized one of the most controversial chapters of state history had been unfolding in central Minnesota.

The power-line protests. Hundreds of people, some family farmers, others sympathizers from the Twin Cities, had been arrested for various forms of civil disorder and property damage.

The confrontation happened long before my days in journalism, but I'd seen some of the old news footage. Tractors driving across frozen farmland, followed by rugged men and women carrying American flags. Normally conservative folks who felt the power companies were trampling their rights like they were bugs.

It was a guerilla war over a four-hundred-mile transmission line from North Dakota to the Twin Cities. Before it was over, surveyors would be attacked, steel towers toppled. But the line would be built.

If Charlie's soul held that kind of passion, wind turbines might make a tempting target.

When I went to Noreen's office, former newspaper political columnist Rolf Hedberg sat across from her desk. They made an odd couple. Next to her facade of Snow White's Evil Queen, he looked like a grizzled dwarf—the grumpy one.

Their conversation appeared cordial, though she wrinkled her nose once and shook her head several times. Rolf had been an occasional guest on our news, expounding on state history and newsmakers. The relationship was reciprocal—it gave us content; it gave the newspaper exposure. But without Rolf's connection to the paper, I was surprised Noreen would even give him the time of day.

I figured it unlikely she would tell me the scoop, so I followed as he left the building, offering to buy him a cup of coffee.

A few minutes later, I'd gotten the story that he was out of work and luck. His wife was tired of him hanging around the house all day, and frankly, he could use the money.

"Your boss turned me down," he said. "Didn't bat an eye."

"She's had a lot of practice. But honestly, Rolf, you didn't really think you'd get a job in television?"

I shouldn't have needed to tell a guy who spent a career working in the media that TV was a young person's game. During the current media slump, young and cheap was the only way to hire. I mean, look at Clay Burrel.

"I could do editorials, Riley," Rolf insisted, "like the station used to do."

"There's a reason the station stopped," I explained. "They didn't like controversy then and they sure don't want controversy now."

"But I have years of experience covering politics. And Minnesotans love politics."

"Channel 3 already has a political reporter, Rolf. Whom the audience has watched age gracefully before their eyes. Neither the viewers nor the station will dump her for you."

He hunched over his mug and didn't say anything. For him to even think Noreen would hire him was, frankly, egotistical. Lots of newspaper reporters think TV is easy and they can just step into the job, but it involves more fieldwork and stranger hours than they generally like.

"Really, Rolf, there's no way you want to go back to street reporting. Covering crime is all pushing and shoving. You're too classy for that."

His face scowled. "Don't assume I don't know anything about crime."

"I'm not saying you *couldn't* do it, Rolf. I'm saying why would you *want* to? I know you have your pride, but have you thought about simply trying to get back on the newspaper?"

He started drumming his fingers against the tabletop.

"I know you and the paper clashed because you didn't want to change beats or hours, but maybe you should think of it as a chance to reinvent yourself."

He didn't answer.

"How about freelance? Be a stringer. Then either of you can walk away if it doesn't work. They're bound to have some money after . . . after the Pierce situation." I really hadn't wanted to bring up Sam's death. "Call them and see what happens."

"I already did. It went bad." His voice had a monotone quality.

"Oh, I'm sorry, Rolf."

"I was certain they'd welcome me back after the . . . the Pierce situation."

I realized I'd misjudged his motive earlier. His job discussion with Noreen wasn't a case of conceit but desperation.

"You'll find something," I told him. "You've got a lot of connections. Something will come through."

"I was certain after Sam's death that they'd welcome me back." Rolf was starting to repeat himself. Not a good sign. "You don't understand, Riley. I even offered to take his job."

"What?" That's all I said out loud, but what I had been thinking was that if any good could come from Sam's death, it would be that the gossip columnist position might be eliminated permanently.

To hear that Rolf was actually willing to fill the role of my nemesis troubled me. Now I was the one scowling.

"Don't worry, Riley," he said. "I was going to be an accurate gossip columnist."

"I don't think there is such a thing. And if you told that to the paper, well, that might explain why they didn't give you the gossip slot. 'Accuracy' isn't part of that job description. The beat is reporting rumor."

"Well, I heard all the same rumors Sam used to hear, I just never reported them. But that could change."

Once upon a time, Rolf had been a confident newsman who routinely swatted the state's politicians. Now a dour man sat across from me, discouraged that the economy had kicked him at a time when he couldn't kick back.

"I need the money," he said.

I decided to change the subject—sort of. So I told him I heard he'd been at Sam's funeral and asked him what it was like.

"How'd you know I was there?"

"I'm a reporter, Rolf. It's my job to know these things." I didn't tell him I'd already seen video of the service. "For obvious reasons, I couldn't go. But I'm curious about your impressions."

"There wasn't much to it, really. A few prayers is all."

"How come you went? Didn't sound like the two of you were particularly close."

That's when he started to look really uncomfortable. And I wondered how much worse his story could get.

"Okay, Riley, this is going to make me seem like a jerk. I went because I thought there was a chance the bosses would be there and I could chat them up."

"You went to a funeral to interview for the deceased's job?" I tried to sound neutral, but it was hard.

"When you say it like that, it sounds bad."

That he recognized his blunder gave me hope he might be able to build a new life sans journalism. But I found myself thinking the Rolf Hedberg I used to respect as an award-winning newshound wasn't the same Rolf Hedberg having coffee with me.

That realization made me anxious to get away from him. So I wished him luck and told him I needed to return to work. As soon as the words left my lips and I saw the hurt look in his eyes, I realized he thought I was gloating about having a job.

"Rolf, that's not how I meant it," I said.

But he just waved me off, staying behind because he had nowhere else he had to be.

One block later, I forgot all about Rolf and his problems when I stumbled on Clay and Chief Capacasa laughing over mustard and relish at a corner hot dog stand.

I hung back across the street to observe the pair. Rather than risk being spotted together and raising suspicion in a dark parking garage like the Deep Throat scene in *All the President's Men*, they made their encounter seem casual and spontaneous. Right down to their parting high five.

I would have liked to go up, letting them know I wasn't fooled. But I thought it best they not know

I knew their secret. Knowledge is power, I reminded myself.

Chief Capacasa headed back toward the cop shop. Clay wiped the corner of his mouth, then looked straight at me and winked.

He was chewing when I walked up, but I think that might have been a ruse to avoid being the first to speak.

"What's up with you and the chief?" I asked nonchalantly.

He shrugged, swallowed, and replied, "Everybody has to eat somewhere."

CHAPTER 21

I grabbed the snail mail from my newsroom box and found a manila envelope with no return address. Inside, an unlabeled CD, wiped clean. Sometimes sourcing pays off, I thought as I kissed it.

I handed the disc to Xiong, who inserted it in his computer, then gave me a thumbs-up when rows of data appeared on the screen. I only had a quick glance, but it sure looked like the gun-permit data.

"How did you come to acquire this?" Xiong asked.

I gave him my Don't Ask look.

Whenever I'd received such a fortuitous package, I never tried to identify my source. Their anonymity kept both of us safer. Once, three years after a particular story ran, I crossed paths with a political aide who let me know she had been my Good Samaritan but that it was a one-shot deal and to never call her again.

Xiong and I huddled over his screen.

Too much information can be overwhelming. Having fifty thousand names is about as helpful as having no names. I gave Xiong my makeshift list of one hundred people who hated Sam Pierce.

"This will take time." He waved me away and hunkered down over his keyboard and monitor, formatting data and programming a search to see if any of the names overlapped. Should any of the Sam haters also show up armed, that could elevate them on the suspects list.

"Thanks." I kept my voice low to avoid distracting him.

He didn't even look up as I walked off.

"Good-bye!" Noreen was slamming down her phone when I entered her office. I hoped the call wasn't about me, or it would be like walking into a trap.

It was about Clay.

"It's the chief again," Noreen said. "Acting like he and I are all pals and wanting to know where Clay's getting his information. I told him it's none of his business."

As she finished ranting, I thought to myself, Nice try, Chief. You may fool my boss, but you don't fool me. I know who Clay's secret source is.

Noreen settled down, so I updated her on the bat situation. Good news, no rabies. Bad news, internal hemorrhaging.

She seemed disappointed about the rabies test results, confused about barotrauma. "So the turbines are smacking the bats out of the sky?"

"No. They kill the bats without even touching them," I said. "Their lungs explode when they fly too close to the blades because the air pressure drops suddenly." She did seem to grasp the analogy about divers getting the bends.

"This hasn't been reported, Noreen, and could be a big story. Especially with the turbines exploding, too."

Noreen drummed her fingers on her desk. I couldn't tell if she was nervous or impatient. I tried to quickly tie elements together like the bombs and bats. Then I divulged that I'd consulted Toby about the story, because I wanted her to hear that from me, on the job. Not from him, over supper.

The mention of Toby seemed to concern her. "How did he react?"

And then I realized what the problem had been all along. Once dead bats showed up, she was worried her animal rights activist husband might somehow be involved in this whole mess. And her fear wasn't all that outlandish. Their marriage was impulsive, two dog lovers tired of living with only their canine companions.

Neither of us knew Toby all that well before their wedding.

"Toby says this is the first he's heard," I said.

My answer soothed her, because usually if I think someone's guilty of something, I come right out and say it—though not on the air. As we discussed the story further, it was clear the bats' obscure cause of death intrigued her. I also pointed out that most national best-seller lists were dominated by vampire books.

"Even if viewers don't like bats," she conceded, "they do like mystery."

Then Noreen observed that Halloween was close and interest in bats might peak. So she gave me the go-ahead to start putting a story together and promised to talk to the promotion department.

I smiled.

> ((PROMO SOT))
> WHY ARE THE BODIES OF
> DEAD BATS BEING FOUND
> NEAR WIND TURBINES? TUNE
> IN TO CHANNEL 3 FOR THE
> ANSWER.

I smiled because promotion meant priority. And also because the station had devised a secret way to get more prime-time promotion slots for local news stories. When a thirty-second promo for a network show was airing during a commercial break, Channel 3 would run one of its own spots over it. Sometimes it rolled a couple seconds late and looked sloppy, but it still meant more viewer eyes on our product.

Of course, if the network ever found out . . . somebody more important than me would have to be fired.

Toby had someone he wanted me to meet. A human, not an animal.

I'd been to Tamarack Nature Center in White Bear Lake earlier that year, on a murder investigation, but this was a much tamer visit.

When Malik and I arrived, Toby introduced me to Serena Connoy, the local leader for Bat Protectors of America, a group concerned about the shrinking population of bat colonies.

"Our followers are few in number but devoted in cause." She explained they tracked hibernating and migratory bats.

A long black braid hung down her back. I imagined that style kept bats from getting tangled in her hair.

"Here's an interesting experiment." She showed us a large flight cage, tucked between some bushes, with several little brown bats inside. Their nest had been destroyed during a remodeling project when the bats were infants, and the group was trying to raise and rehabilitate them for release back in the wild.

Toby praised their mission. "Bats deserve freedom."

"Bats deserve life," Serena replied.

Malik shot some video of the tiny creatures, huddled together on the side of the cage. A fluorescent lantern hung in the middle to attract flying insects for them to eat at night.

Another bat volunteer stepped up and shook my hand. "Just call me Batman." He was long and lanky, with an angular face. I couldn't help but think the Batman logo on his black-and-yellow Bat Protectors T-shirt was a bit cliché as well as a copyright infringement.

"Bats are nature's superheroes," he said in defense of his attire. Then he cited several examples of their valor, including how the flying mammals can consume nearly a thousand mosquitoes an hour.

Our conversation took an interesting twist when Serena divulged that their group was the one collecting bat bodies under the Wide Open Spaces wind turbines as part of a scientific study. Other bat zealots made similar pilgrimages in California, Pennsylvania, and Maryland.

They'd observed the same thing I had: dead bats without visible signs of injury.

Most of them were hoary bats, red bats, or silver-haired bats—which all migrate through the Midwest in the fall. I asked if we could clip a wireless microphone on her for an interview and she agreed.

"Because so little is known about the species'

population size," she said, "these wind deaths could have far-reaching consequences."

After the barotrauma threat became known, national leaders of Bat Protectors had asked wind farms from coast to coast to stop the spinning, but the owners were insisting on more research.

That upset the Batman volunteer. "They say a few dead bats is not too great a price for going green."

I thought it unlikely they phrased their response so bluntly, but Toby was outraged. "This is about prejudice against bats."

Serena stayed calm, explaining that bats seldom collide with turbines because they use a sonar navigation system called echolocation. "While they can sense the actual turbine, the atmospheric pressure drop around the blades is an invisible hazard." She also stressed that both sides—wind farms and researchers—were working to negotiate some sort of compromise. "Perhaps using sound to deter the bats, or halting the turbines at certain times of night."

"What do you think of the bombings?" I had to ask.

"Our organization is peaceful and opposes breaking any laws, including the destruction of property. We believe education is a more productive route."

I was pleased to have corroboration that the bat casualties were not an isolated circumstance.

((RILEY, STANDUP))
CHANNEL 3 WASN'T ALONE
IN GATHERING BAT BODIES
. . . AN ENVIRONMENTAL
GROUP HAS FOUND A
PATTERN IN THE DEATHS AT
WIND FARMS HERE AND IN
OTHER STATES.

I had what TV news calls an "enterprise" story—one not easily duplicated by the competition. I figured I could have it on Noreen's desk tomorrow afternoon.

By day's end, work was work.

Besides the wind farm story, I was still trying to secretly investigate the gossip murder.

To stay alert, I scanned the walls of my office, noticing the surveillance photo of the woman and child, along with my flower note. *"Thanks Alot, Riley, Give Everyone The Disturbing Information Regarding That Bad Ass Gossip."*

I decided to compare the handwriting on my missive to the one on the condolence flowers.

From my computer, I pulled up the Sam Pierce funeral video, freezing the shot of the wildflower sympathy card. The message seemed strained: *"Be Assured Sam Took A Righteous Direction."* But the penmanship matched. I printed a copy, pinning it next to its bulletin board mate.

More promising, Xiong sent an email containing four names that overlapped both lists: possible armed suspects in the killing of Sam Pierce. I grabbed my archive file and pulled those particular gossip columns. Certainly there was no guarantee that the person who murdered Sam would have gone through the trouble of getting a gun-carry permit. But because these four had weapons and motives, it was a place to start.

Buzz Stolee—a pro basketball player who had walked, nude below the waist, behind a sports reporter going live from the locker room. The athlete claimed he didn't realize his image was being broadcast to more than a hundred thousand viewers. Instead of teasing him for being a dumb jock, Sam criticized the size of his . . . you know.

Ashley Lind—a former reporter for a competing station whom Sam literally ran off the air. He hated her hair. He hated her clothes. And he kept asking when the baby was due when she wasn't pregnant. Her contract wasn't renewed.

Ryan Meister—a local politician who lost re-election after Sam kept writing that he threw like a girl when he threw out a feeble first pitch for a Twins game.

And Tad Fallon—his society wife, Phedra, committed suicide by taking pills after Sam suggested she had an alcohol problem. She didn't. But she had a depression problem. Her husband had a gun. And the paperwork suggested he got it barely a week before Sam was gunned down.

I made a wall chart with all four names, putting Tad's first. But I reminded myself not to develop tunnel vision, like the cops sometimes did with suspects. I left space in between each name to add clues, should they develop. Then I leaned back to admire the short list.

I was reluctant to bring any of the names to the attention of the police, because in a recent missing person case I had suggested two suspects. They both ended up being in the clear; I ended up looking like an idiot.

And almost getting killed by the real murderer.

Matters were further complicated in the gossip case because the cops undoubtedly had their own short list of suspects. I just hoped it wasn't so short that my name was the only one on it.

Because Noreen had ordered me to stay away from Sam's homicide, any investigating I did had to be inconspicuous. I couldn't just call up the people on my list, identify myself as a Channel 3 reporter, and blurt out questions. Because if any of them called the station to complain, I was doomed.

Ashley Lind was the easiest of the four to find. I'd phoned a rival at Channel 7, where she used to work, and casually inquired if they ever heard from her.

"Good timing," I was told. "Or did you already hear?"

"Hear what?" I answered, hoping they weren't on the verge of breaking a story about her being arrested for murdering anybody. Not only would they have the news first, they'd have the best suspect file tape.

The only clue I got was a vague comment that a picture was on the way.

Seconds later, I clicked on an email attachment and instead of a mug shot, I saw a photo of a beaming Ashley in a hospital bed holding a bundled baby. She apparently really had been pregnant this time.

The birth announcement gave me a pang as I read the details about baby Neal's length and weight. Hugh had so wanted to be a father. But I'd wanted to wait. I wondered what our kids would have looked like.

I felt a different pang when I reached the date and time of Neal's birth and realized Ashley Lind had a seven-pound, ten-ounce unalterable alibi for Sam's homicide.

I crossed her name off the list. Then I reached in a card file I kept in my desk and mailed her some baby congratulations, telling her how lucky she was to be out of this sinking news business.

Most days, Channel 3's sports department holds little allure for me.

It's unusual for a market the size of Minneapolis–St. Paul to be home to so many major professional sports franchises. Twins baseball. Vikings football. Wild hockey. Timberwolves basketball. There's continuous debate on whether we can support them all; one team or another is always threatening to leave unless it gets a new stadium. The North Stars followed through and became the Dallas Stars. Now the Vikings are making similar noises.

What the players do on the field or ice or court doesn't particularly interest me; out of uniform is when they generally create news. Breaking laws versus breaking records. And over the years, various athletes have hit the front pages with driving transgressions, drug offenses, and sex crimes. But so far, not homicide.

I wandered back to the sports corner of the building to try to ferret out leads where Buzz Stolee might be found off the court. I didn't use his name specifically, because I didn't want any of the Channel 3 jocks giving him a heads-up. I merely asked if there was a downtown bar where the NBA guys hung out.

"Why do you want to know, Riley?" countered one of the sports producers.

"Yeah, you a groupie wannabe?" said another, leering.

I should have guessed this would be a waste of time. The sports staff liked to shield athletes from the news department. For Buzz, I imagined they'd be even more protective. He was a frequent guest on their *Sports Night* show. I'd run into him in the green room a couple of times, but he'd never given me a second look.

"I'd like to pick their brains on a possible story," I said.

"Any story *you* want to talk to them about can't be a story they want to show up in."

"And they're not used to women being interested in their brains."

I ignored him and the implication. He responded by throwing a basketball at me, then seemed surprised when I caught it.

To further the decoy ruse, I mentioned wanting to chat up football players as well. "I just want to run some info by them about the pro sports world and gauge their reaction."

"You're such a hot investigator, Riley, you don't need our help."

"Well, I guess that's good," I replied. " 'Cause I'm sure not getting it." I threw the ball back at him and turned away.

Normally the sports staff wouldn't be so snarly to my face, but they probably sensed I was not riding as high as usual. And sports journalists resent how when last-minute news breaks, their section of the newscast is often compressed to make room for political intrigue like a governor's Argentine mistress, or even just a fire as long as there's good video of actual flames and not just smoke.

• • •

The conversation was a lot shorter, and a lot more cooperative, when I called a political source and asked where former legislator Ryan Meister was working these days.

"Iraq," she answered.

"What?" I responded.

"Former National Guard sergeant, called up for service again. But now that the U.S. is talking of pulling out, look for him home next year and running for election again the first chance he gets."

"This time as a war hero?" I pictured him walking in a Fourth of July parade dressed in uniform, a combat ribbon on his chest.

"Better than throwing like a girl," she laughed.

A star-spangled alibi.

I crossed Ryan Meister off the list. And decided I needed to go barhopping.

CHAPTER 22

At six foot eight . . . I figured Buzz Stolee would be fairly easy to spot in the neighborhood around the basketball arena.

For organization, I'd starred the sports bars and nightspots on a downtown Minneapolis map. I started at Rosen's Bar and Grill because Hugh used to like to hang out there with his buddies after games. When that lead came up empty, I moved from bar to bar.

I was about to give up when I saw a line winding around the block outside a neon-lit nightclub. Like a lemming, I followed the herd as they slowly moved to the door. As I got closer, I realized that not everyone was waved inside. There seemed to be some sort of screening going on.

I saw the bouncers approve a pair of cute blondes in short skirts and low-cut tops despite the autumn weather. Two older women in business attire received frowns. I paid closer attention and noticed the gatekeepers didn't seem so picky about the menfolk. A man with a pudgy belly and a bald spot was waved inside.

As the line got closer to the door, I rolled up the waistband of my skirt like a parochial school girl and unfastened a few buttons on my blouse like a slut.

The two guards at the door looked at me, looked at each other, shook their heads simultaneously, and motioned for me to step aside.

"What do you mean?" I pressed them.

I'd stood in line for more than twenty minutes and I wanted inside, or an explanation of why not. But it didn't seem like the thugs were going to yield either.

"I deserve to go in just as much as anyone else," I insisted.

They blocked the door but ignored my questions. The crowd was starting to notice.

A woman in spandex tights looked at me funny, then shouted, "Hey, I've seen her on TV."

The bouncers looked at me again, but again they shook their heads. "No way. Not her."

I considered pulling out my media pass to try to bigfoot my way through the door. Especially now that I didn't have to worry about winding up as a headline in the "Piercing Eyes" gossip column.

But suddenly I realized my neckline was open far wider than felt comfortable. As I was adjusting my wardrobe malfunction, the two thugs each grabbed one of my arms and flung me off the curb and out of the way. Off balance, I was facedown in the grime of a Minneapolis street.

The crowd gasped and seemed to take a step backward. Just as I pushed myself to my knees, someone tall hoisted me to my feet.

"What's a nice lady like you doing in the gutter?" he asked.

My head only reached his chest, but I didn't need his jersey number to recognize Buzz Stolee's blue eyes and wavy blond hair.

"A little too much booze, I think, boss," a sidekick said.

"No." I shook my head. "Them." I pointed to the pair of bouncers, who were conspicuously facing the opposite direction. "Those guys didn't want me inside."

"Well, I've been in plenty of times and you're not missing anything," Buzz said. "Loud music. Loud people."

A red-haired woman in tight jeans and an even tighter halter top nudged him suggestively. But he ignored her and bent down to stare at me more closely.

"You look familiar," he said. "We met before?"

The way he said it made me think he was trying to figure out if we'd ever slept together. I explained that I was a television reporter and people sometimes recognized me from the air. "We might have passed each other in the hall at Channel 3."

His female companion scoffed at that information and flashed her midriff to possessively show either a tattoo or an autograph of Buzz's signature and jersey number above her navel. That gave me an idea.

"I bet people recognize you all the time from the basketball court," I said, trying to get the focus off me. "I'd love your autograph."

I pawed through my purse, pulled out a narrow reporter's notebook, and flipped the cover open to a blank page. Then I fumbled for a pen.

"Oh, sure," he said. "What's your name?"

"Riley Spartz." Oops, I hadn't meant to be that specific just yet. Sometimes my name scared people, but usually only if they were guilty of something. "But could you make it out to my dad instead?"

"Now I know who you are," he said. "You're the chick who threw the drink at that gossip goon." He started chuckling.

No point in denying the episode, especially since, eventually, that's where I wanted our conversation to go.

"I'm not usually so rude." I tried to sound apologetic and harmless.

"Hey, no worries." He leaned close and whispered in my ear. "Far as I'm concerned, the rat deserved it." Then he gave me a wink.

Now we were getting somewhere.

"That's a relief," I murmured back.

He smiled at our private joke.

"How about you let me buy you a drink," I said, "and I'll prove I'm fit for decent company by *not* throwing it in your face."

It was probably just a habit professional athletes acquire, but his eyes seemed to scan my entire figure, lingering on my still disheveled bust.

"Unless you give me a really good reason." I gave him a playful punch in the arm and fastened two buttons.

"No way I'm turning down such an interesting offer. This way, boys." He gestured toward a couple of guys hanging nearby.

"Hey, what about me?" The woman waiting at his side posed with her hands on her hips and a pout on her face.

"Later, honey."

Then Buzz put his hand against my back and directed me inside the club I'd just been barred from. I flashed a triumphant glare at the bouncers, but instead of looking apologetic, they pretended we'd never met. Buzz and I were shown to a corner booth, and his pals took a table nearby. While we waited for our drinks I wondered if he was packing the gun he was licensed to conceal and carry.

I was curious but not particularly worried. Even if Buzz had shot Sam, I didn't fear a bullet in the chest any more than he seemed to fear a martini in the face.

"So how'd it go down between you and Sam?" he asked. "Did his eyes go all wide and crazy?"

It seemed an odd question. But I thought back to that day at the newspaper bar where the real trouble started. My pinot noir versus Sam Pierce.

"He was definitely surprised," I said. "But he had been sort of asking for it." I was rationalizing my actions by blaming the victim, something I'd noticed suspects often do during camera interviews.

Buzz nodded sympathetically. "Were you glad you did it?"

"No." That was the truth and I meant it. "It was just one of those times when you snap."

"Was there much blood?"

"Blood?" I recalled the red stain on Sam's sweater. "There wasn't any blood. It was wine."

"Wine? I was talking about the shooting," Buzz said.

"I wasn't." From the look on his face, I realized that what I viewed as amiable chitchat, he took as a murder confession.

"I didn't kill the guy," I laughed. "In fact, I was starting to wonder if you might have."

"Me?" Buzz seemed amused by the idea. "Why me?"

"Well, you own a gun, and I don't."

He seemed startled that I knew that piece of information. And without saying anything, Buzz patted the outside of his jacket as if reaffirming the presence of a hidden weapon.

"So where were you the night he died?" I asked.

"None of your business," he answered. "But you're the one everybody thinks did it. You need an alibi more than me."

"But you hated the guy, too. After what he said in his column about your . . . you know." Suspecting Buzz was armed made me cautious about how I phrased the statement.

"Well, he was wrong about that." Buzz's voice dropped and took on an edgy tone. "And I got plenty of chicks who'll testify for me."

Seemed kind of early to be talking about testifying, but I wanted to avoid an argument.

"I don't doubt it for a minute, Buzz. Most of Sam's column was a lie—day after day. He lied about me and he lied about you. And he never ran a correction."

"Yeah." Buzz calmed down. "Guess the day finally came when he lied about the wrong person."

"Most likely that's what happened," I said in agreement. Besides the initial embarrassment, I knew Buzz still got razzed about Sam's article. At away games, it wasn't unusual for fans to yell "Pants! Pants!" at him when he came on the court.

I raised a glass and made a toast to the two of us. Buzz clinked his against mine. We each took a swallow. When I looked up next, he seemed to be gazing straight into my eyes. I blinked. He didn't. Nor did he turn away. I cleared my throat, took another sip, then stared back at him.

"You reporters, you're always after the truth, right?"

Those were the last words I expected to hear from his mouth. And he said it like he was looking for confirmation . . . not confrontation.

"Certainly, Buzz. Truth is the essence of my profession."

He stammered a bit, as if working up the courage to tell me something. "Getting back to that 'Piercing Eyes' column Sam wrote about me . . ."

"Yes." I spoke softly, in case he might be poised to confess.

"Gossip columnists aren't the same as regular reporters, right?"

"Absolutely. Our standards are quite different when it comes to truth."

"I was pretty upset with him."

"I don't blame you."

I wish I'd have thought to roll a tape recorder from inside my pocket, but I'd never considered our conversation might go this easily.

"I'm comfortable letting you be the judge," he said.

Now didn't seem the time to point out that juries, not judges, and certainly not journalists, decide guilt or innocence in murder cases.

"Go on, Buzz." I smiled to encourage him.

"Not here." He shook his head. "How about we go to my place, and I'll prove the truth about the size of my . . . you know." He patted himself down there to make sure I understood his proposition.

If my glass wasn't empty, I'd probably have flung the contents at his face—or crotch.

But I needed to keep open the possibility of future rapport, so I decided to appear flattered rather than disgusted by his offer. And maybe on one level I was. After all, the room was full of younger women who'd have loved to be sitting across the table from Buzz Stolee and going home with him later. And, I reminded myself, athletes act like all men would act if they could get away with it. So I extracted myself from a delicate situation by explaining that journalists can't have physical relationships with sources.

Tempted as I was.

"Honest, Buzz, I could get fired."

He seemed to accept my explanation as the only logical reason a woman would turn down such an invitation—and didn't appear to even consider I might be reluctant to be alone with a man I thought capable of murder.

When I got back to the station, I put a question mark by his name on the "Suspects with Carry Permits" chart. Under my theory, that left just Buzz and Tab Fallon. Both men had guns. Both had strong revenge motives. Whether either had an alibi, I didn't know. But I'd made some progress today.

So I went home—alone as usual.

On the drive, I swung by Wirth Park, where the headless body had been dumped. I'd seen the crime-scene video, but that was shot during the day. I wanted to feel the killer's world by moonlight.

The moon was actually hidden behind the clouds. But there were plenty of streetlights in the parking lot. Woods and tall grass covered the park grounds of more than seven hundred acres. If the murderer had wanted to hide the body, plenty of places beckoned where it probably wouldn't have been discovered until spring.

Instead, the homicide was a stop and drop. Almost as if the maniac wanted his ghoulish work found. Was he just passing through town? Fantasizing about the discovery of his horror? Or was he a local? Watching the news coverage with satisfaction?

I imagined tires rolling, a door opening, a torso hitting the pavement.

CHAPTER 23

A dead man is more newsworthy than a dead bat. So when Ozzie interrupted the morning meeting to say someone had been killed at the wind farm, I knew my story was gaining in respect under the TV news code of "If it bleeds, it leads."

Even Clay looked interested at the mention of death.

I grabbed the phone Ozzie was waving and heard my dad explain how all the neighbors were abuzz about the dead body in the weeds by one of the turbines.

"Did somebody shoot somebody?" Wouldn't have surprised me after all the trigger talk the other day.

"No," he said. "There was another explosion. Nobody knows anything more. Your mom and I are safe."

The bombers apparently decided to escalate matters with a human casualty. Chances were, I knew the victim. We could have been related. The bloodlines along that Minnesota-Iowa-state-line neighborhood were intertwined pretty deep. Everybody was a cousin of everybody else. This story had the potential to jerk some tears. Even mine.

"We're on our way, Dad," I said. "Tell folks not to talk to other media."

A bad break for me, the weather was clear but the chopper was in for maintenance. That meant it lay in pieces on the floor of the hangar. Sometimes the station rents a small plane for out-of-town shoots, but that only works if there's an airport runway nearby. And the aerials are never any good; the fixed wings get in the way. So once again Malik and I drove south even though news was breaking.

"No comment."

The county sheriff wouldn't release any details over the phone about the mysterious death. I hoped by the time we arrived, he'd have a statement. But in the meantime, their tight lips might mean the rest of the media pack was unaware of this latest development.

To save gas money, both the St. Paul and Minneapolis newspapers were attempting to conduct poignant telephone interviews about distant tragedies. Our television competitors hadn't been covering the wind explosions much because they happened on the far edge of the viewing area and because, unlike Channel 3, they didn't have dramatic video of a falling turbine.

But a dead body could change everything.

By the time we arrived at the wind farm, we'd missed the critical shot of the corpse being moved. Yellow and black crime-scene tape surrounded about two acres of land. In the distance, Scout and his handler, Larry, were sweeping the field.

My bachelor farmer pal Gil Halvorson had discovered the body. Or parts of it. I wasn't going to risk another live interview with Gil, so Malik rolled tape as we talked.

"What happened?" I asked.

"Still dark this morning. Heard a blast. No huge crash like when the turbines fell. But a big noise."

Prudently, Gil grabbed a rifle before going outside. "Didn't want to walk into an ambush."

At first nothing seemed wrong, except for a burning odor. All the turbines looked fine under the moonlight. And he didn't see any unusual movement. Then his dog started barking. Gil headed over and saw the animal carrying something—a human arm. Ends up the body was in pieces.

"That's when I called the cops."

Malik shot cover video of Gil and his black Lab walking around the farmyard. Every once in a while, the animal would head toward the police line, but Gil would call him back.

"It could be worse," he said, probably because he didn't know what else to say.

I could see scattered paint marks on the freshly cut straw field where a crew from the state crime lab moved around, gathering evidence. I tried calling the station before realizing I had no cell service. I figured authorities were again blocking calls until they cleared the area.

Initially, the neighbors feared what I'd feared. That one of their own had taken a hit, victim of the mad wind bomber. But nobody from the surrounding farms seemed to be missing. Most were rubbernecking from the road. As for the dead man, being blown apart made visual identification impossible.

Locals also concluded he must have been an intruder because no one they knew would ever do anything so violent. Or stupid. Their consensus: the evil bomb builder had accidentally blasted himself. They'd dismissed suicide bombing because he didn't take anyone or anything else with him.

"Are there any unknown vehicles parked in the area?" I asked.

That might have indicated whether the trespasser worked alone, and might also have helped with identification through motor vehicle records.

Gil shook his head. "Not unless it's hidden in the corn." Several of the surrounding fields still hadn't been harvested because it had been such a wet fall.

By then a small crowd had gathered around us. I wasn't sure if they were trying to be helpful or just trying to get on TV now that the bad guy was dead.

"That terrorist got what he had coming to him," one of the farmers said.

"Must have gotten a little sloppy with those explosives," another added.

They all nodded, relieved danger had passed and order had been restored.

The sheriff went on camera saying the death was under investigation and he would release more details on Operation Aeolus as they became available. I was surprised to hear him use that term.

Then the sheriff walked away, with me and Malik following. "Do you think the deceased was trying to bomb a turbine and accidentally detonated the explosives?" I asked.

"Too soon to say."

"What kind of evidence were you able to recover?"

"No comment."

"Could you tell if the man had partners?" I asked. "Someone must have driven a getaway car."

"That's enough questions for now," he said.

Not a whole lot of usable sound. The sheriff was much chattier when there wasn't blood and gore to explain to his constituents. Today, he was all law and order. Then I saw the FBI guy waiting for him at the command center and figured that was where he got his media coaching on Operation Aeolus.

Charlie Perkins stood off by himself, watching the show unfold but not mingling. I pointed him out to Malik and told him to casually get some video even though he wouldn't do an on-camera interview. I wanted a shot in case Charlie ended up being important. And now seemed as good a time as any to chat Charlie up about his past experiences as a power-line protester.

"Does this remind you of anything?" I asked.

He shrugged. "Not particularly."

"How about maybe thirty years ago and three hundred miles north?"

Immediately he knew what I knew. "That was a different time and place."

"Forgive me, Charlie, but I do see some similarities. Transmission towers falling. Turbines falling."

"But there're some major differences." He started walking away. "There the energy companies took people's land against their will. Here everybody in wanted in."

"Care to talk more in an interview?" I asked.

But without saying anything more, he climbed into his car and drove back toward his place.

With Charlie's cooperation, a story comparing the wind farm bombings with the power-line protests would be fascinating. Without him, it would still be interesting. Two energy wars. Decades apart. But the news of the day was the dead man. So Malik and I shot a standup with the few facts we had.

((RILEY, STANDUP))
LAW ENFORCEMENT TEAMS
ARE SEARCHING THE AREA

FOR CLUES, BUT THE BLAST
DESTROYED MOST OF THE
EVIDENCE . . . INCLUDING
MUCH OF THE MAN'S BODY.

I was just telling Malik we needed to swing by my parents' place before heading north when I spotted a familiar face.

Part of me wanted to rush over and wrap my arms around Nick Garnett. Our being apart made me realize I missed him. But people were watching, and other media were arriving, so after the mean dirt Sam Pierce had written about me being a bad wife, part of me just wanted to stick to the plan of pretending Nick and I had never met.

"What brings you here?" I wondered if his mysterious assignment was over or if this was it and he didn't want to tell me.

Because we were out in public, I compromised by playing our relationship cool and professional. My businesslike attitude annoyed him, but he followed my lead.

"I've been assigned to this case," he said. "The Department of Homeland Security is helping coordinate the various agencies involved in the bombing investigation."

"Anything you can share about today's explosion?"

"We're still in the early stages and will release information as it becomes appropriate."

"Now that there's a dead body involved," I teased, "the public might demand answers a bit faster."

Garnett glared at me.

"Honest," I whispered, "you're sounding like a government bureaucrat."

"And you're sounding like a media asshole."

"That's not the kind of cop talk I like."

Malik looked straight ahead, climbed into the van, and turned on the radio to give us some space. I leaned against the driver's door to block his view of our conversation.

"Really, Nick, you know I've been covering this story since day one; you should have given me a heads-up you'd be here."

"In this situation it would have been awkward. But now that we're both here, how about we make peace?"

I gave him a two-fingered peace sign, but he had something else in mind.

"Sounds like you're heading over to your folks' farm," he said. "This might be a good day for us to meet."

Garnett had been pushing to meet my parents for the last few months. The geography was complicated. Because he lived in Washington, I was in Minneapolis, and my mom and dad were almost in Iowa . . . this convergence had been easy to stall.

"Don't they live just a couple miles down the road?" Garnett pointed east. He knew what my family's farm looked like from an old aerial photo that hung in my kitchen. If I nixed the meeting, I wouldn't have put it past him to drive over and introduce himself without me.

"Well, yes, they live nearby. But I think I need to prepare them first. Especially after that 'Piercing Eyes' newspaper column and Sam's murder. Please understand, Nick, this is sort of tricky."

He didn't look like he understood. "Speaking of tricks, Riley, I'm starting to think you want to keep our relationship secret forever."

"I just don't want to flaunt it right now."

"Flaunting sounds negative. Are you ashamed of us?"

"Absolutely not, but I feel like a lot of eyes are watching me, and I need you to keep a low profile because the last thing I need is more gossip."

His face did not sport the look of a happy boyfriend.

"Come with me." I gave him a playful shove.

Our voices were getting louder and I didn't want Malik overhearing any more than he already had. I motioned Garnett toward some end rows of corn left standing for the pheasants. We walked and talked.

I remained convinced that his timing regarding my parents was all wrong. I knew them, and I knew once we got past the formality of their meeting Garnett, they'd grill me about our "plans." That future was still too vague for such a debate. I thought it might be better to wait for a traditional holiday, like Christmas. Travel could always be delayed by weather.

Garnett maintained it was now or never. And he made it sound like an ultimatum.

"What's the rush, Nick? It's not like you're asking my father for my hand in marriage."

"What would be the point? You're clearly married to your job."

I could have said the same about him, but I didn't. "This is not a conversation I want to have in a cornfield."

"Well, I'm tired of sneaking around."

"For a guy who doesn't like sneaking, why don't you tell me what you were doing in Minnesota the day before you came to see me?"

I stopped walking because I wanted to look at his eyes when he answered. I wished I hadn't, because they looked hurt.

"What do you mean?"

"I saw your boarding pass," I said. "I know you flew in a day early."

"You can't turn off that reporter urge to snoop, can you?"

"You left it in my house."

"I'm pretty sure I would have put it in the trash. Are you nosing through my garbage? Maybe that judge was right about you journalists."

That settled it for me. "I don't want you to meet

my parents today. And I want my house key back. You call me when you want to apologize."

That apparently settled it for him, too. "You call me when you want to have a normal courtship. The kind where we can hold hands someplace besides a dark movie theater."

"What we've got here is failure to communicate," I said, thinking Strother Martin's 1967 quote from *Cool Hand Luke* might lighten things up.

Garnett didn't respond, just turned and walked toward the crime scene without looking back. So either he didn't know the line, or he was too mad to play our game.

I climbed into the van, telling Malik to head to the station and not ask any questions. I didn't want to visit my parents in this foul frame of mind. This was becoming a very bad day. I tried to keep perspective by telling myself it could be worse.

Malik was also in a bad mood because the station had implemented an overtime freeze; usually he racked up enough overtime during a ratings month so that his wife could buy a new household appliance. With the cost cutbacks, they'd have to settle for a two-slice toaster.

When my cell phone started working again, I called the farm to tell my parents we had to rush back to make deadline.

"Any ideas about the dead body?" I asked my dad. "Him being a stranger nixes any theory of a neighbor angry over a ruined view or jealous they missed out on the wind money."

Unless they were working together, I suddenly thought.

"Nobody around here knows what to think anymore," Dad answered. "Nothing like this has happened here before."

That sure was the truth. This environment grew crops, not news. There, when someone asks, "Where's the beef?" they actually are talking about cattle, not substance. Same thing with pork. They mean pigs, not government waste.

To keep my mind off my fight with Garnett, I wrote the story on the drive back. I'd been told I was the lead. And for the first time all day, I smiled.

> ((SOPHIE LEAD CU))
> A DEAD BODY IS THE LATEST
> CLUE IN THE STRANGE
> BOMBING OF WIND TURBINES
> IN SOUTHERN MINNESOTA.
> RILEY SPARTZ BRINGS BACK
> THIS REPORT.

Plugging in a set of earbuds, I played the interviews back from Malik's camera and pulled sound bites in the car, complete with time code.

I transcribed Gil's answer about hearing a loud noise and going for his gun. I liked the part about how he didn't think anything was wrong until his dog found human remains.

"Make sure you use a shot of him and the dog," I told Malik. "Noreen will like that."

> ((RILEY, TRACK))
> SO FAR, INVESTIGATORS ARE
> KEEPING QUIET ABOUT
> POSSIBLE MOTIVES FOR THE
> BOMBINGS.

I closed the piece by saying that no means of transportation had been found for the dead man, thus leading to speculation he might not have been working alone.

CHAPTER 24

The next morning I was staring at the suspects chart in my office, trying to figure out a good way to cross paths with the last name on my Sam Pierce suspects list—rich widower Tad Fallon—when an announcement came overhead asking all news staff to report to the assignment desk immediately.

Our general manager stood in the middle of the newsroom next to a guy who looked about twelve years old, except he wore a suit and tie. Probably to command respect. Noreen stood on his other side with an inscrutable look on her face.

I had a bad feeling that our mystery man might be a new anchor, brought in to shake things up in a failing economy. But I was wrong. It was much worse.

"I'd like everyone to know just how lucky we are here at Channel 3," the GM said. "We've brought in one of the hottest news consultants in the industry to help us blend old media with new."

Then he introduced Fitz Opheim, explaining how he'd become a legend turning around an East Coast, medium-market station practically overnight. "We expect his uncanny instincts to guide us through these turbulent times of ratings change. Feel free to ask any questions."

The GM applauded his own remarks, prompting Noreen to join in, more enthusiastically than the rest of us. News consultants are often the bane of journalism, and I was more comfortable taking a wait-and-see attitude before expressing glee.

Then Fitz shared his vision. "In troubled times, happy news rules. People want to feel better after the day's news."

His voice was squeaky. At first I thought he must be nervous, but as he continued to describe how viewers watch the news for reassurance, I realized his natural pitch resembled that of Jay Leno.

I also realized we had a major philosophical difference on the role of media. "I thought people watched the news to be informed," I said.

"That idea doesn't hold anymore," he said. "With so many places to get information, viewers are overwhelmed with choices. To make sure they choose Channel 3, we need to give them hometown heroes and happy endings. Then their own lives will feel more stable."

Fitz paused, like he was waiting for feedback. The GM, Noreen, and much of the rest of the staff offered another round of applause. I couldn't bring myself to fake it, so I pretended I had a cell call and fumbled to turn off my phone.

"But we'll still be covering the news, won't we?" I asked.

"Certainly," he answered. "Crime. Politics. Those remain an essential core of television news. But instead of depressing viewers, we want to start offering them hope. Mitigating bad news with good news."

"Like the bad news is someone was killed today. The good news is it wasn't you?"

"Not that obvious. More subtle. For example, yes, there was a murder, but overall violent crime is down."

"But what if violent crime is actually up?"

"Then we empower viewers with ways they can stay safe. We play on their core fears."

He could tell not all the staff were following him. So he explained that core fears are universal terrors we all share. For example, dying in a house fire.

"We can use reporter involvement to show them how to get out alive. Crawling on the floor. Staying under the smoke. Feeling the doorknob for heat." He paused for dramatic effect. "We give them news they can use."

That wasn't such a novel concept; news organizations have been using that News You Can Use technique for years. So I nodded my head like I was a team player and wondered how much the station was paying this guy.

Then he talked about how on-air staff—reporters and anchors—needed to reach out to viewers with social networking.

"Like partying?" one of the sports guys asked.

"Cyber-partying," Fitz answered. "I want everyone to join Facebook to attract younger viewers. They are the ones who advertisers value. This way that demographic will feel more in touch with Channel 3 talent. That's the first step to breaking down the wall between us and our audience."

Such sites allow people to share pictures and personal trivia with other members who became their cyber "friends." I'd purposely steered away for a variety of reasons: the MySpace suicide, in which a teenage girl in Missouri was bullied by neighbors posing as a teenage boy and subsequently killed herself; just plain old suspicion about computer hackers; and a simple desire to keep a privacy wall between myself and the viewers.

But Fitz assured us safeguards existed, and he'd already discussed implementing this system with Noreen, and she was on board big-time. Our boss gave a thumbs-up but didn't say anything.

"She'll go into more details with you later, but keep in mind, your next job review will take into account how many Facebook friends you accumulate, especially in our viewing area."

I already felt job reviews focused too much on story count and not enough on story quality. To hear that my value as a journalist was going to be judged on the number of superficial "friends" I made online seemed insulting. Plus, it was likely to be a big time-suck. More time online meant less time in the field, scrapping for exclusives.

Maybe Fitz could read my mind; more likely he noticed me rolling my eyes . . . but he looked right at me while explaining that social networking sites would be a new way of building sources and breaking news.

"This will be the future of journalism." Then he cautioned us: "Channel 3 has a glorious history, but you can't live on your past accolades."

We all knew the motto of any news manager: What Have You Done for Me Lately? And I certainly didn't need Fitz lecturing me on the similarities between the word "news" and "new."

But Fitz recognized that television is a visual medium, and he was not all talk and no action. He had a live demonstration planned for us, with props. Suddenly two men, wearing coveralls, carrying a ladder and buckets of paint, walked into the meeting.

"To symbolize a fresh start," Fitz said, "we are painting the newsroom!"

The newsroom walls certainly needed paint. But the policy of most television stations is to not care how anything looks that doesn't show on the air. In fact, you can often see a visible line near the anchor set of new and old paint that illustrates where the camera shot ends. So while it was surprising to me that Channel 3 would spend money on a purely cosmetic change, I didn't particularly care one way or another.

That changed a couple hours later, when Xiong stuck his head in my office to complain that the painters were advancing on the green room with their rollers.

"Hey, you can't paint in there," I shouted as I raced down the hall to protect the signatures that symbolized Channel 3's collection of famous guests.

The crew had already rolled a couple of strips of fresh green across the wall by the Hollywood mirror. Part of former vice president Walter Mondale's name was gone. So was baseball legend Kirby Puckett's.

"Stop," I pleaded.

"We're just following orders," one of the workers insisted as he pulled the dripping roller from the tray.

Fitz heard the commotion and came to see what the fuss was about. Without hesitation, he insisted the deed be finished.

"Channel 3 will make new history. There'll be new names on that wall before you know it."

Walter Cronkite's signature was the next to go under the roller.

I found myself wishing there was a gossip columnist I could call to shame my employer. Unable to bear watching Paul Wellstone's name disappear, I left.

The last thing I heard was Fitz asking Xiong how many Facebook friends he'd acquired so far.

CHAPTER 25

I kept walking 'til I reached my car, then drove west out of downtown Minneapolis to the old-money neighborhood of Minnetonka. I typed an address I'd pulled from property tax records into my GPS, because the tangled streets around Minnesota's largest urban lake were a maze to outsiders like me.

The mansions on the water, those that could be seen from the road, conformed to an elite standard of stone, brick, and cedar. The one I was seeking was surrounded by a high iron fence. I parked across from the locked gate framed by two concrete statues of lions and stared at Tad Fallon's estate. Trees blocked much of the acreage, but I noted that the cobblestone road turned into a circular driveway in front of a massive structure.

I considered my tongue glib but couldn't figure a way to talk myself inside through the intercom. And thinking about it, I wasn't sure I even wanted to get inside if Fallon was a killer. So rather than press the red speaker button and give away my position, I pulled around the corner, where I could still observe anyone entering or leaving the stately home.

My hope was Fallon would leave in a fancy car, and I'd follow and then engage him in public once he reached his destination. A long-shot plan because parked cars attract attention in posh neighborhoods. But since I'd driven all this way, I decided to wait.

Ten minutes passed. Nothing. Fifteen. I started trolling the Internet on my cell phone, reading background about him, his deceased wife, and their various businesses.

Her obituary summed up their public lives. He and Phedra married and merged two very different Minnesota fortunes of new money and old. Her family had come from timber, then started a grocery empire. His owned a nice chunk of a lucrative medical patent. They'd attended the same exclusive prep school. No children. As a hobby, they raised pedigreed bulldogs.

Happiness eluded them.

No cause of death was listed in the paid newspaper obit, but I'd seen the death certificate. Officially it concluded accidental poisoning by overdose of prescription drugs. But plenty of high-society and law enforcement sources thought her husband had interceded to keep the word "suicide" off the paperwork.

Tad blamed a column Sam wrote a few days before her death, alleging Phedra had a drinking problem.

And while Tad still donated money to all the various charities they'd embraced, he no longer attended any of the gala events. Society crowds considered him an intriguing recluse. That made any hope of following him even more of a long shot, because most of his vehicles remained garaged.

But I could relate to losing a spouse and was optimistic Tad and I might connect once we connected.

I was contemplating approaching the fortress, posing as someone in need of a good bulldog, when a squad car pulled up behind me. I rolled down my window as the policeman approached.

"Can I help you, Officer?" I always liked to get the first word in.

"May I see some ID?"

"Have I committed any offenses?" Journalists also like asking questions.

"Do you have a driver's license?"

I considered balking, maybe pressing him further on whether I'd broken any laws, but I figured he'd already run my vehicle plates and had my name, so I handed over my identification.

"Riley Spartz," he said. "You that TV reporter?"

I nodded.

"What brings you out here?"

I had been there about an hour and figured a neighbor considered me suspicious and called the cops. It often happened on surveillance. More often with men parked in residential areas. Staking out a house was easier if there was a garage sale down the block. Or perhaps an open house under way. But this was such a swanky street, strangers wouldn't be tolerated.

"Just enjoying the neighborhood," I answered. "Might want to live here someday."

The officer looked over my older-model Toyota and shook his head in doubt. Even though I was parked legally, I didn't want to make a big deal out of my presence, so I told him I was just leaving.

He wished me a pleasant day and followed me to their city limits.

When I stuck my head in the green room back at the station, the walls looked like the Kentucky bluegrass sod on the Minnesota Twins' new outdoor baseball stadium.

And Clay Burrel's name was the first to decorate the Channel 3 turf.

I opened a Facebook account to keep my job.

It was discouraging to see that Clay was already an established player on the social network. He had hundreds of "friends" and had made a big deal out of friending the rest of the newsroom—including me.

Ditched by his wife, alone in a strange city, I could see how cyber friends might help fill an empty gap for him. To be honest, I preferred flesh-and-blood company. But since Noreen was monitoring our friends inventory, I didn't feel I had much choice.

Garnett and I hadn't talked since our fight. He was clearly waiting for me to apologize. And I did feel some guilt about the way our conversation had ended. Still tormented by Hugh's death, still feeling judged about my marriage, I had overreacted to him wanting to meet my parents.

I reached for my phone to call him and grovel. When he took my call, I hoped that meant we could pretend the other day hadn't happened. I started off by explaining my latest workplace dilemma.

"Maybe you could join Facebook and be my cyber friend?" I asked.

He nixed that idea. "I'm not content being merely your friend, much less cyber friend. You want online buddies, click on that Clay Burrel guy."

"I thought you considered him a jerk."

"I do." Then he unveiled his strategy. "Remember, Riley, keep your friends close, keep your enemies closer."

"Very funny. Al Pacino, *The Godfather: Part Two*, 1974."

The year Richard Nixon resigned. The year newspaper heiress Patty Hearst was kidnapped. The year I was born.

So I clicked the computer mouse on Clay Burrel's name and made him my first Facebook friend.

"Done," I told Garnett. "Now are we cool? Can we be normal again?"

"Not until we take the next step."

Next step? I hoped he wasn't hinting at shopping for a ring. While I didn't want us fighting, I also didn't want us married. Or at least I didn't think I did. But he had a different measure of our relationship in mind.

"Not until I meet your folks," he said, clarifying the terms.

Then he hung up. And when I tried calling back, he didn't answer.

CHAPTER 26

Doing laundry, I found the business card my parents got at Sam's funeral, so I went to the man's corporate office the next morning, asking to see him. No, I explained to the receptionist, I didn't have an appointment, but I was willing to wait. After all, the building was only about five blocks from the station.

When I told her I'd come for some advice, she assumed it was financial advice, since that was his job, and asked me to take a seat. After making a call, she stepped down a hallway. Minutes later, she told me it could be a while, and it might be better to come back another day.

"I don't mind waiting." I smiled to assure her I wouldn't be a problem.

This was not an unfamiliar technique in news gathering. It's the strategy of Sitting Until They Feel Sorry for You. If that doesn't work, you Sit Until They'll Do Anything to Get You to Leave.

Rookie newsies sometimes worry about causing scenes, but that only happens if business owners escalate things. They may threaten to call the cops but seldom do. The downside to having police chase away the media is that then owners have to explain to their business neighbors, customers, or employees why the media was there in the first place. And those discussions can sometimes be touchy. This wasn't one of those times, but bystanders can't always be sure what to believe.

About forty minutes later, Jeremy Gage stepped into the lobby, dressed much the same as he had been at the funeral—dark suit and tie. Appropriate attire whether mourning friends or consulting clients. I recognized him from the videotape. He recognized me from the news. I held out my hand, but he didn't take it. I doubted his snub had anything to do with avoiding the H1N1 flu.

"I know who you are," Jeremy said, "and you have a lot of nerve coming here."

"I'm sorry," I replied. "I just want to clear up a misunderstanding from Sam Pierce's funeral."

"What would you know about his funeral?"

"This gets a bit complicated, but you gave your condolences and business card to an elderly couple. They were my parents, not his."

"What?" He looked displeased.

"Several people made the same mistake," I said. "His parents apparently weren't there. It sounded like they might have been at odds with him."

"And your parents were there because . . . ?" The tenor of his voice made me think my answer better be good, or this meeting was over.

"I'll be honest. Because they're busybodies. But you seemed like a friend of his, and I didn't want you left with the impression his family ignored your offer."

"What offer was that?"

"To share some memories with them."

Jeremy paused briefly, like my remark might even have jogged a special memory. "You definitely weren't a friend of his," he said. "So why would you care?"

"Because you clearly *were* a friend. And I didn't want you to think his parents didn't care."

"Except now I know for *sure* they didn't care," he said. "Until your visit, I thought they attended the ceremony but just gave me the cold shoulder. Can you imagine actually boycotting your son's funeral?"

I shook my head, knowing from conducting numerous television interviews with grieving parents that there's nothing worse than burying your own child. Especially following an act of violence.

"Do you mind if we continue this discussion in your office?" I asked. The receptionist pretended to be filing papers, but I could tell she was following our conversation. And I thought he might loosen up more without witnesses.

"Sorry, Ms. Spartz, you may look harmless, but I'm uneasy being alone with you," Jeremy said. "At best you're a reporter. At worst, you're a murderer. Neither is the kind of character I care to associate with."

At those words, the receptionist stopped even pretending to file and followed our squabble with her mouth partly open.

"How about we compromise and I take you out to lunch?"

"Why would I want to spend an hour with you?" he asked.

"Because I didn't kill Sam."

I hated having to justify the rumor with a denial. And I wasn't certain he believed me. The receptionist definitely didn't.

Even though the joke was getting old, I promised we'd remain in public view the entire time and that I wouldn't throw my drink in his face.

A server stepped over to take our orders. I'd let Jeremy pick the lunch spot and he opted for Murray's, a historic downtown steakhouse. We didn't know each other well enough to share their famed silver-butter-knife steak for two. Jeremy went for a top sirloin; I went for the cobb salad because I've eaten enough beef to last the rest of my life.

As we waited, Jeremy opened up about Sam. He seemed to appreciate being able to talk about his friend. Reporters sometimes play the role of listener when others are uncomfortable talking about a murder victim with his friends or family. They think they're helping by changing the subject. But that's not how grief works.

Sam Pierce grew up in a tight family in the Little Italy neighborhood of Chicago, where his mother had grown up. To my surprise, he graduated from Northwestern's prestigious school of journalism. Which made the fact that he'd become a gossip hack even more woeful.

When he moved to Minneapolis for an entry-level newspaper job, he stayed in touch by sending flowers to his mother every other week. Such devotion seemed a contrast to the unpleasant man I'd known, so I was interested in hearing more about his background.

"He became friendly with an area florist and over time their relationship bloomed." Jeremy smiled at his pun.

"You've used that line before," I said. "Or do you vary it with 'blossomed'?"

"Actually, I'm stealing his line. He was good with words. I'm a numbers man."

Jeremy went on to tell how Sam brought his lady friend home to Chicago to meet his parents. They were jubilant. All was well. There was talk of a big wedding. With magnificent floral arrangements.

"Whenever she sent flowers to anyone personally, his betrothed used a signature bouquet of Minnesota wildflowers. Quite eye-catching."

I thought back to the vase on the funeral video and had an idea of who might have sent my mystery bouquet to the station. But our food arrived, so our table grew quiet except for knives and forks scraping china.

Jeremy resumed talk of the sunny future ahead for Sam and his bride. A honeymoon in Tuscany. The secret family recipe for lasagna. And especially grandchildren, to please his parents.

But there was one complication. Sam was gay, though deeply conflicted.

"He was seeing a man on the side," Jeremy said. "His best man."

His betrothed caught them entangled one week before the wedding. Wilted with shame, she called the engagement off. His parents were mortified by the scandal. Extremely religious, they disowned him when they learned the details of the breakup.

Shunned by his family, they hadn't spoken since. And now they could never speak to him again.

"Not that they particularly cared, as we've already established." Jeremy sounded harsh.

"Where do you fit in all this?" I asked, even though I had my hunch.

Jeremy was the other man. And by his side, Sam embraced his sexuality. Sleeping with women, as well as men, had been his way of denying being gay. Staying in a comfortable closet.

"But you know what they say," Jeremy said. "Bi today, gay tomorrow."

So circumstances outed Sam to friends and family. I couldn't help but think this new facet of Sam's life offered some insight into why he was so interested in the size of Buzz's . . . you know.

"His parents refused to ever meet me," Jeremy said.

This was beginning to sound comparable to me not wanting Garnett to meet my parents. Comparable enough to make me feel guilty. But I wasn't going to discuss my personal mistakes with Jeremy.

"Because we'd never met," he said, "I simply assumed they were the older couple at the funeral. Especially when they acted uncomfortable with my questions."

"If Sam had been as close to his mother as you described, the rejection by his family must have been distressing."

"An understatement," he replied. "They made him bitter about life."

"Some people might argue that's a good quality for a gossip columnist," I said. "What did you think of his writing?"

Jeremy told me he read only the newspaper's business section, while Sam never read the business section unless it featured a juicy bankruptcy or corporate scandal he could glean for his "Piercing Eyes" column.

"Sam's work routinely made people angry," he said. "Sometimes so angry it scared him."

"That's happened to me a time or two on the job."

"Did anyone ever egg your car? Or leave a dead animal on your porch? Or throw a drink in your face?"

Jeremy picked up his glass of water and shook the ice. Now he was mocking me. And since his lover was the one who was dead, I didn't dredge up details of nasty things story subjects have done to me. I also didn't point out that a lot of what Sam Pierce wrote was unfair or just plain wrong.

"I suspect Sam wasn't nearly as insulted about our little tussle as he let on," I said.

"Delighted with the exposure," Jeremy answered.

"You must be devastated by his death."

"Actually, we ended things a couple months ago."

Now I was curious but stayed quiet in case he'd keep talking. But he didn't. It made me wonder if I was starting to lose my touch for getting people to bare their souls, but then I realized this entire conversation was a giant coup since I was considered a suspect in the homicide of the man we were discussing.

"May I ask what happened?"

He said no. "It's personal."

To be fair, he had shared plenty, and we didn't even have the check yet.

"Do you love Sam or hate him?" I asked, thinking his answer might yield a clue about the breakup.

"I respected what we had together," he said. "That's why I came to his funeral."

"His old girlfriend wasn't there, was she?" I asked.

"No, but she sent flowers. Her trademark arrangement. You'd recognize it if you knew what to look for."

I had no doubt. "Wildflowers, did you say? Sounds beautiful. I might have some business for her. What's her name?"

But he saw through my ruse and stayed mum. So I changed the subject.

"What did she think of Sam's column?" I had considered him one of the most unlovable media figures in the market and was impressed two people could both have adored him.

"I'm not sure she read him either," Jeremy said. "She only bought the newspaper for the crossword puzzle. She's an aficionado of word games."

Just as I was handing my credit card to our waitress, she turned away and rushed to an empty table, where she picked up a bill. She glanced around, then headed toward the front door, nudging the restaurant maître d'. They both stepped outside, then came back, shaking their heads in disgust. I realized the dine-and-dash thief, or an ingesting imitator, had struck again.

• • •

Later, I thought back on Sam's life. Lonely or not, if anyone else's family had spurned them, Sam would have put it in the newspaper. Perhaps carrying pain of his own made it easier to inflict it on others. And inflicting it on others made it easier for someone to put a bullet in him. But who?

CHAPTER 27

Sam's parents still lived in Chicago. But there was no way Noreen would ever let me go after them. Even phoning them myself might backfire. True, they parted on bad terms with their son, but that didn't mean they wanted him dead.

During the afternoon news meeting, I brought up the idea of contacting them for a possible interview.

"You were saying, Noreen, how crime seems to be selling. And not even the newspaper has had an interview with them."

"You're not getting one either," she replied. "I told you, Riley, you're staying far away from that story."

"Yeah, stop trying to butt in on my beat," Clay said.

"I'm not insisting I have to do the interview, I just thought it might be a new angle to develop. I'm trying to be a team player. Who knows, they might even have a lead on who killed their son."

"Well, I'll develop any leads," he said.

"Make some calls, Clay," Noreen said, "and see what they have to say, but no trip to Chicago unless we know they'll talk, and it better be good."

A job well done, I thought. But then Noreen called for news updates since the morning meeting, and that's when things got interesting.

"Such a shame," Ozzie said.

"What?" I asked.

"All the money in the world can't buy happiness."

"We're here to discuss news, not philosophy," Noreen snapped. "Unless this can help fill a newscast, save it for after work."

Ozzie explained that a police call this morning for a medical examiner out in Minnetonka ended up being a suicide.

"Rich guy, too. Tad Fallon apparently shot himself."

Xiong and I looked at each other. "What?" I asked again.

"Wealthy philanthropist—"

"We all know who he is," Noreen said. "What happened?"

"Still waiting for details," Ozzie said. "Self-inflicted gunshot wound. Dead nearly a week. Nasty."

The media doesn't normally cover suicides—unless the case involves another crime or a high-profile individual, or occurs in a public place—so while Noreen debated how to handle this death, I grabbed a calendar to count back whether Fallon was still alive when Sam was shot.

He was. Could this have been a murder-suicide?

"Clearly he was mentally ill," Noreen said. "So we have to be careful not to encourage copycats. But when one of the wealthiest men in the state kills himself, it's some kind of story."

While the news huddle discussed what kind, the question on my mind was, would Fallon's gun match the weapon used in the gossip homicide?

Because the shootings happened in different jurisdictions, the cops would have no reason to bother checking the bullet patterns unless someone suggested it. If they matched, case solved. If they didn't, the person who even suggested such a thing might look like a real jerk.

Several hours and phone calls later, we learned that the weekly housekeeper had found Fallon's body, along with a note. The contents weren't disclosed but supported the suicide theory.

Noreen decided the station would report the death in the context of educating viewers about depression. No flashy live trucks at the scene. No pushy interviews with horrified neighbors. Merely something factual that put us on the record as being in the know. Nothing more unless a disagreeable legal battle over the estate went to court.

((ANCHOR, BOX FALLON PIX))
PHILANTHROPIST TAD FALLON
WAS FOUND DEAD TODAY IN
HIS LAKE MINNETONKA HOME.
AUTHORITIES BELIEVE HE
DIED LAST WEEK FROM A
SELF-INFLICTED GUNSHOT
WOUND.
FAMILY MEMBERS SAY HE WAS
BATTLING DEPRESSION.
FALLON WAS BEST KNOWN
FOR DONATIONS TO
MINNESOTA COLLEGES,
MUSEUMS, AND HOSPITALS.

I called the detective handling the Fallon case just to ask if he had any doubts about the cause of death. He and I had chatted a couple times in the past about drunk boaters on Lake Minnetonka, and there was still time for changes before the story would air.

"Hey, we were just talking about you," he said. "You want to tell me what you were doing parked in front of Tad Fallon's house yesterday?"

That wasn't exactly how I'd hoped to work the conversation. But hanging up the phone wasn't an option since, technically, I was the caller. Neither was feigning perplexity, since the traffic cop had obviously ratted me out.

"Had a couple questions I hoped to ask him," I said. "But our paths never crossed."

" 'Cause he was dead," he replied.

"Well, that does explain a lot." And made me glad I hadn't wasted more time on futile surveillance or left my fingerprints on the front gate.

"What kind of questions did you have for him?" he asked.

"How about you tell me about the note?" I tried to sound confident, like I had something to bargain with.

He wasn't buying it. "Maybe if you tell me why for the second time in a week, somebody's shot and your name has come up."

That was the problem with working in television. Everybody knew your business. So I explained Fallon's resentment of Sam and ownership of a handgun.

"I just wanted to find out where he was that night and if there might be a revenge motive out there."

The cop made a comment about homicide investigation not being my job.

"Since that's the case," I said, "have you thought about calling Minneapolis police and comparing your suicide gun to their murder bullets to try linking the two crime scenes?"

A strong sigh of exasperation came over the phone as he explained that my connection had already prompted his curiosity, and not over murder-suicide, but rather double homicide. Lucky for me, he explained, the shootings came from two entirely different makes of guns; Sam was killed with a Glock and Fallon with a Sig Sauer. And Fallon's weapon was lying next to his dead body.

"So when it comes to our suicide and murder victims," he said, "I think we can rule out any direct tie between *them*."

I didn't like the emphasis he put on "them" but thanked him for his help. As for me, I was starting to wish he hadn't called Minneapolis homicide, because every time another Sam suspect was eliminated it made me stick out more.

The only name still standing on my list of people who hated Sam and carried guns was Buzz Stolee. And no way was I offering any new suspect to the cops without a taped confession or eyewitness interview. And frankly, while Buzz certainly ranked as an NBA scamp, I wasn't sure anymore whether he had a killer instinct off court.

This hypothesis that I could search computer records to find the killer was hitting a dead end. In the movies, when journalists embark down a path to solve a murder, a combination of brilliant insight and dumb luck does the job. Hollywood leaves out all the wasted paths that lead nowhere.

My office seemed dark and stuffy, so I wandered over to the assignment-desk board to see if anything big had happened in the last hour that I'd missed. It hadn't.

Clay waved me over to his desk, told me he'd reached Sam's father, and said no way was he going to Chicago to interview such creepy church people.

"Not even going to ask the boss for an out-of-town trip," he said. "So I reckon you and me have nothing to feud about."

"That bad?" As long as they'd be willing to go on camera, it seemed like they must have had something to say.

Oh, they did. "Between you and me, missy, that old man seems to think his boy's better off dead."

Sounded like Texan hyperbole. "What did he actually say?"

Clay looked down at some scrawled notes. " 'Homosexuality is a sin. Our son has taken a path against the natural order. As we speak, he is burning in hell for his perversions.' "

If those quotes hadn't jived with how Jeremy described Sam's folks over lunch, I would have accused Clay of making them up. He might have sensed my skepticism because he pointed out he had it all written down in black and white.

"I'm telling you," Clay insisted, "we Texans aren't big on all this gay marriage talk, but this dad's mean as a rattlesnake."

I was just starting to admire Clay's wild metaphors when a thought hit me. "Do you think he might have killed Sam?"

My blurting that out surprised Clay. Even me. Honest, I don't know where it came from. Probably from him comparing Sam's father to a venomous reptile.

Filicide, the murder of one's own child, usually is an impulsive act with young children as victims. For Sam's parents to travel more than four hundred miles to gun down their adult son because they were homophobic seemed a trifle cold-blooded for such a supposedly God-fearing couple.

But Clay still hadn't answered. I should have just let it drop and pretended I was kidding; instead, I pushed too far.

"Well, crime reporter, what do you think?" I asked. "You're the one who talked to them."

"What do I think? I think you're crazy as a loon. That's your state bird, right? Now I know why."

That's when I started fearing that clearing my name of Sam's murder might be a losing battle, similar to Don Quixote tilting at windmills.

CHAPTER 28

Toby left a message asking to meet me at the dog park north of Minneapolis–St. Paul International Airport. He didn't say why, but it was a relief to get outside.

It wasn't an official city park, rather eighty acres of land where the Metropolitan Airports Commission let owners exercise their pets off leashes because the activity helped deter car break-ins in their parking lots.

Toby was already playing catch with two of his dogs, Husky and Blackie, when I arrived. He handed me a tennis ball, and I threw a bouncy toss for Husky. He fetched, I piled on some "good doggie" praise, and we repeated the maneuver.

After a week of cool, gloomy days, I welcomed the warmth of Indian summer. Colorful yellow, red, and orange trees lined one side of the property by a small lake. An airport runway bordered the opposite end. Visitors could almost forget they were in the middle of a major city, except for commercial airplanes taking off and landing constantly.

The property wasn't completely fenced, so owners were cautioned not to let their pets run loose unless they could be recalled. That and scooping poop were the only real rules. About a dozen other dogs were frolicking in the area.

"How are you doing these days, Toby?" Toby had the type of face that always looked sad, even on his wedding day. But on this day his whole being slumped, from his shoulders to his walk to his voice.

"Same as always," he replied.

I felt obligated to ask but was actually relieved he didn't volunteer any details. I figured he and Noreen might be having marital issues and I didn't want to play mediator. Working for her was bad enough; I couldn't imagine being married to her.

Toby was starting to sweat and laid his jacket over a fence. He cautioned me to avoid tossing the ball into a marshy corner because he didn't want muddy dogs in his Jeep.

Then Toby got to the point of our visit. "I have another wind-bombing lead for you."

I paused, wondering where this might lead.

"Worms," he answered.

"Worms?" I wasn't sure I'd heard him right. "Like crawling in the dirt? Earthworms?"

He nodded, explaining that worms till the soil and help plants grow.

"I'm a farm girl, Toby. I know all about worms, but what does this have to do with the wind farms?"

"I met an animal activist who believes the vibrations from wind turbines harm worms."

Toby had always been strange, and some of the people he hung around with were even stranger.

"It's true." Toby sensed I had some doubt. "He believes worms are a vital link in the food chain but are overlooked because they dwell underground."

That probably was true, but it might also have something to do with worms being slimy. "You should have brought him along, Toby. When can we meet?"

That's when Toby told me the man preferred to keep his work quiet "until the time was right."

"What does that mean?" I asked.

"He wants to finish his research first."

Toby was coy when I asked for contact information. I knew how protective these animal rights folk were of each other. I might have pushed harder, but in the distance we noticed a K-9 van pulling into the parking lot.

A uniformed officer stepped out with his canine companion, a chocolate Labrador. Various law enforcement agencies used the park to exercise their four-legged partners. The man unleashed the dog and he raced off in the field.

As they got closer, I recognized Larry Moore, the deputy searching the wind farm with his explosives-detection dog, Scout.

"Anything new happening with the turbine investigation?" I didn't expect him to reveal anything juicy, and he didn't.

"Scout and I just take it one smell at a time. Hoping we never have another day like that last one at the wind farm."

I introduced Larry to Toby and pointed out his pooch pair, playing in dog heaven as the red tail of a DC-9 roared overhead. "Toby is one of the most sincere animal lovers I know," I said. "Not just dogs, but all creatures."

Larry called Scout over. On slow days, he dropped by the park to give his Lab a workout, for her body and her nose. The deputy tossed a spent shell casing far into the grass and ordered her to seek.

Scout took off like the bullet she was chasing. In just over a minute she was sitting patiently on target. We all walked over and spotted the shiny object on the ground. She looked up expectantly with faint drool on her jaw; Larry reached into his pocket and rewarded her with a snack and praise.

"She's fed when she finds explosives," I explained to Toby.

Larry nodded and threw another shell casing, this time farther out, in fallen leaves. Again, he gave the command. Scout took off.

"That's remarkable training," Toby replied as we walked in her direction. He was impressed by working dogs and had even donated my favorite, Shep, to the St. Paul Police narcotics unit, where his powerful nose for drugs made him a star. "Some dogs thrive on the excitement and structure of working for law enforcement."

"Scout was being trained as a guide dog for the blind," Larry said. "But she was too curious. This job is a better fit."

The men chatted some more as we approached Scout. Toby respected her as a professional too much to try to pet her. Larry pulled out another treat, and we offered our verbal admiration for her hit.

Toby needed to return home, so he grabbed his coat, called Husky and Blackie, and came back to say good-bye.

Scout approached Toby, smelled his jacket, and sat down in front of him.

"She can tell you're a true pal, Toby," I said. "She likes you much better than me."

While Toby smiled and headed back to his pickup truck, Larry passed a snack to Scout.

"I'm surprised your friend is a hunter," he said. "Him being so fond of animals."

"Toby's no hunter," I answered.

"Scout alerted at his coat. I figured it must smell like gunpowder."

• • •

Toby. Explosives. I couldn't get the thought out of my mind on the way back to the station. It might just have been a coincidence, or it might have been more. I knew some members of the Animal Liberation Front believed a blast was the best way to deliver a message, but I had always told myself Toby was more reasonable. And I truly believed he understood the power of the media. After all, we first met when he suspected a veterinarian of a pet cremation scam. Toby didn't bomb the guy's office—he came to me.

I couldn't approach his friends. They didn't trust me. I couldn't approach his wife. He didn't trust her. Well, not enough to confide this kind of a blowup. And if I did share my doubts with Noreen, ended up wrong, and ruined their marriage . . . I'd be out of a job.

CHAPTER 29

As I stepped into the station elevator, one of the guys from sales followed me just as the doors closed. News and sales staffs generally don't mix, so I ignored him. But he didn't take the hint.

Over the last few months, I'd developed a consumer series that involved reporting restaurant scores by city health inspectors. Viewers loved the hundred-point system, and the series didn't require much work or expense and landed respectable ratings. Just the kind of story bosses eat up.

"Are you planning another of those food inspector stories?" the sales guy asked.

"I don't discuss what projects I'm working on." Actually, new restaurant data would be available in another week, and Xiong would start crunching the numbers. "Especially not to your department."

"Well, in the interests of the struggling media climate these days, you should be aware of the need to stay on good terms with station clients." Then he listed three large restaurant chains that advertise on Channel 3. "Just to help you use some discretion."

It was a blatant attempt at advertising coercion. What made it unusual was it came from within the station. Usually the advertisers issued their own ultimatums to reporters.

"You're not allowed to talk to me," I told him.

I got off the elevator and took the steps downstairs straight to Noreen's office and repeated our conversation.

"Can you imagine, Noreen, what it would do to our credibility if we left advertisers who scored poorly off the list?"

Then I sat back and waited for her to call his boss and raise hell. But that didn't happen.

"Riley, the budget is very tight right now." So Noreen suggested that for the time being, instead of airing restaurant inspections, it might be better if I focused on investigating government agencies.

She didn't bother explaining why and didn't even have to . . . I already knew it was because the government doesn't advertise and can't sue the media. It makes them an easy mark for journalists.

"I understand completely," I said. "Do you?" She didn't answer, but I noted that she couldn't look me in the eye.

I'd always been proud that Channel 3, historically, didn't take guff from anyone.

A former station general manager, whom I adored, was once confronted by a shifty car dealer who threatened to pull his ads unless a fraud story about his dealership was killed.

The GM simply told him he wasn't *allowed* to advertise on their air anymore. "Airing your ads would be a disservice to our viewers."

Back then, there were enough advertisers that a station could take such a stand. And the deep pockets of advertisers funded good journalism. Now, with the economy forcing a media meltdown and two years out from huge political campaign buys, the few remaining advertisers apparently had more clout.

I certainly had less. Although I couldn't be sure how much of that slump had to do with the economy versus the Sam Pierce scandal. Either way, I was hosed. And Noreen knew it.

I decided to make one last pitch for the monarch migration trip to Mexico. It was visual and uncontroversial.

"It's the kind of good news that our consultant talked about, Noreen. I know viewers would tune in to see that fluttering wall of orange and black."

Then my boss reminded me about a reality of local TV news. Foreign travel can only be justified on anchor trips. No big budgets for reporters. Just talent. And those days, it had to be a hard-hitting story, like Iraq or Afghanistan.

"So forget the butterflies, Riley. I want an investigative story, and I want it to lead tonight's ten," Noreen said. "So get busy."

The assignment was an in-the-face reminder from my boss that the days of long-form news investigations were over. Newsrooms used to brag about how long they spent on an investigation.

((ANCHOR, SOT))
TONIGHT AT TEN, THE
RESULTS OF A SIX-MONTH
CHANNEL 3 INVESTIGATION
INTO HOW FLOOD CARS ARE
MOVED ACROSS STATE
LINES AND RESOLD TO
UNSUSPECTING CONSUMERS.

Time used to mean quality. Now time meant wasted time. Quick-turn stories were where the profession was headed.

So I shuffled back to my office to call sources and see who had something ready to go that Channel 3 could promote as an *investigation*.

I got lucky with an email from one of my favorite lunch spots. The manager of Peter's Grill sent me a photo he had taken with his cell phone. This picture, he claimed, was worth jail time. It showed a man, perhaps in his thirties, having lunch alone.

"He's the dine-and-dash thief," he wrote with pride.

So far, the restaurant's most famous lunch guest had been President Bill Clinton in 1995, but that could change if this led to an arrest.

I grabbed Malik and headed on over to the restaurant to get some sound. Because few restaurants have surveillance cameras, the manager had discreetly snapped photos during the last two weeks of all solo male diners—the modus operandi of the culinary crook who'd been walking on the check in Minneapolis restaurants. Click. Click. Click.

Finally, one who disappeared without paying his bill.

"He stuck us with a twenty-dollar tab," he said. "But he picked the wrong place to chew and screw."

The suspect was clean-shaven, with brown hair, a suit and tie. A briefcase lay on the table across from his plate. He blended in with the hundreds of other businessmen in the downtown skyways each day. That's why the description from previous restaurants had been so vague. But now, armed with a photo, I suspected identification was not far away.

"I'll have to show it to other places where he skipped out," I said. "Just to see if they recognize him."

Peter's Grill had already given the picture to the police. So Malik and I swung by the cop shop for verification that they, indeed, considered this man to be a suspect in many of the recent meal thefts.

Over the past month, police had logged more than two dozen restaurant complaints of filched food, from upscale eateries as well as greasy spoons. And they'd already gotten confirmation from three other dining establishments that this was the same walkout guy who'd hit them. The PIO gave me a tip-line number for viewers to call, as well as a nifty sound bite.

"If we have our way," he said, "the next meal this jerk eats will be jail food."

This is where television news excels. Broadcast a suspect photo. Promote it during prime time. Wait for the tip calls. Take credit the following day.

> ((ANCHOR SOT))
> TUNE IN TONIGHT AT TEN,
> WHEN CHANNEL 3 BREAKS
> OPEN THE DINE-AND-DASH
> LUNCH CASE WITH AN
> EXCLUSIVE PHOTO OF THE
> ALLEGED FOOD VILLAIN.
> ((PETER'S GRILL/SOT))
> HE PICKED THE WRONG PLACE
> TO CHEW AND SCREW.

No mention was made in the station promotion about the amount of time we'd invested in the story.

CHAPTER 30

Ten minutes before airtime, I found a surprise in the green room when I went to check my hair and makeup before breaking my dine-and-dash exclusive.

Buzz Stolee was primping for a live interview on *Sports Night,* which followed the late news. Apparently he'd been the star player in that day's basketball game with a last-second three-pointer to win.

"Weren't you watching?" he asked.

"I'm afraid I was working."

"Bummer."

We both stood in front of the Hollywood mirror, fixing our hair. Buzz had to scrunch down a little because of his height. I considered leaving, but I didn't want him to think he unnerved me. And I was still hoping he might let something incriminating slip about Sam.

"Hey, can just anyone write their name on this wall?" he asked.

"Anyone who's a guest on our air," I replied.

So he did. With his jersey number next to it. One more autograph for posterity on the pristine green room wall.

Apparently Buzz had been talking with the Channel 3 sports team about our encounter the other night. And they'd assured him that hitting on me was worth his while by clarifying the definition of a reporter-source relationship.

"You see, you and me, babe, we aren't working on a story together," he said. "So I'm not your source. So we could do a little messing around, and you wouldn't get fired."

He smiled and nodded as if glad to have cleared up that business for me. "So you stick around until after *Sports Night*, we can pick up where we left off." And just in case I'd forgotten, he grasped his crotch.

"A wink would have been enough, Buzz."

"Okay then, meet you back here later." He winked. "See, I can please a lady."

"I'm sorry, but I already have plans tonight."

"Course you do, so do I. I'm the team hero. Groupies are waiting for me."

He then shared his philosophy of plans being made to be broken when something better comes along. He seemed to think that would flatter me.

So I owned up that I was Seeing Someone Special, even though Garnett and I were still on the skids. "And I sort of have a policy, Buzz, of not socializing with celebrities, because you could become news at the drop of your pants. And that could be awkward."

"Listen," he said, lowering his voice, "if this is about my . . . you know. I say we settle things here and now." He shut the green room door and glanced over at the couch.

"There's nothing to settle, Buzz." I glanced at my watch. "I'm four minutes from airing my restaurant rustler story. The floor director's probably looking to mic me now."

"Oh, I get it. You don't want to be rushed." He winked again.

"No. I don't want to be alone with you. You and me are never going to happen. End of story."

Buzz looked disturbed. "Endings can be tricky. Sometimes fans think a game is over and leave early. Then the game turns." He bent down so we were eye to eye. His gaze made me anxious. "You and me are just getting started. Certainly too soon to be talking about ending anything."

I tried pushing past him to get to the door. But he pivoted and guarded it like we were on a basketball court and my escape path led to the hoop.

"Knock it off, Buzz. I have to get to the set."

He pretended to be shooting a layup as he continued to block the door with his wide reach. "The buzzer hasn't sounded yet, we got plenty of time."

I didn't answer, just tried acting bored.

"Get it? BUZZer," he said.

Because of our proximity to a live television newscast, I wasn't afraid for my life, but I was starting to fear Buzz. Some jocks have a sense of entitlement that comes from sold-out arenas.

"I bet you'd cheer when the BUZZer sounds." He pressed up against me in what surely would be called a foul.

I weighed whether to kick his shin or knee him in the groin but decided the latter contact would only encourage him to think I was interested in touching that part of his body. Just as I kicked, the door opened and slammed him from behind.

Buzz swore, crunched over, and looked down at Clay Burrel's cowboy boots.

"You two aces okay in here?" Clay asked. "I was just fixin' to check my face."

"I'm heading to the studio," I said. "Take all the time you need."

And as I left, I heard Clay give Buzz a high five and congratulate him on his game-winning shot.

After finishing my set piece, I headed past the assignment desk, the back way to my office, to avoid any lurking sports guests. On the way, I stopped to thank Clay for his timely intervention.

"The guy's a jerk, and I was glad to get out of there," I said.

Apparently the simple curiosity of a news-hound made him open the green room door. "Never seen it closed before. Wondered what I was missing out on."

So that night I decided to let first impressions be bygones, be friends with Clay Burrel, and stop trying to steal his headless homicide story. After all, we were both part of the Channel 3 family.

I even offered to buy him a drink, but he declined because he was already going out for a beer with Buzz.

"Sorry, little lady." Clay smiled as he pressed his index finger against my forehead. "But he asked me first."

I decided to forget being friends with Clay. Who needed him, anyway? Noreen was thrilled with my dine-and-dash story. So were the police.

Before the newscast even signed off, they'd received half a dozen calls, all claiming to know the identity of the meal moocher. And the best part was they all gave the same name.

John Borgeson was picked up that night and taken to jail.

I got his mug shot in time for the morning news the next day, then did a noon-news interview with a neighbor who described him as a quiet man who had kept to himself after losing his job as a bank loan officer a few months earlier.

A couple of the tipsters were former coworkers of his; others recalled him answering employment ads for their company. Apparently, whenever Borgeson had a job interview downtown, he would steal a meal, purloin sirloin, take steak . . . I had fun with the script, and viewers called in with more suggestions. David Letterman even included a joke in his late-night monologue.

Noreen gave me an I Told You So lecture. "See, Riley, it doesn't have to take weeks or months to produce top investigations. Let's hit the streets and find some more like this."

I didn't want to get into what would only be a pointless discussion about journalism's role in "serving the public," working for the "greater good," and being a "voice for the voiceless."

I just nodded and told her I'd do my best. And said a silent prayer that the news profession didn't completely lose its swagger before going bust.

CHAPTER 31

With one connection, the blown-up body by the wind turbines became a major news story. Enough of the man's remains remained to match his fingerprints to a name on a terrorist watch list.

Authorities released a photo of Lucas Harlan, the dead bomber, taken from an old passport or driver's license. Dark eyes. Bald head. Couldn't tell if it was natural or shaved. None of the farmers I spoke to recognized him. Yet something seemed familiar.

He was an American citizen, thus a domestic terrorist. But he'd also been tagged because he'd traveled to the Middle East about a decade ago and participated in what was now suspected of being a terrorist training camp.

He'd moved around the United States, never staying anywhere long. He often worked temporary office jobs, keeping under the radar. The Department of Homeland Security was asking anyone with information about the bomber to contact them.

Nick Garnett was on the case, handling questions at a news conference open to all media. I was disappointed not to get a one-on-one interview. He was introduced at the podium by Mr. FBI Guy, who summed up the importance of Operation Aeolus.

((GARNETT/CU))
OUR BEST EVIDENCE THAT
LUCAS HARLAN WAS A
TERRORIST IS HIS DEATH BY A
CELL PHONE BOMB . . .
NORMAL EVERYDAY
FOLKS DON'T TEND TO BLOW
THEMSELVES UP.
WHETHER HE HAD
ACCOMPLICES . . . REMAINS
UNDER INVESTIGATION.

The farmers were anxious, and I could understand why. Located in America's flyover land, they'd never had big trouble before because they'd never had anything anyone wanted before. Now, because wind is a valuable resource, they felt like targets. All their bluster about fighting off Islamic extremists was gone.

Some told the wind company they wanted out. But Wide Open Spaces said it was too late. They had signed contracts. They had spinning turbines. They wanted their electricity.

Until now, the wind farm owners had given me the brush-off when it came to doing a sit-down camera interview. All I'd gotten was some walking video of them on-site and a short sound bite saying they were cooperating with the authorities in the investigation of the explosions. But now, with a feeling of mutiny in the wind, they wanted to come across as in charge. So they invited me to tour Wide Open Spaces headquarters.

"Before these bombings," said the company manager, "our biggest challenge as an industry was getting electricity from the soybean fields to urban areas."

"A new power grid is being planned for rural Minnesota," his assistant said. "But now turbine security is diverting our attention and finances."

They showed Malik and me a large computer monitor that had small wind turbine graphics across the screen that represented each of the real things. It resembled a war room, except instead of a map of nukes, they had windmills. Three flashed red. They appeared in the same geographic location as the blasts.

"We can watch if there are disruptions." The manager pointed to the red flashes. "This is what happens if a turbine has a problem."

"Except that's after the fact," I said. "Do you have any plans to prevent trouble?"

I could tell this was a question he dreaded.

He explained that law enforcement couldn't constantly jam cell signals in the area, unless they had reason to believe a threat was imminent. And even then, terrorists could always use a cell phone timer to detonate the bomb without making an actual call.

Starting this week, Wide Open Spaces was bringing in patrol guards after dark. And hoping to hire an explosives-detection canine of their own. They felt going public with all their precautions would reassure the residents living around the wind farm and discourage troublemakers.

> ((WIND MANAGER SOT))
> WITH THE DEATH OF THE
> BOMBER, WE EXPECT THIS
> MESS TO BLOW OVER SOON
> AND OPERATIONS TO BE
> BACK TO NORMAL.

National media were now interested in the explosions. The *New York Times* sent a reporter to do a "Troubles in Lake Wobegon" kind of story. And *60 Minutes* had Katie Couric on the way.

When Malik and I arrived to interview the farmers and their families about living with fear, Malik's presence behind the camera now made them nervous. Certainly they were less eager to be featured on TV than they had been earlier.

Then my dad told me about whispers around the neighborhood that Malik might be connected with the bombers and passing information to them.

"That's crazy," I said to anyone who would listen, dismissing that kind of talk.

I actually thought I'd done a good job of convincing folks about the folly of stereotypes and not to prejudge people, until something hit our van windshield at the only stop sign in town.

"What was that?" Malik said.

Another egg splashed the driver's window, and we turned and saw my old schoolmate Billy Mueller with a proud smile on his face.

"Just ignore him," I said.

"Easy for you to say," Malik replied. "He's basically calling me a terrorist based on my ethnic background."

"I don't think Billy is that sophisticated. I think he's calling you a terrorist simply because your name sounds different from his. Malik Rahman. You know how messed-up the watch list is; for all we know, you're on it."

"I do have difficulty with airport security," he acknowledged.

Over the last few years, it's been widely reported that the government terrorist watch list is a joke, stacked with numerous duplicates, respected politicians, even children and dead people.

When word started to leak that the wind farm bombing victim/perpetrator was part of the terror file, I called the only real federal source I had, Nick Garnett, to see if it might all be a mistake. He took my call but kept the conversation all business.

"It's a hit," he said, verifying the rumors. Then he told me the time and location of the news conference and hung up.

These developments didn't go over big in the Twin Cities Muslim community. (Minnesota has one of only two Muslim congressmen in the country.) Upset with any hint that Islamic extremists were behind the wind bombings, they protested the coverage outside the station, dismissing Lucas Harlan as a Muslim wannabe.

We were targeted because in the minds of the public, Channel 3 owned the wind story. The protesters simply marched up and down the block, some in regular street clothes, some wearing more traditional garb. Quite a few waved signs reading "Channel 3 is unfair!" or "Islam Loves Green," and even "Turbans for Turbines."

Malik and I were on our way back to Wide Open Spaces to shoot another standup. He'd asked me to take a different photographer to the wind farm because all the eyes watching him suspiciously made him uncomfortable.

But just as Sancho was Don Quixote's traveling straight man, I felt like Malik was mine.

"Forget it," I said. "Then we're just letting them win. We need to show them how wrong bigotry can be."

As a compromise, I offered to drive and let him nap. He could even pick the radio station. About an hour into the trip I glanced in the rearview mirror, and my face looked so horrible I wanted to close my eyes but couldn't since I was behind the wheel.

"Why didn't you tell me my skin was so splotchy?" I shook Malik awake.

He mumbled something about trying to sleep.

"But you're my cameraman; you're supposed to have my face, if not my back."

"Not my job," he replied. "I shoot what's in front of me. Real life. Real people."

"I stopped being a real person the day I became a TV reporter. Noreen will kill me if I show up on camera like this."

I pawed through my purse before I realized I'd left my makeup bag in the green room, so I pulled off the highway in Rochester so I could pick up some foundation and powder at a mall department store.

On the other end of the counter two women in veils were buying several bottles of expensive perfume. They appeared to be part of the royal entourage, accompanied by a bodyguard and a flunky carrying packages. The Rochester newspaper had recently run a front-page story that the Saudis had pumped two million dollars into the local economy.

"I wish I could report the news from behind a veil," I told Malik. "Then no one would care what I looked like."

"Be glad for your freedoms." I looked up and grasped that, from behind her cloak and veil, one of the women had spoken English.

Malik drifted away and the two of us chatted briefly and cordially about her stay in Minnesota and how well the Mayo Clinic was treating them. She alluded to women's rights being nonexistent in Saudi Arabia. Then her shopping party grew restless, so I said good-bye, and they moved on to the shoe department.

After they were out of earshot, Malik whispered, "There's a problem."

"Please don't let it be a newsworthy problem. We have enough headaches."

The two men apparently had been chatting in an Arabic dialect, unaware that Malik was somewhat familiar with it. His father, a university professor, had made sure various tongues were spoken at home. "They were talking about bombs."

"What was the context?" I asked. This was crucial.

But Malik couldn't follow the details. It's possible, he conceded, they might just have been discussing the wind farm explosions. Or might even have recognized me as the reporter covering the story and been gossiping. Or they might have been discussing building bombs.

I recalled a speech President Obama had made a few months earlier, vowing to stop importing oil from the Middle East in ten years. I wondered if that national goal could be motivation for oil-producing countries to stall the green movement, maybe by urging extremists to blow up American wind farms. Could the terrorists' motive be economics, not ideology?

I kept the Saudi shoppers in sight as I called Garnett to share the theory.

"It's me," I said.

"You really need to call the Homeland Security press office," he replied. "I have work to do."

"This might be the best tip you get all day." I reminded him that the Saudi royal family was in town for medical checkups and explained what Malik might have heard. "What do you think? Any chance some of their team might be involved in the wind blasts?"

Garnett advised me to drop it.

"That's all? Drop it? What happened to your sense of curiosity?"

Then he gave me a lesson in foreign relations while I watched a clerk bring my Saudi sister nearly a dozen boxes of heels.

"The Saudi entourage is able to travel with diplomatic immunity," he said. "Completely exempt from criminal prosecution. Neither they nor their families can be arrested or detained, nor their residences entered or searched by authorities."

He waited to let that settle in my brain. "So what are you saying, Nick? There's no point in investigating them because if they did it, they'll just get away with it anyway?"

"I'm saying they aren't even on the hook for parking tickets. Let me repeat myself. They have diplomatic immunity. So drop it. This is not a direction the federal government wants to explore. Or that you're capable of exploring."

"What if this is all about discouraging farmers from leasing land to energy companies? What if the bombings are part of a plan to keep America dependent on foreign oil?"

"Just drop it."

I don't know who hung up first, me or Nick. It might have been a tie.

Malik and I shot our wind follow-up story, but without much enthusiasm. On the way home, I swung into Rochester again, this time driving by the Kahler Hotel, where Saudi Arabia's monarch was staying on the lavish eleventh floor across from the Mayo Clinic.

Malik nudged me and pointed down the block. A handful of demonstrators plagued our international guests. Their signs read "Wind Instead of Oil" and "Blow Sand at Them."

When we got back to the station, our own protesters were still on the march. Channel 3 had moved all the newscasts to the inside studio away from the set that looked onto the mall. This way the crowd couldn't wave signs in the background at our viewers.

Noreen considered all this negative attention too high a price for any exclusive, especially one that wasn't moving the people meters in our direction. She told me to tone down the wind coverage unless national security was at stake.

I didn't mention the business about the royal entourage because I didn't know what to say.

CHAPTER 32

I went into my office, shut the door, and laid my head on my desk for a few minutes. When I opened my eyes, I noticed the gun-carry permit disc stuck in between some papers. So far, my Sam revenge theory was a bust, but that didn't mean the disc might not contain other news.

I loaded it in my computer and started scanning for gold amid the data. All I needed was a handful of interesting people viewers might not expect to be armed; then I'd have a story. And my boss would be off my back.

After a couple minutes, I realized I'd never get through the tens of thousands of names. Especially since so many were named Anderson and Johnson, typical of Minnesota's Scandinavian roots.

I headed to Xiong's desk. He still had the data downloaded on his computer and agreed to try a search.

"Scrolling will be a time waste," he declared.

I didn't argue because I'd already wasted

enough time coming to that conclusion on my own. That Xiong knew that, and other clandestine computer stuff, instantly confirmed him as an alpha geek.

He suggested trying to match the carry-permit database to others the station owned. The sexiest—convicted felons—might have been a long shot because county sheriffs were already supposed to be screening out those applications. But any hits there would be pay dirt.

"Obviously we do them," I said. "What other computerized files do we have names for?"

"State employees and campaign contributors are promising," he said. "And we have your local-celebrity file still on hold."

Last year, on a slow day, I'd gathered a few interns to help draw up a spreadsheet of famous Minnesotans—rosters of politicians; business leaders; pro athletes; radio, television, and newspaper names; musicians; even best-selling authors—just for a handy computer shortcut to separating newsmakers from ordinary folk, because newsmakers make the most news. I'd even added birthdays and addresses when we knew them, because that can often help match computer data.

So far, we hadn't come up with the proper project to harvest them . . . but I thought this might have been it.

"I will get started," Xiong said.

I left him to do his computer magic.

• • •

By now I had nearly a hundred Facebook friends. And I could lurk on their pages and delve into their cyber lives. If I cared.

Clay still had the most, though Sophie was catching up. She seemed to attract men. Single men. I seemed to attract people with problems. Some felt they'd been ripped off by car dealers or insurance agents. Others wanted me to investigate their neighbors for not separating their recyclables or for letting their dogs run loose across their yards.

Facebook was proving almost as annoying as the Channel 3 tip line. Except here, the crazies had a direct hook to me.

Before Fitz Opheim had left Channel 3 to consult at his next station of news dupes, he urged us to use the social network to promote our stories, but also to let viewers have a glimpse of our personal lives.

"Tell them what you had for lunch," he said. "Share what you're reading. Let them see how you're different from them, but also let them see how you're the same."

Noreen had friended all of us in the newsroom so she could monitor how well we interacted with viewers and how many friends we'd acquired.

"I notice you didn't post your birthday, Riley," she said.

"I'm worried about identity thieves."

That seemed to throw her, as if she'd never considered the idea before.

"Well, work on your numbers then. Instead of just waiting for people to friend you, you should friend them. Making friends is making viewers."

I didn't necessarily believe her reasoning, but I also didn't want to argue. I looked at Clay's Facebook page to see how a man with a ten-gallon mouth had become so popular.

He'd listed his status as "Clay is drooling for steak on the grill tonight." Several folks had already commented on his good taste. Earlier in the day, he'd encouraged viewers to tune in to see his report on why the H1N1 flu vaccine was so slow in arriving. Normally that would have been covered by our medical reporter, but she was home sick.

Clay and I had a few Facebook friends in common—local media junkies. But he had loads of his own. True, some were from back in Texas. But a surprising number heralded from the Minneapolis–St. Paul network. So in a flash of jealousy, I invited all Clay's friends to be mine. In this computer age, stealing friends was lots easier than stealing a story.

Then I went back to Sophie's page and did the same thing.

Within an hour, a couple dozen people I had never heard of had embraced our cyber friendship.

The next morning Xiong showed me the list of a couple hundred computer matches of people who carried guns. I scanned them for news.

One of the sports figures was familiar, Buzz. I also noted a couple of other athletes—a football player hardly anyone had heard of and a baseball player everyone had heard of.

One politician had supported gun-control legislation but now carried a firearm. That had some potential.

As for media personalities, no shock to see that a highly rated local radio talk-show host packed heat. He'd already bragged plenty about being a gun-totin' American and was true to his dogma.

But a big surprise hit me in the gut when I saw Rolf Hedberg's name on the list. To my knowledge, Rolf had never written about the right to bear arms, expressed a fondness for hunting season, or even worn camouflage. But Rolf was surprising me in a plethora of ways. Or maybe "frightening me" would be more accurate.

"He is not working for the newspaper anymore," Xiong said, "so we do not care about him."

Before I could refute my computer sidekick's conclusion, he moved down the list efficiently until he reached the prize he'd unearthed—ten felons, who shouldn't have been able to own guns, had been granted carry permits. A lead story, once we got reactions from the various sheriffs' offices. And even better if we could get sound and video of the nefarious weapon owners.

Several had been convicted of domestic abuse. Another had stolen cars. Yet another had a DWI felony. The prize: one had shot a man in the chest during an argument.

All had been issued permits to secretly carry a loaded gun.

Normally, I'd have been excited at the prospect of such a story. But all I could think about was Rolf Hedberg. Normally, I wouldn't have been afraid of him. In a fight, I figured I could take him. Unarmed.

But now I knew that Rolf owned a gun. And Rolf had displayed some very visible feelings that, even from the grave, Sam was ruining his life.

I wasn't sure just then whether to be more worried that Rolf might have killed Sam or that Rolf might kill himself.

I decided to keep quiet about Rolf until I learned more.

But when I showed Noreen what Xiong and I had on the gun-permit felons, she called Miles to come down and talk since, technically, the story involved nonpublic data. And with all the fuss the NRA was likely to make, she wanted to be sure it was solid enough for the station to go to the wall.

Malik was in the photo lounge, so I briefed him quickly and pulled him and Xiong into the meeting.

"What are you going to say when the cops ask where you got this information?" Miles asked.

"It's not a question of declining to reveal my source," I said. "I don't even know the source." I told him it had arrived in the mail without a return address.

"Then how can you be certain it's authentic?" Miles had a valid point, but I explained that I'd already verified that some of the people with carry permits owned guns. Tad Fallon and Buzz Stolee, for example.

"As part of the felon story, I'll seek reactions from the sheriffs' offices issuing the permits about how this could have happened, but first I'll see if I can get the felons to confirm it."

"How are you going to do that?" Noreen asked.

"We'll make it good TV," I promised. I told them my plan was for Malik and me to walk up to the felons and see if we could get them to show us their guns on camera. "I'll explain we're working on a story about the conceal-and-carry system and ask how well they think permitting works."

"Stop right there," Noreen said. "What if one of them shoots you?"

"Or me?" Malik had been quiet until then. "Sometimes they hate the camera more than the microphone."

"This could be a huge worker's comp claim," Noreen said. "We can't afford that. I think you should just contact them by telephone. Run their mug shots for the story. Mug shots generally look scarier anyway."

CHAPTER 33

Thinking back on the low turnout for Sam's funeral, I decided to visit his grave instead of going to lunch.

Since I knew I didn't kill him and figured he must know I didn't kill him, I thought he'd probably appreciate some company. And I felt it was the decent thing to do, considering how he and I had left things. And part of me just wanted to get out of the newsroom.

The Lakewood cemetery office warned me his headstone wasn't up yet but gave me directions to his plot and the names of other people buried nearby for landmarks.

The landscaping was lovely along the path to Sam's final resting place, but when I reached the hill overlooking his grave, I saw I was not alone. And neither was Sam. An older woman sat on the ground by his burial site, dabbing her eyes on her sleeve and praying. Then she picked up a handful of loose soil and put it clumsily in a plastic bag and kissed it.

I hung back, not wanting to disturb her grief, yet curious about her relationship with the deceased. After a couple of minutes of watching her struggle to her knees, I realized she was having trouble getting up. I walked over, gave her a hand, and pulled her upright.

Tears streaked her wrinkled face, so I offered my condolences. She burst into noisy sobs, literally crying on my shoulder.

While I consoled her, I noticed a bouquet of wildflowers propped in the dirt of Sam's grave. The vase held an unsigned sympathy card reading, *"God Overpowers Those Outside His Extended Limitless Love."*

I had no idea what the message meant, but discreetly, I snapped a picture on my cell phone for later.

"Now, now," I told her, directing her to a bench under autumn oaks. "Come sit a minute and rest."

Neither of us spoke right away. Then she asked me if I'd ever lost a child. And I realized I must have been speaking to Sam's mother.

"No," I replied. "I'm not a mom."

Answering her question out loud made me face a truth I'd been trying to push to the back of my mind since Hugh's death. That I might never have a child. Most days I could live with that realization, but here, next to a grieving parent, it hurt. Seeing the pain of her loss made me understand how much I was missing. It was even harder than looking at the photo of Ashley Lind and her brand-new baby.

"Would you like to see a picture of him?" she asked.

"Sure."

She pulled a photo of a much younger Sam out of her purse and handed it to me.

This was a determining moment. I had to admit I knew him or pretend I didn't. Whatever choice I decided on would determine the course of our conversation.

"He's a good-looking boy," I said, stalling for time.

She wiped away a tear. "He deserved a better mother."

I wanted to hear more, so that meant pretending Sam was a stranger. "I'm sure you did the best you could."

She shook her head. "I had to choose between him and his father. I chose his father."

Wild-eyed, she outlined a story similar to what Jeremy Gage had told me, that they cut Sam off because they objected to his lifestyle. Considered it sinful, even. "We didn't go to his funeral. My husband said it would be like turning our backs on our beliefs."

That seemed harsh, but I didn't want to join their debate. "You came here today," I said. "And that counts for something. You even brought flowers." I didn't really think the flowers were from her but just wanted to get that on the record and see where the trail led.

"They must be from his ex-fiancée," she said. "She owns a floral shop in the uptown neighborhood and used to arrange blooms like that."

She'd narrowed the geographical location of the flower shop, not realizing what a favor she'd done for me.

"Have you spoken to her since your son's death?" I asked. "Perhaps that might bring you some comfort."

"No. But my husband and I will see her later this afternoon at a law office for the settling of Sam's estate."

She had my attention now. "I'm sure that'll be difficult. Will it just be the three of you and his attorney?"

"Not exactly. We always liked Daisy and would have welcomed her into the family." Daisy, I thought to myself. An apt name for a florist. "But our son's"—she paused briefly—"male friend will also be there. We've never cared to meet him and I fear it could be awkward."

"Your husband will be with you?"

She nodded, explaining that he was waiting in their car, outside the cemetery gate, for her to return. To me, that seemed awfully cold, being that his only son was buried a couple hundred yards away.

She could tell I was thinking something along that line and started to become agitated. "We compromised. He agreed to drive the four hundred miles but wouldn't stand by our son's grave."

I didn't know how to respond, so I kept quiet.

"I'd best be heading back before he worries," she said.

"Worries" wouldn't have been the word I used, but I helped pull her up from the bench. I brushed some leaves from her jacket, then walked out beside her, amid her thanks. As I watched her climb into a blue sedan next to a white-haired gentleman, I made a mental note of the Illinois license plate.

In movies, the reading of the will is a fictional device to create suspense and surprise. In real life, there's no legal requirement that the estate attorney read it aloud before the named parties, but the fact that Sam's attorney was assembling a crowd gave me the feeling something unexpected was under way.

I glanced upward, telling Sam I'd come back for a proper visit later. Then I got behind my steering wheel and kept his parents' vehicle in my sight line for the next two hours.

For the first fifteen minutes, they drove like they were lost. And they probably were. Normally, it takes multiple vehicles for a successful surveillance, but when it comes to elderly drivers, fewer can work.

Sam's parents parked by a nondescript hamburger joint in Minneapolis called Matt's Bar and went inside. Even though I was tempted to follow them and order a famous Juicy Lucy burger, I stayed outside, a newspaper in front of my face.

I always kept a paper in the car for camouflage should surveillance needs arise; unfortunately this one was about a month old, so I got to read a "Piercing Eyes" column blasting a high school coach for suspending a couple of football players for stealing pumpkins.

"Every boy should steal a pumpkin in his youth," Sam had written.

I was just thinking that if I had been a public pumpkin pincher, Sam would have run a graphic of a jack-o'-lantern with my face on it. Just then his parents got back in their car, and I tailed them to the parking lot of a law firm. They appeared to argue for a few minutes before going inside.

I hooked a tape recorder up to my cell phone and used the next hour to call some of the gun felons. I identified myself as a Channel 3 reporter and said I was surveying some firearm owners about how well they thought the carry permit system worked. Already three had confirmed they owned guns.

I hung up on a fourth when a young woman carrying a toddler pushed through the front door of the law firm and headed for the parking lot. They looked like the same mother-child pair who had dropped the flowers off for me at the station.

Sam's parents chased them through the parking lot. His mother and father moved fairly slowly, but the woman had to buckle her child into a car seat. So the contest for them to reach her vehicle before she started the ignition was essentially a tie.

Sam's mother seemed to be pleading. I unrolled my car window and tried to listen.

"Let me hold him," she begged. "I'm his nana!"

The child was crying. His mom was telling Sam's mom to keep back.

Sam's dad pulled at his wife's arm. "You're scaring him," he told her, then said something about "later" and "lawyer."

The young woman, Daisy, I presumed, gunned the accelerator, leaving them standing alone.

I turned my key, intending to follow someone, though I hadn't yet decided which one. Then I saw Jeremy Gage leaving the building. I pulled up alongside him, unlocked the door, and gestured for him to get in.

He hesitated, surprised to see me, considering that the happenings inside were technically none of my business.

"Come on, Jeremy," I urged him with a smile. "We need to talk."

He sighed and climbed in, but the first words out of his mouth were not promising. "It's complicated."

Just then, Sam's parents' car started to move, and I found my attention torn between the man in the seat next to me and the couple getting away. I gave their vehicle a two-block lead out of the parking lot, then took off after them.

"Hey, stop the car," Jeremy said. "Let me out."

"Later. I need to keep them in sight."

Again, Sam's parents drove conservatively, making them easy to follow. Rush hour was just starting, so I stuck to their bumper to avoid getting caught at a light.

"Scrunch down a little bit," I advised Jeremy. "Just in case they recognize you."

He refused, so I handed him a Notre Dame baseball cap I kept in the car just for undercover emergencies. He gave an exasperated sigh but donned it.

"So what happened in there?" I asked.

"It's complicated," he repeated.

"I'm a smart reporter," I told Jeremy. "No matter how complicated this mess is, I'm confident I can follow it."

He paused, like he was trying to figure out just where to begin.

"How about if you start out telling me whose kid that was?" I said. "Or should I save time and suggest it was Sam's?"

He shrugged but didn't say anything.

"Don't make me play twenty questions, Jeremy. Or you'll never get home in time for dinner."

Two months ago, he explained, Sam had stopped at Daisy's flower shop for the first time since they'd broken up nearly two years ago. He needed a bouquet delivered and thought enough time had passed that he could give her the business without a fuss. The baby was asleep in a playpen by the cash register.

"Sam did the math and decided he was the father," Jeremy said. "But Daisy refused to discuss it."

"The Sam Pierce I knew didn't seem the paternal type."

"He felt it might be his only chance to raise a child. He thought he could do a better job than his own parents did." He said Sam hired a lawyer, demanded a DNA test, and vowed a custody fight for visitation.

I followed Sam's dad onto a freeway ramp, hoping they weren't driving the six hours back to Chicago tonight.

"Is this why you two broke up?" I asked.

"He felt his odds in family court were improved without me."

"Brutal."

Jeremy nodded.

"So why were you at this legal meeting?" I asked.

"I handled Sam's finances."

He explained that Sam died without a will. Under the law, if baby Jimmy was his son, Jimmy would inherit the entire estate. If Sam was not his father, the estate would go to his parents. Estranged or not.

"Sam's mother is praying for a DNA match," he said. "She'd rather have a grandchild than the money."

"Can't be much money," I said. After all, Sam worked for a newspaper—a dying industry. I noted some symmetry.

Then Jeremy informed me that Sam actually had a considerable estate from all his speechwriting.

"What speeches?" Occasionally I spoke before civic groups or journalism classes, and all that usually netted me was a thank-you and perhaps a luncheon buffet. The long-term hope was that the audience would become Channel 3 viewers.

"Sam wrote speeches for many corporate executives. General Mills. Best Buy. Medtronic. 3M. His rate was ten grand."

The number was such a surprise, I almost rear-ended the vehicle driven by Sam's dad. I slammed on my brakes, skidded to safety, then looked to see if Jeremy was joking. He wasn't.

"That rate seems on the high end to me," I said.

"I've seen the checks. Apparently he was worth it."

I asked who, for example, Sam had written for recently and was impressed when Jeremy named a top CEO.

"He also wrote speeches for some politicians, but not very often."

I was about to point out that such moonlighting might have posed a serious conflict of interest for Sam's "Piercing Eyes" column when his parents suddenly slowed down for an exit off the freeway. I hung back as they turned onto a frontage road. When they pulled into a hotel parking lot, I pulled into a gas station across the street and watched them carry luggage inside.

Jeremy used that opportunity to open the car door and tell me he was catching a cab.

CHAPTER 34

For the next ten minutes, I tried to come up with a believable way to approach Sam's parents for an interview. Generally, I pride myself on being creative in the field, but my earlier graveyard rendezvous with Sam's mother made another encounter impossible.

I considered cruising by uptown florists to look for Daisy but decided she had probably closed the shop by now and would likely be in a more approachable mood tomorrow.

Instead, I headed back downtown to the station. Traffic was now flowing better in that direction. The newscast was ending as I walked in the back security door. Nobody asked me where I'd been. So I ducked into my office before anyone thought about it.

I called another of the pistol-packing felons on my list. "Hello, I'm conducting a news survey about Minnesota's conceal-and-carry permit system and whether any improvements might be made—"

He hung up on me as abruptly as if I was hawking magazines or asking for used clothing donations.

Just for the heck of it, I called the CEO whose speech Jeremy said Sam had written. I was connected to the company communications director and told her I'd like to talk to her boss about Sam Pierce's speechwriting abilities.

I didn't have much hope of getting a call back. So when it happened almost immediately, I was flustered, especially by his angry tone.

"What kind of a shakedown is this?" the head of one of Minnesota's Fortune 500 companies screamed in my ear. "First him, now you."

"Excuse me?" I said, trying to understand what he was talking about.

"Don't play dumb with me. Just know if I hear from you again, I will call the police." Then he hung up.

A half hour later, I got a call from one of the name partners of Minneapolis's largest law firm. Because he handled corporate, not criminal, law, we didn't know each other, but he had something he wanted to discuss.

I smelled a story. I needed a story. I offered to come over right away.

When I walked in, even though it was after business hours, I saw legal associates hunched over their desks, desperately working to make partner. The economic downturn was causing many companies to balk at the concept of straight bill-able hours from their attorneys, and the only legal business on the upswing was bankruptcy filings.

The first thing Bryan Streit told me was that he was representing Mr. CEO about "our matter."

"My client is sorry he lost his temper and asked me to assure you he doesn't want to involve the police."

Sometimes when I don't know what a source is talking about, I bluff that I do, hoping to get clarification. This wasn't one of those times. I was blunt. "I don't know what you're talking about."

"Let's stop playing coy. Mr. Pierce may have preferred referring to it as a 'speech,' but hush money is hush money. What's your price for keeping this quiet?"

Suddenly I suspected Sam was not just a catty gossip but also a calculating extortionist. And I decided to try my bluff tactic.

"So Sam wrote a 'speech' about your client's personal life and sold it to him?"

"Don't play dumb," he said. "All that talk about how much my client thought the 'speech' was worth? And if my client didn't want the 'speech,' maybe it would make a good newspaper column. Pierce called it a speech to make it sound like a business transaction, but it was straight-up blackmail."

It sure was.

"We don't know exactly how you came to have

possession of this confidential information." The lawyer seemed to be hinting I must have stolen some file after killing Sam. "But my client continues to want to keep the issue about his life private."

"This is a misunderstanding." I explained about running across his client's name while doing research about Sam Pierce and being curious about the payment. "I have no idea what secret your client is hiding, and frankly, I don't want to know."

That last bit wasn't actually true. But if his client's skeleton was newsworthy, and if I ever unearthed it, buying my silence wasn't an option. My hunch was it probably had something to do with sex. Maybe Sam's target was a closeted gay.

Mr. CEO's attorney seemed unsure whether or not to believe my professed ignorance. He was skeptical when I refused to accept a check for "my discretion."

As I walked back to the station, I wondered how Sam decided which people to sell "speeches" and which to simply surprise with an item in the newspaper. I'd been featured numerous times in "Piercing Eyes," and he'd never offered me the speech deal. Of course, I'd have gone straight to his boss before paying him ten grand.

Sam was taking a risk each time he played his game. If he approached the wrong mark, he could have wound up fired.

Or dead.

CHAPTER 35

The next morning, while eating burnt toast and drinking juice, I heard a heavy knock and loud, unwelcome words: "Police officer. Search warrant."

When I opened the door, Minneapolis police frisked me through my frizzy bathrobe, then waved a warrant for my home and car. They didn't include my desk at Channel 3, most likely to avoid a First Amendment battle.

This meant legal work for Benny, not Miles.

My criminal attorney rushed over and reviewed the probable-cause affidavit attached to the warrant. He noted the cops had already subpoenaed my phone records and discovered several calls to both my house line and cell phone that went unanswered the night of Sam Pierce's murder—despite my telling police that I'd been home during that entire evening.

"See, Riley, this is why I didn't want you to let them interview you," Benny said. "Not only do you not have an alibi for the night of Sam Pierce's murder, your whereabouts seem inconsistent with your official statement."

"I was too upset to talk to anyone that night. I crawled into bed and ignored the phone."

"Well, the cops think the calls went unanswered because you were busy killing Sam."

In the affidavit, the court bailiff also verified tension and sharp words between the gossip columnist and me hours before the homicide. Of course, the police made much of my guilty plea for assault.

"Luckily, none of this is enough to actually charge you with murder," Benny said. "Please assure me they won't find any evidence while searching your house or car."

"Absolutely not. It's going to be a waste of their time. I'm innocent. So I have nothing to fear."

We both sat on the porch—him in a lawyer suit because he was a lawyer, me still in my bathrobe because the cops wouldn't let me upstairs to change into something less comfortable. Some neighbors glanced over at the squad cars, one marked, one unmarked, as they left for their jobs. An elderly couple undertook yard work, probably as an excuse to keep a curious watch on the happenings outside.

Meanwhile, the cops examined my car and house. The main item they were looking for was a Glock handgun. They came up empty but took other items like my hairbrush, toothbrush, and some clothing.

"They're hoping to link your DNA to the crime scene," Benny said.

I shook my head. "Not going to happen, but at least this way they can eliminate me."

"I like confidence in a client, but promise me you won't do any media interviews. Nada. All that does is make my job harder."

I understood Benny's point, but there's a public relations strategy that journalists call getting out in front of bad news. That means announcing your own trouble before the media finds out. Sort of like late-night host David Letterman gaining sympathy for sexual high jinks by sharing his extortion tale in front of a live studio audience.

"What if I just give a statement?" I asked Benny. "No questions."

"Any statements to be made, I'll make them."

Because I wanted to keep top defense attorney Benny Walsh as my lawyer, I raised my palm in a solemn pledge.

Until then, I'd been observing the police proceedings with more professional interest than personal worry. Calling Noreen, I told her why I'd be late, and she told me the station didn't need any more of this kind of publicity. Then she quoted more clauses from my personal services contract about "public morals" and actions that "reflect unfavorably on her employer."

I just sat there and took it because I didn't have a choice and figured it wouldn't last for long.

"Are our competitors likely to find out?" Noreen asked.

Typically the media doesn't learn about search warrants being executed until after the fact, when the paperwork is filed with the court. So any beat reporter who made daily rounds would eventually find the story. Of course, with the recent newsroom cutbacks, those checks often get nixed in favor of more easily obtained fresh content.

"Chances are, someone inside the cop shop will leak it," I said. "Maybe even the chief."

"In that case," she said, "we better be first. I'll put Clay on it."

I had no objection to Channel 3 going on the record with the story. Best that the station didn't appear to be hiding negative news. But even though Clay and I were starting to get along, he was the last reporter I wanted covering me. He'd likely try to turn it into the lead story. I know I would, if the newsmaker wasn't me.

"Because the search isn't going to yield anything useful for prosecution, maybe it's best, Noreen, to just make the story an anchor reader rather than assign a reporter."

"No, Riley, Clay's been covering the gossip homicide from the start. He's got the big-picture perspective."

He's also got a big mouth, but I held back sharing that view with Noreen because the homicide investigator in charge came over. I told my boss I had to run but would be in the office shortly. The cop handed me a copy of the paperwork outlining what their team had confiscated.

"Hey, why'd you take my pink jacket?" I asked. It wasn't like it had bloodstains or anything. And I'd started to appreciate the color for standups. "When am I going to get it back?"

He didn't answer, simply pointed to the blank line that needed my signature and date.

Less than an hour later, I arrived at Channel 3 and, under orders from Noreen, made Clay a copy of the pages, which he eagerly grabbed from my hands.

He shook his head as he scanned the search warrant. "Well, little lady, seems to me you have more of a talent for making news than covering it."

"And you have no talent at all," I responded. "Seems to me if you're such a well-connected crime reporter, you'd have aired an exclusive on this search warrant already without my help."

"Maybe I promised my sources not to reveal anything until this business at your house was finished up," Clay said. "They might have worried you'd destroy incriminating evidence if you got a heads-up."

Actually, that was exactly the kind of thing the chief might have made Clay agree to before telling him about the warrant.

"But there isn't any evidence," I said.

"That's what half the bums in prison say."

"Clay, you're just afraid I'll find Sam's killer before you do."

"Honey, you couldn't find your head with both hands."

"I'm getting sick of your Texanisms."

"How about that Minnesota accent of yours, you betcha?"

"Never mock a TV market you're new in," I advised him. "The audience won't forget or forgive."

I decided a lesson in talking Minnesotan might be just what Clay needed. After all, moving from the Lone Star State to the North Star State couldn't have been easy. So I started explaining how we drink pop, not soda, and eat a hot dish, not a casserole.

But he wasn't the least bit grateful and accused me of trying to change the subject. "Missy, you give aspirin a headache."

"Headache? Me? You're the biggest headache who's ever worked here."

"Does that mean you're declining an on-camera interview?"

"You betcha." I stomped away.

So much for Minnesota Nice.

((CLAY, LIVE))
THIS HOUSE . . . WHERE
CHANNEL 3'S OWN RILEY
SPARTZ LIVES . . . IS WHERE
MINNEAPOLIS HOMICIDE

> INVESTIGATORS SPENT THE
> MORNING SEARCHING FOR
> CLUES IN THE MURDER OF
> GOSSIP COLUMNIST SAM
> PIERCE.

When I turned on the noon news an hour later, Clay had a wide grin across his face as he broadcast a live shot in front of my home. I didn't like that he walked across my yard instead of standing in the public street. If he hadn't been live on the air, I would have called his cell phone and screamed, "Trespasser!"

> ((CLAY, LIVE))
> SPARTZ REFUSED TO
> COMMENT OR GIVE AN ON-
> CAMERA INTERVIEW . . . AND
> HER ATTORNEY DISMISSED
> THE POLICE ACTION AS
> "POLITICAL
> GRANDSTANDING" . . .
> SAYING HIS CLIENT WAS
> "MOST DEFINITELY NOT
> GUILTY."

Infuriated, I threw a dictionary at the television set, forgetting it wasn't really hitting Clay. He'd used an old broadcast trick of talking fast and swallowing the "not" in "not guilty" to create the impression for casual viewers that even my own attorney thought I was guilty.

Even though I should probably have called my parents right then and reassured them that things were not as bad as they sounded, instead I marched to Noreen's office for a showdown.

My boss was leafing through budget papers and didn't even have the volume turned up on her wall of television screens. The noon was Channel 3's lowest-priority newscast in terms of content, ratings, and advertising. The audience was largely older viewers—demos the sales staff didn't think spent much money. Much of the advertising comes from the Cremation Society of Minnesota and various hearing aid companies.

"Did you watch his report?" I asked. "Clay made it look like I was uncooperative when I was the one who gave him the story. Noreen, you need to talk to him."

"Was what he said accurate, Riley?"

"His words may have been accurate, but his tone was obnoxious and the notion he gave viewers was false."

"And how many times have you done the same thing?"

How could she take that attitude? Clay must have brainwashed her.

"This is me we're talking about, Noreen. You're supposed to have my back. The deal was the station was simply going to be first on the record with the search warrant. That's it. Let the newspaper be the one to gang up on me."

My boss sighed and promised she'd look at his report once the newscast was over. Then she bent over a spreadsheet and ignored me.

When I got back to my desk, the newspaper's crime reporter had left a phone message asking me to call him back. I passed the number on to Benny. Getting quoted in the paper was one of his favorite parts of being an attorney. He called it free advertising.

CHAPTER 36

Within an hour, I had my own breaking news and no time to worry about Clay.

((ANCHOR/PIX))
IF YOU'VE SEEN THIS
CAR . . . AUTHORITIES WANT
TO KNOW.

Abandoned in a north Minneapolis neighborhood, a green station wagon was towed to a storage yard after thieves made off with the tires and stereo. But the cops didn't care about the vandals, they cared about the owner: Lucas Harlan, the dead wind bomber.

One of the lot workers, a news junkie, had recognized the name.

((CAR GUY/SOT))
I RAN THE PLATES AND
THOUGHT, ISN'T HE THAT

WIND BOMBER GUY
WHO BLEW HIMSELF UP?

A forensics team examined the vehicle and discovered, on the hood, traces of blood and tissue—Lucas Harlan's blood and tissue. That crucial clue placed the vehicle at the location of the blast and proved the existence—but not the identity—of a coconspirator.

((POLICE, SOT))
SOMEONE MOVED THAT CAR
MORE THAN A HUNDRED
MILES AND WE WANT TO
FIND HIM.

The feds also released another photo of the wind bomber. In this one, he had hair.

Maybe it was his angular cheeks or the way he held his chin. But in a flash of clarity, I recalled Batman's dark eyes and shaggy mane. I looked back at the video from the Bat Protector interview but Malik had saved no shots of him from the video card, only Serena. And I was uncertain where to look for her just now.

I thought of one other person who might have been able to make an ID. I phoned Toby and left a message that I wanted to show him something. I headed out to his and Noreen's animal house in the country while the sky was drizzling. But after I handed him the photo, I wished I hadn't. Because Toby needed a lawyer more than I did.

The weather was clearing, so we sat on Toby's covered porch. Husky and Blackie lay by our feet. Toby stared at the photo of Lucas Harlan like he'd thought he would never see him again.

"Batman said I could be the lookout," he said. "It seemed like excellent training. And I believed his cause worthy."

Then Toby said something that changed our personal dynamics forever. He'd been a source. He'd even been a friend. But I didn't know what to call him anymore when he told me he was watching when Batman exploded.

"One second he was there, the next he was gone."

Shivers went up my back. "How horrible. Obviously, for him, but for you, too, Toby." I meant it. I'd never actually seen human remains after a bombing, but I'd heard enough descriptions to know how gruesome it can be for those in the vicinity. And Toby had a sensitive soul. A dog whisperer's, even.

"I know you're blaming yourself, Toby. You probably have survivor's guilt. But something clearly went wrong and Batman accidentally blew himself up. I'm just glad you're safe." I meant it. And for the first time since we'd met, I hugged him because I thought he needed it.

I didn't know what else to say, so we sat silently together for a few minutes.

"It was no accident."

"What do you mean, Toby? Of course it was. You don't think Batman was a suicide bomber, do you? He gained nothing by his death."

He shook his head. "It was no suicide."

"Toby, you're not making any sense."

He looked at me with his long droopy basset-hound face. "I detonated the bomb."

I felt my stomach cramp. But I didn't doubt his confession for a minute. He'd been oozing regret over something. I'd just assumed it was Noreen. Now the whole episode was starting to make sense.

"What happened, Toby? Did you hit the wrong button?"

Toby said they parked about a hundred yards away in a farm field driveway to hide the car. Batman turned off the headlights and handed a flashlight to his new eco partner. Toby described how Batman removed a cell phone motor, hooked it up to a blasting cap, then put it in a small package with explosives—a crude remote-control trigger.

"He gave me a disposable phone with the bomb phone number programmed on the screen and told me I could be in charge of pushing the send button as we drove away."

Toby took a deep breath, like he was reliving that particular moment of power. Then he confided how much he'd been looking forward to witnessing the blast and feeling the crash when the turbine hit the ground.

The pair walked toward the windmill, but instead of stopping at their destination, Batman moved past. "I asked where he was going, and he said the time had come to send a real message to the owners, farmers, and world."

Blowing up turbines wasn't getting fast enough results, he said. The blades still spun; bats still died.

"He kept talking about how the deaths could have far-reaching consequences because so little is known about their population size," Toby said. "I agreed with everything he said, except his plan."

"What was his plan?" I suspected I already knew, but I wanted to hear it from Toby.

"He wanted to blow up a house. Dead bats. Dead people. He was convinced it was only fair."

"What did you do?"

"I tried to change his mind. But he wouldn't listen."

I stayed quiet and let Toby talk.

"I told Batman to leave the bomb by the turbine, but he ignored me and kept creeping toward the house. There was a light upstairs, so I knew people were home. Maybe children. Maybe even their pets. I stayed behind, but his shadow grew closer to the house. I saw a tire swing in the moonlight and knew time was running out."

That's when Toby hit send. And Batman went boom.

Toby whimpered like a puppy. "I'm an activist. Not a terrorist." Then he started to snivel softly. "But now, they're going to call me a murderer."

I gave him a few minutes to calm down. Blackie and Husky tried licking his face. "Who else knows about this?" I asked.

"Nobody," he answered.

I asked him about Serena, the local leader of Bat Protectors. And he told me she wasn't involved in the explosions. Batman operated solo.

"I don't want to get in the middle of your marriage, Toby, but what about Noreen?"

"She knows I was gone that night. She's upset."

"What are you going to do?"

"I don't know," he said. "What are you going to do?"

"I don't know either."

Nobody else had this story. So I didn't have to worry about Channel 7 or any other media beating me. I wasn't even sure if my boss would let it hit the air once she knew the ramifications.

Garnett would be angry if he ever heard I knew the details of the bombing death and kept quiet.

I mentioned to Toby that there might be forensic evidence linking him to the getaway car. Maybe even fingerprints. I told him he needed to consult an attorney. And level with his wife. He didn't let on whether he was going to follow through on either idea.

He'd been arrested for various animal rights protests and once on suspicion of abducting Minnesota's record largemouth bass. But nothing was as serious as what he faced now. I shouldn't have been surprised that such a development was festering. Toby had been acting staggeringly unhappy, even for Toby.

Clouds were rolling in again. As I avoided stepping in a puddle on the sidewalk, I saw a worm stretched across the cement. "Toby, what about the worm guy?"

He seemed to blush, though the sky was getting too dark to tell. "I made him up. I wanted to divert your attention from bats."

I didn't answer but decided to go home and sit on the dilemma until tomorrow. But the tomorrow I was expecting never came.

CHAPTER 37

The police didn't wait until morning to arrest me. But they did allow me to change out of my pajamas and into some normal clothes before hauling me off to jail that night on homicide charges for the murder of Sam Pierce.

"Can't I just turn myself in?" I knew courts routinely made deals like this with white-collar criminals.

They shook their heads. "Chief gave the order himself to bring you in."

That I could believe.

The two blues recommended I leave my purse at home, because it would just be put in jail inventory.

"How about my cell phone? Can I take that?"

They shook their heads, herding me toward the door.

"Don't I get to call my attorney?"

"Later," one of them replied. "Jail has phones."

Then I learned the main reason they didn't

want me to bring anything along was because they intended to handcuff me.

"What if I promise to behave?" I asked.

"Sorry, it's procedure."

Obediently, I held my wrists in front of me, hoping cooperation might win me some points. But they insisted on cuffing me from behind, again resorting to that same excuse of police procedure.

Off balance, I nearly tripped on my way to the squad car and one of them had to steady me. The handcuffs cut into my wrists. They loaded me into their Crown Vic, where a barrier separated me in the backseat from them in the front seat. I wondered if any famous criminals had ridden there before me.

The cops didn't seem in the mood to talk. And for once, I wasn't in the mood to ask questions. I was afraid of the answers.

As we drove away, I thought I saw a still photographer across the street and hoped the newspaper hadn't been given advance warning about my arrest.

The two miles to downtown had never seemed so long. I was torn between wanting to get there fast to fix this crazy mess, and wanting to never get there in case they never let me out.

The car drove down a ramp to an underground garage and I was escorted into the booking area of the Hennepin County jail. Years ago, I recalled Channel 3 airing a story about what a fabulous jail this was—accredited even. But from my perspective just then, the only good part was that the cuffs came off.

The intake officer confiscated my clothes, even my underwear, trading me for plastic sandals, jailhouse bra and panties, and an orange jumpsuit. Neither the color nor the fit pleased me, but wardrobe is not a priority in the pokey.

"When can I call my attorney?" I asked.

"Later."

While I waited in a plastic chair, a video played in a wall monitor, outlining the rules of jail. The production quality was only so-so, but I thought it best not to criticize.

"Riley Spartz." A man called my name. I stood and a couple other inmates stared at me as if trying to recall where we'd met. I was waved into a booth and admonished not to smile.

I'd seen plenty of bad mug shots on the job. Most of those people were drunk or high. Being sober and scared, I knew how important it was not to look guilty. Or creepy. Because a mug shot follows you the rest of your life. Ask Lindsay Lohan.

At one extreme are the meth addicts with wild hair, bloodshot eyes, open facial sores, and rotting teeth. At the other is bathroom foot-tapper Larry Craig, whose mug shot looked exactly like the photo on his official U.S. Senate ID.

That's the look I was aiming for. A mug shot so neutral it could be used on a press pass. An in-custody image that minimized just how bad a legal jam I was in.

As they prepared to snap my picture, I had to balance on two white shoe outlines spaced fairly far apart on the floor. I wondered how a drunk could be expected to perform such a feat. The reason for the maneuver was to record an inmate's height and weight. So in addition to my being accused of murder, everyone would know how much I weighed. Just the kind of obnoxious detail Sam would have relished for his column.

As I braced myself for the camera click, a crazy inmate started singing "Jailhouse Rock."

I couldn't help it. I started laughing. Along with everybody in the whole cell block.

So instead of an earnest mug shot that reflected how seriously I viewed the whole situation, I looked like I was snickering at the law.

I asked to do a retake but was told, "One mug per mug." Then I was motioned down the hall, where a couple of goons kept "Hey baby"–ing me while I waited for the deputies to take my fingerprints.

The days of inky fingers are gone. The jail used a biometric computer that allowed them to electronically compare fingerprints with others in the system. The acquisition came after a minor scandal at another jail when an accused rapist was confused with a shoplifter and accidentally turned loose. Now jailers check an inmate's finger upon booking and release to make sure they match.

"Hey, sweetheart." Another jerk hooted at me and made kissy sounds as he was escorted down the hall.

Finally, a jailer gave me permission to use one of the wall phones. I dialed Benny because Noreen had been so pissy lately. I figured instead of notifying my attorney, she'd just interrupt regular scheduled programming with the breaking news of my arrest. As for Benny, I knew he'd call the station because he likes appearing on television.

"Get me out of here," I said as soon as I heard his voice on the other end of the line.

When Benny heard where I was calling from, he bellowed so loudly I thought he might rip a vocal cord. He promised me he was on his way and hung up.

I continued to hold the phone by my ear, pretending to listen so I could delay rejoining the jail scene. The guy next to me was ordering someone to bring cash now. The woman on my other side was crying and apologizing. Then I got the signal my time was up.

I was taken to a tiny holding room with a cement bench and a metal sink and toilet. I swore I would rather pee my pants than sit on that throne. No clock was in sight, probably so inmates would lose track of time.

Benny arrived hollering about probable cause and them not having grounds to hold me. Detective Delmonico let him settle down, then mentioned having other questions he'd like to ask me since my attorney was present.

"Absolutely not," Benny said. "Any questions you have for her can go through me first."

Then Chief Capacasa stuck his head through the door. The last time we'd talked he was mad about a serial killer, targeting women named Susan, whom I'd tangled with a year before. "Hello, Ms. Spartz, Mr. Walsh. Thanks for joining us downtown today."

"Back at you, Chief," I responded, even though it grated on me to use his title just then. One piece of street strategy I've adopted is to call police chiefs "Chief." It's like standing up when they enter the room. Or saluting. "You didn't have to send a car, Chief. You could have just called. I'd have come down."

"We thought we ought to do it by the book." Chief Capacasa smiled. "In case the media's watching."

"Stop talking to them," Benny told me. "That's my job. Let me earn my bill." Then he turned to the chief. "As for you, we both know you're playing politics here. I'd like us to have a word alone."

They left me in my cell to alternate staring at the metal toilet and concrete walls.

About a half hour later, they moved me to a larger room where Benny was waiting.

"You know how the button works, Mr. Walsh." The jailer pointed to a large, red button on the wall over the table.

"That won't be necessary," Benny replied.

Then the two of us were alone.

"What's with the button?" I asked.

"I'm supposed to hit it if you attack me," he said. "Then they come running with clubs."

"If you don't get me out of here, that might be necessary," I joked. But Benny didn't crack a smile. "What aren't you telling me?"

"It's complicated," he answered. "You're going to face homicide charges."

"Are you crazy, Benny? Let me talk to them."

"You'll only make things worse. Tomorrow you're going to appear in front of a judge."

"Tomorrow? What about today? What about tonight?"

"You're going to spend tonight in jail, Riley."

"Jail? You're my lawyer. You're supposed to get me out of here. What about bail?"

"Your arrest is a publicity stunt. Normally they'd just have you turn yourself in, get processed, and show up in court. In this case, they want you to cool your heels in the slammer."

He'd started to explain how the defense argues for bail, the prosecution argues against it, and the judge makes the final decision before I cut him off.

"I'm a reporter. I know how bail works. And I also know they can't charge me without probable cause. So something's not right."

That's when he told me we needed to talk. "You first, Riley."

"Me first? Benny, I've got nothing to say I haven't already said."

That's when he told me the cops found gunshot residue on my pink jacket, the one I was wearing at the assault hearing just hours before the gossip murder. And even worse, a couple of my hairs were on Sam's dead body.

If true, this was serious. "That's not possible."

"Along with your drink-in-the-face altercation, the gossip column in the victim's mouth, and you with no alibi . . . they're liking their case before a jury."

I had no answer and instead thought hard to come up with a reasonable explanation. The cops couldn't be this stupid. All I could think was that I'd been framed.

The guard banged on our door and told us time was up.

"Give us a minute," Benny yelled. "They're going to make me leave now. I'll be back tomorrow before court."

Just then the answer came to me—or part of it anyway. "I fired at the shooting range with Nick Garnett the other night. I wore the pink jacket."

"You fired bullets?" Benny asked. "With a real gun?"

"He loaned me his. I shot terribly."

"Let's hope he'll testify to both facts."

Benny had briefly represented Garnett once in a criminal matter, and knew both his aim and word to be true.

• • •

The Hennepin County jail has one of the tougher law enforcement media policies in the state—no camera interviews, no in-person media visits. Inmates may return a reporter's phone call, collect. Few do. But those who do call back are tape-recorded by the news organization so Their Side of the Story can be heard. Often the cops tape-record those calls, too. Just in case something surprising comes out.

For all those reasons, I was careful about what I said to Noreen, didn't detail the new evidence, and assured her it was all a big misunderstanding.

She tried to cheer me up by assuring me Channel 3 had broken the news of my arrest first.

The Minneapolis newspaper's crime reporter left a message for me with the jailers, but I didn't return it. The other TV stations didn't bother, but I figured their lights and cameras would be waiting for me tomorrow.

Instead of reminding myself I was a prisoner, I tried pretending I was undercover in jail trying to get an exclusive so I could win a major journalism award.

I'd been incarcerated for hours but still hadn't seen any actual bars. Just the same concrete benches. The same metal toilets. This was a modern jail.

I'd been moved to another temporary, but larger, holding area, with ten other women who had recently been arrested. None of us had been convicted of anything. The jailers had no say in who gets in and who gets out. Those decisions are made by the cops and the courts. I wished I had business cards to hand out in case any of my fellow detainees became newsworthy.

One woman was asleep on the cold cement floor, having spread toilet paper for a rug.

Another, more animated cell mate walked up to the window, unsnapped her jumpsuit, and flashed her breasts at a male prisoner standing in the hall. He hooted with appreciation.

I recognized a pretty blond woman accused of sneaking into schools, stealing teachers' purses, and using their credit cards. Her picture had been publicized the past two days, and the cops must have picked her up earlier in the day. Already she seemed popular with our peers.

I was trying to decide if it was better to just lay low and hope no one noticed me, or whether it might be nice if someone recognized me and wanted to be my friend. Then I heard my name.

"Hey, you that TV chick?" A chubby woman with wavy black hair looked me over from top to bottom.

I pretended I didn't hear her. Yet she insisted I was Riley Spartz from Channel 3.

"Really, you're on TV?" Another inmate seemed suspicious. "What are you in for?"

"Parking tickets, I bet," said a third woman, piping up.

"Maybe it's one of them First Amendment things like not revealing a source," another prisoner suggested.

"What if she's here to spy on us?" asked a scowling woman with lots of tattoos. "Maybe she's wearing a wire."

Several of them formed a circle and started to move toward me, like a wall of orange.

"Murder," I blurted out. "That's what I'm in for. Homicide."

They all pulled back, steering clear of me, and returned to their jailhouse business. I felt like I was in high school again, rejected by the popular girls.

All except the chubby one, who shook her head and laughed. "I don't believe you're a killer. I think you just messing with us to sound important."

"Then I hope you're on my jury," I said.

"Felons don't get jury duty," she said. "Courts don't trust us to be impartial."

"So what are you in for?" I asked. It seemed only polite to show an interest in her life.

"Hooking." She smiled, like a night in jail was all in a day's work, then flashed a shimmery set of fingernails in front of her face. "My customers call me Sparkles but you can call me Maureen."

She told me to stick by her 'til morning and I'd be fine. I wondered if she had a Facebook page. Maybe we could be cyber friends as well as jailhouse buddies.

"This your first night inside?" she asked.

I nodded.

"Don't worry, it goes fast."

Over the next few hours, some of our band were moved out and new ones were added. I was tempted to encourage them to call me collect from jail if they ran across any good story ideas, but I realized they might get out first. The tattoo woman snarled at me a few times, but Maureen snarled back.

I dozed once, but a loud noise outside our cell woke me. My new best-friend-forever told me to go back to sleep, that it was only a couple of guys across the hall slugging each other.

"Gang issues," Maureen explained. "Routine."

By then, I had to go to the bathroom so bad I abandoned dignity and headed for the metal toilet. And that's when I knew my life had hit bottom.

TV news is a business in which success is often measured by seconds. Even tenths of a second. The highs are high and the lows are low, and while the lows are long and slow, the highs are brief and fleeting. Sometimes a minute of professional jubilation has to carry you for what seems like an entire career.

I turned toward a corner in the holding cell, dabbing my eyes with toilet paper because I didn't want the other girls to see me cry.

CHAPTER 38

In fiction, jail tunnels represent the hope of escape. I'd always known there was a winding tunnel under the street from the jail to the courthouse, but for security reasons, the area is restricted.

For some inmates, perhaps, the tunnel does symbolize a chance at freedom should a judge pound a gavel and order them released. Me? I'd given up on hope, so the tunnel simply led to a more public humiliation: open court.

Before our march to the halls of justice, jailers handed out combs and toothbrushes. The jailhouse green room was a holding cell with a shiny piece of unbreakable metal fastened to the wall, supposedly to function as a mirror. Those of us with first appearances primped as best we could. If my mug shot had been taken then, I'm not sure my mother would have recognized me.

This time, they handcuffed our wrists in front of us, a concession to the lengthy walk ahead. This was the first time during my incarceration that

women and men were mingled together. Maybe
because they'd had time to sober up, heckling was
minimal. About thirty of us made up the perp parade. The guards leading the way were unarmed;
the ones following the inmates had holstered
weapons. I remembered Garnett telling me once
that cops use this technique because it's easier for
a prisoner to steal a gun from an officer if they
don't have to turn around.

We were herded into the tunnel, turning cor-
ners like lemmings in a maze. When I brushed up
against a wall of textured stone, I realized we were
directly under Minneapolis city hall.

That's when I hit the ground backward, pum-
meled by a man in a jumpsuit matching mine. We
rolled together on the cold floor. He landed on
top of me, his handcuffs around my neck. I could
hardly see or breathe.

Then Maureen wrapped her handcuffs around
his neck, trying to yank him off. She seemed to be
swearing encouragement to me the entire time; he
didn't say a word.

I'm sure only seconds passed, but it was one
of those long, slow lows that last forever in your
mind.

Guards yanked Maureen off him and him off
me before pulling me to my feet.

"You okay, honey?" Maureen asked.

Even though I was no longer being strangled,
I still couldn't talk. But I could see well enough to

recognize my attacker. The dine-and-dash thief. And he kept muttering "You, you" in my direction.

I was shaky, and there was some debate about whether I should delay my court appearance and go to the infirmary. The last thing I wanted was another night in jail, so I mustered enough words to convince the folks in charge to stick to the schedule. And since I wasn't actually bleeding, they agreed.

When we reached the basement of the courthouse, men and women were put in separate holding areas while we waited for our turn to appear before the judge.

A few names were called before mine. But then they put me in an elevator that opened to a normal-looking hallway. My hands were unlocked. I knew that meant showtime because there's a legal rule that unless an inmate is proven dangerous, no one should appear in court while handcuffed.

A door opened. I saw a full courtroom and heard muffled gasps as I was seated next to Benny in a chair at a table. I remember thinking how good it felt to sit on something cushioned instead of cement or plastic.

"Riley, you look horrible," Benny whispered.

"I've had a really bad night," I answered, and left it at that.

The bailiff was still getting the courtroom settled before announcing the judge.

"What were you up to last night?" Benny continued. "The chief tells me first thing this morning that some inmate offered to testify against you if they'd drop her charges."

No doubt he was talking about snarly lady. "What could she possibly have to testify about?" I asked.

"She claimed you were bragging about killing a guy. I hope that's not true."

"Come on, Benny, she's some scammer trying to land a snitch deal."

"Well, the sooner we get you out of here the better."

He got no quarrel from me. I was tired of being tired.

"Are those scratches on your neck?" he asked.

I simply shrugged.

"Our goal is not to argue you didn't do it," he continued. "That comes later. Today we argue for your release from custody."

"I know how the legal process works."

"That's what worries me. I mean it, Riley. The only thing I want to hear from your mouth is, 'Not guilty.'"

His lecture stopped because the judge entered. The only break for me was that Hennepin court judges rotate handling the criminal calendar each week, so my media-hating, grandstanding nemesis Judge Tregobov was not on the bench.

Benny waived reading of the criminal complaint. No need to have the assembled crowd hear the word "murder" said out loud in the same sentence as my name any more often than necessary. There'd be plenty of journalists doing that later.

I know it sounds egotistical, but during my simple assault hearing involving Sam, I had felt more like a peer than a defendant. That's why I was so unsettled when things went against me. Now I actually believed that Minnesota truism—it could be worse.

I knew I should muster hope, but frankly, hope had been beaten out of me somewhere between a dingy toilet seat and a violent choke hold.

A courtroom artist sat in the front row sketching me. I could hear the scratchy sound of her colored pencils on paper.

Minnesota has one of the strictest rules in the country regarding cameras in the courtroom. All parties—defense, prosecution, and judge—must agree or no go. And they never agree. So there's never any video. Unlike across the river in Wisconsin, where cameras flourish during court proceedings.

This was the first time I was okay with the no-camera policy. Especially since the rules also required I wear my orange jumpsuit, and I look bad in orange.

As a matter of legal procedure, the judge let the criminal complaint stand. I didn't expect otherwise, especially with a full media pack watching. To be fair, the prosecution's case looked strong

on paper. Forensics. Hair follicles. Gunshot residue. Motive. No alibi. If I was part of the working
media right then, I'd probably have viewed me as a
slam-dunk conviction.

"Killer!" The shout came from the back of the
courtroom. We all turned to see an older woman
standing and waving her arms wildly.

"Order." The judge pounded his gavel a few
times. "We'll have order."

"Sam's mother," I whispered to Benny. His
parents must have decided to stay in town while
they sorted out their grandchild situation.

"Don't worry," Benny whispered back. "No jury
to influence."

"She deserves the death penalty!" Sam's father
was trying to quiet his wife's shouts but not having
much success.

"Don't worry," Benny whispered again. "Minnesota doesn't have the death penalty."

A bailiff hurried down the row of spectators toward them.

"You came to his grave!" Sam's mother yelled.
"How dare you come to my son's grave."

"Please tell me that's not true," Benny said.

Before I could answer, both of Sam's parents were escorted out the door, but not before
his mother burst into noisy tears. "She thinks
it's funny she killed him. I saw her picture on the
news this morning. Laughing like it was all a big
joke."

Benny had no legal response to her description of my smirking mug shot. He probably agreed she had a point. The judge called for order a few more times to quiet the buzz of courtroom spectators who don't generally get this kind of show, certainly not in Minneapolis.

"The state requests no bail," the prosecutor said. "The defendant clearly poses a danger to the community and should remain incarcerated until trial."

Benny glanced toward her as if he'd like to snort but didn't want to be cited for contempt.

"This is America. Defendants have rights. And in this case, the defendant asks to be released on her own recognizance. Not only is Ms. Spartz a highly respected member of the community, she is a highly *recognized* member of the community. Her chance of fleeing unnoticed is virtually nonexistent. She also is a skilled investigative reporter, capable of assisting in her own defense—and we argue she is most certainly innocent."

"Save that for another day," the judge said. "We're here to discuss bail."

"Two million dollars," the prosecutor said. Her voice was beginning to sound like an auctioneer's.

"In this economy?" Benny said. "Get real. Bail is not supposed to be unattainable, merely to ensure the appearance of the defendant."

As the two growled lawyer talk, I scanned the audience for friendly faces. Father Mountain sat next to my parents, and I felt shame at being ac-

cused of such a mortal sin as murder in front of
the man who had baptized me.

My mom held a hankie; my dad held her hand.
I held my breath.

I felt a pang in my heart when I didn't see Garnett. I scoured the courtroom again, but nope. I
didn't know whether to be sad or mad, so I decided
to be both. Sad, for what we'd lost. Mad, for what a
jerk he was to shun me. This was lousy timing for
me to grasp that we were through. I found myself
hoping his plane was late and wishing he'd walk
through the courtroom door, flashing a supportive
grin in my direction. I glanced over my shoulder,
just in case, but Benny nudged me to keep my eyes
straight ahead out of respect for the judge.

The audience held plenty of unfriendly faces.
Noreen, in a rare appearance outside the newsroom, sat next to Clay Burrel, who scribbled something on his notebook. He threw me a wink, which
I ignored. Competing media filled many of the
rows. Some looked almost gleeful, others merely
curious.

Then Rolf Hedberg caught my eye. He'd shown
up at Sam's funeral. And here he was at the murder
hearing. True, he had a lot of time on his hands.
But his interest seemed atypical.

By then the judge tired of the attorney squab-
bling and announced bail would be set at half a
million dollars on the condition I didn't leave the
state. He pounded his gavel.

"I'm working on it," Benny said as guards herded me out the side door.

I had a mess ahead. Either pay a bail bond of 10 percent—fifty grand—or put up a half million bucks as insurance I wouldn't flee.

If I had to, I could muster fifty grand, but I hated to kiss away that kind of cash. Especially since Benny was costing me a fortune. As for half a million bucks, I didn't know the immediate value of my stocks, pension, 401(k), and checking account . . . but after the black stock market crash, I knew I'd come up short.

A few hours later, I was handed my street clothes. But the price for emancipation was higher than I thought I'd ever have to pay.

"No, lock me back up," I begged. Benny had just told me my parents had signed over the family farm to bail me out of jail.

"Don't worry," he said. "No land changes hands unless you skip town. It's just a formality."

He didn't understand my mortification . . . or my parents.

With that kind of money invested in my freedom, they would feel like majority shareholders in my life.

CHAPTER 39

Paparazzi waited outside the jail for my release. I tried to think of a literary description of them so they'd seem less a tabloid threat.

They moved like a windstorm across the prairie, throwing muddled questions in the air.

It didn't work. I almost turned back inside, but Chief Capacasa gave me a taunting wave good-bye, shutting the door behind me.

Benny grabbed my arm and pushed through the thicket of microphones, calling for order. "Give us space. Give us silence. Or no sound."

That was language the media mob understood. They fell back and quieted, waiting for the reward of a quote or sound bite.

"My client is innocent of all charges." Benny looked good in a dark lawyer suit. "The victim had numerous enemies. The police have yet to fully investigate this case."

Now my turn. "I welcome my day in court."

Benny had drafted my line and told me to utter it and nothing else.

When it became clear that was all I was going to say, questions exploded from behind the camera lenses.

"Was it a crime of passion?"

"What about all the forensic evidence?"

"Is the station going to fire you?"

I was curious about that last question myself.

Murder wasn't part of my job description. Whenever my bosses had praised me for landing a "killer" story, this wasn't what they meant.

Noreen had come to jail earlier to tell me in person—through the glass visitor window—how badly she felt about my "situation," yet the station couldn't help me out with bail money. She insisted that decision had nothing to do with our shrinking ad revenue, and that probably was the truth. Noreen also thought it best I not be photographed leaving jail and climbing into any vehicle with a Channel 3 logo. So I'd need to arrange my own transportation as well as bail.

"It'd be different if you'd been arrested during some freedom-of-the-press stunt," she said. "Then we'd back you. As it is, the station is still weighing how best to handle your predicament."

Her words had the same ominous tone she used during job reviews.

Benny ignored all the paparazzi questions, shoving me toward the curb, where a dark sedan pulled up. My attorney opened the front door and pushed me inside. Before he slammed it shut, he warned me—remember, no interviews.

Father Mountain was behind the wheel and my parents were in the backseat. Once the news throng was smaller in the rearview mirror, I was able to start to relax and thank them for the rescue.

Father Mountain explained he'd always wanted to drive a getaway car. "This way I get to say 'I'm on a mission from God.'"

If those words had come from Nick Garnett's mouth, I'd have answered, "Dan Aykroyd. *The Blues Brothers*, 1980." Suddenly I felt even lonelier than I had in jail, and I knew our romance was officially over.

"We would have driven ourselves," Dad said.

"But we get nervous in all the downtown traffic," Mom said.

"And we worried we might get lost," Dad explained.

"So we left our car at your place," Mom said, finishing up.

Clay Burrel and a photographer were sitting on my front steps when we pulled into the driveway. A Channel 3 live truck was front and center. The other stations had vehicles parked along the curb but none of their reporters had the guts to step onto my property. Maybe fear that I really was a murderer had something to do with them keeping their distance.

Clay's cameraman hoisted his gear to his shoulder. I noticed it was one of the new HD cameras and rued how bad my complexion would look on the air.

Clay held out a wireless microphone for me to clip on. "We can do it out here real fast," he said, "or inside nice and easy."

"Sorry, Clay, my attorney told me no media interviews. Not even Channel 3."

"You just don't want me to get another exclusive." He pointed his finger at me like it was a gun. And even though it wasn't, I worried he might have the real thing tucked in his jacket. "Admit it, Riley. You've been threatened by me since the day I started work at the station."

"That's not true," I responded. This was an awkward conversation to have in front of my mom, dad, and especially priest.

Father Mountain spoke on my behalf. "Riley is a good mentor. Perhaps you could learn from her."

"You've never seen her in action," Clay said. "She hates competition like the devil hates holy water."

"Competition doesn't prohibit cooperation," Father Mountain said. "Catholics and Lutherans compete for souls, but we all love the same God and fear the same hell. That puts us on the same life team. Just like you and Riley are on the same news team."

"I didn't come here for a sermon," Clay said. "I came here for an interview."

He left without one, heading back to the truck

to prepare for his live shot. His parting words: a whiny threat to tell Noreen about my lack of co-operation. I couldn't imagine she'd be surprised or pleased.

"Is there anything we can do to help?" my mom asked.

"You already have," I answered. "All of you. Being here means so much."

For a whole lot of reasons, I was close to tears. And for a whole lot more reasons, I did not want my parents to see me cry. I thought if they saw me cry, it would mean I still had some growing up to do. And no thirty-six-year-old woman wants to feel that way.

"And thank you for the bail money, you didn't have to do that." I held my fingers over my eyes because I could feel tears poised to fall.

Mom and Dad gave me a group hug, which was unusual in the normally stoic Spartz family. That gesture was enough to put dampness on my cheeks.

"It's just signatures on a piece of paper, Riley," Dad said.

"Father Mountain wanted to help, too," Mom said, motioning for him to join the hug. "But he has that vow of poverty."

"How about if *we* offered to do the media interviews?" Dad asked.

"No." Zero hesitation from me. That one suggestion immediately halted any need to cry.

I couldn't be sure, once they were out of my sight, whether my parents would follow my wishes. The last time I had told them I didn't need their help, they crashed a funeral. Now, if given the chance, I had a hunch they'd show up on *Oprah* to tell my side of the story.

Father Mountain gave me a good-bye blessing as he headed out the door. I encouraged him to wait until the news crews left, but since no one knew exactly when that might happen, he decided to put his faith in God that none of his parishioners would see his picture on television in connection with a heinous crime. Then he urged me to turn to the Bible for reassurance in how the righteous triumph over the wicked.

A commotion of wicked camera lights, flashes, and microphones followed him to his car. But he drove away in triumph, demonstrating to me that it can be done.

My parents headed for the kitchen, because kitchens are the most normal part of any house, and we needed to feel normal.

"That reporter guy kind of looked familiar," Mom told Dad. They were talking about Clay.

"Yeah, didn't we meet him at the funeral?" he answered.

"Maybe," she said. "Or maybe we just saw him on TV."

Mom opened the refrigerator to see what I had to cook. The pickings were sparse. She moved on to the freezer, disappointed not to see a frozen wild rice hot dish waiting for company.

"You can eat whatever you can find," I said.

The doorbell rang while she was looking through the cupboards. I went to tell Clay that if he came back again, he was trespassing. I didn't imagine that threat would carry much clout because, under the circumstances, I couldn't really call the police.

But instead of my TV colleague, the newspaper's former political columnist stood under the shadow of my porch light, looking even older than he had in court.

Ends up, Rolf wanted an interview, too.

"No, Rolf. N-O. If I'm not doing an interview with my own newsroom, why would I talk to you?"

"Well, Riley, you were the one who encouraged me to try freelancing for the paper, to see if they'd take me back. My first assignment is to interview you. If I don't bring back the story, my career is over."

"Rolf, your career is already over, and mine isn't far behind."

Then I slammed the door in his face, not caring whether he had a gun. Or Clay had a gun. Or that I was the only journalist in the state armed only with my wits. Then I found myself wishing neither of them knew where I lived.

In the other room, I heard my parents discussing whether Rolf looked familiar or whether they were just getting old.

CHAPTER 40

My folks wanted to watch the news. It was their bedtime ritual. But I nixed that idea and hid the TV remote control. No good would have come of them seeing me branded a criminal on all four network affiliates, even my own.

Finally, I had time to shower away the smell of jail. I warned my mom and dad not to answer the telephone or the door while I was upstairs. I wished some special soap was invented that could wash away humiliation, or at least the vulgar image of that intoxicated inmate vomiting next to me in the holding cell.

A half hour later, I wrapped a towel around my head, threw on my frizzy bathrobe, and went to check on my parents. Dad was reading what few car ads remained in the newspaper.

"Where's Mom?"

"She went out to the pickup to get her sweater."

I wished she'd stayed inside, away from possible paparazzi. But through the window, it looked like all the live trucks had pulled cable and left, now that the newscasts were over. So the path to the curb was probably clear for her.

I was just filling a glass when suddenly we heard a scream that sounded like Mom. Then another scream that didn't. I dropped ice cubes on the kitchen floor as I rushed outside. Mom stood empty-handed in the driveway. I speculated that someone might have grabbed her purse. Dad followed seconds later because of his bad knees.

"A tall man," she said. "He jumped out at me."

"What did he look like?" I asked.

"It was dark. I couldn't see. He was really tall."

"Where did he go?"

She pointed down the block. "He said we had unfinished business."

I wondered what he meant. And then I wondered if, perhaps in the dark and because I lived alone, he'd mistaken my mother for me.

His next actions made his intentions and identity clear.

"Then he turned on a flashlight and pulled down his pants," Mom said.

"He what?" I asked.

"It was like he wanted to show me his . . . you know."

Any guy who'd walk naked in front of a live television camera would think nothing of flashing a woman on a street corner. But this was my mother, so Buzz was going to hear plenty from me.

"It wasn't anything special," she said. "I've seen many men over the years."

"Don't say it like that, Mom. You sound like a prostitute."

She was a retired hospital nurse, dating back to the days when they wore white caps.

"Well, it wasn't anything special," she insisted. "You'd think such a tall man would have a bigger—"

"Mom, I don't want to hear about it."

"Then he shined the light in my face, and that's when he started screaming, too."

Buzz must have been watching the news, elated that all the channels reported which corner I lived on and showed what my house looked like. I could only imagine his dismay when he realized his throbbing manhood was face-to-face with someone old enough to be his grandmother.

All Dad could muster was, "It could have been worse."

And he was right. I had a nagging suspicion that Buzz Stolee might not be the only thing lurking in the dark, waiting for me.

CHAPTER 41

Again, I slept poorly. My ears strained for suspicious noises, my eyes for mysterious shapes outside the window. I wished I didn't live in the same jurisdiction where I was a murder suspect, because right now I couldn't really think of the cops as my protectors.

I'd decided that whoever was framing me couldn't be a complete stranger. The strongest evidence against me was my hair on Sam's body. That was difficult to explain away. He and I had been in court together the day he was killed. But we'd stayed an arm's length apart.

The murderer somehow had access to my hair. Thus access to me or my home.

That night, as I lay in bed, I'd decided it was best to keep my parents there where I could keep an eye on them.

By the next morning, however, I'd decided to send them back to the farm, rationalizing that they'd be safer next to wind turbines than next to me. I promised I'd call. They didn't argue, seeming to want to pretend things were fine, too. Mom made fluffy pancakes and smiled like nothing was wrong, even though I caught her and Dad exchanging parental glances. None of us mentioned anything, and we all waved as their pickup pulled away.

I didn't want to be home alone, so I dragged myself into work even though I wasn't sure I'd be welcome.

Turns out, Noreen wanted to see me in her office ASAP.

"I wouldn't be doing this if the economy wasn't so shaky," she told me. "You know how far our numbers have dropped."

I nodded, dreading where our conversation was going. I'd been suspended a couple times before, but those transgressions were nothing compared to being charged with murder.

"I'm more torn up over this decision than any I've ever made as a news director. But Fitz, our consultant, is insisting on it."

I believed her. Fitz knew I dissed him. And even though Noreen and I had clashed and snarled over the last couple years, we'd also developed a certain camaraderie that comes from teetering on the edge of the abyss.

"You've always been one of our strongest reporters, and your instincts in the field are unmatched, but I have to do what's best for the station."

It was too difficult to look her in the eye while she said the words, so I reached down for my bag in order to make a quick getaway once the deed was done.

"To be perfectly blunt, Riley, if the ratings fall any farther, my own job is on the line. So I have to follow orders."

I nodded that I understood. The morals clause in my contract was clear. But instead of commiserating about what a jam she was in, I just wanted Noreen to get it over with so I could slink away.

"So, Riley, starting tonight, I'm making you the lead anchor here at Channel 3."

I've never aspired to the anchor desk. Sitting under hot lights, reading what the rest of the newsroom staff did in the trenches all day isn't my idea of a challenge. And it isn't why I went into the news business.

But it's sure better than being canned.

Upper management at Channel 3 had decided to view my arrest as a gift, not a curse. Starting that afternoon, the station was launching a massive promotion campaign urging viewers to tune in to our newscasts for an opportunity to look me in the eye and decide for themselves whether or not I was a cold-blooded killer.

It was a bold scheme to abandon honor for ratings.

If it worked, and the numbers spiked . . . I'd be glued to the anchor desk until the cops dragged me off to prison.

If it tanked, and viewers turned away in revulsion . . . I'd be thrown out the door to wait in isolation for my court date.

I had no idea how the overnight ratings would read in the morning but realized Noreen was taking a big gamble on the morbid curiosity of Minnesota television viewers.

"What about Sophie?" I had asked my boss. Technically the anchor desk belonged to her. Her cadence was sound, her smile adorable. She may have been a good sport about the bat altercation, but there was no way she wasn't going to blame me for ousting her from her princess throne.

"We could face viewer backlash," I said.

"Never overestimate viewer loyalty," Noreen countered.

If that's what they taught news directors in management school, well, that explained a lot about the state of journalism.

"Anyway, it's not your call, or even really mine." Noreen explained that Sophie would have a chance to do some reporting.

Then I really felt guilty.

Sophie wasn't the kind of anchor who could report anything beyond baby dolphins born at the zoo. But because she was under contract, Noreen couldn't just yank her off the anchor desk; my guess was our boss had blackmailed her with threats about a tough renegotiation.

Then Noreen had ordered me off to the green room, where a makeup artist was waiting to work me over for my big anchor debut.

Since the switch from analog to digital, every pore on a television journalist's face popped off the screen and into viewers' homes. More and more TV talent were using airbrush makeup to make their complexions more uniform.

So were certain politicians, my makeup expert said with a wink. Male and female. "Now close your eyes."

I'd watched her squirt a few drops of liquid foundation labeled "olive beige" into a pen fastened to a narrow hose that plugged into a small machine. I heard a strange whooshing sound and felt cool air against my skin.

"Feels good," I said.

"Looks even better," she answered. "Open your eyes."

I'd scoffed at the concept of high-tech makeup. But darn if my face didn't look flawless.

She was just explaining it would stay that way for a good ten hours without getting splotchy when I blurted out, "I'm beautiful." Something I hadn't thought in a very long time.

My confidence was so high, I even practiced

my model walk as I moved down the hall toward the newsroom. Then I turned a corner and suddenly was face-to-face with Sophie.

She was carrying an overnight bag, like she'd cleaned out her desk. She was also clearly in a hurry to leave.

She's quit, I thought. It's all my fault. She hates me for taking her job.

But Sophie flashed me that huge trademark grin of hers.

"Guess what, Riley?" She threw her arms in the air in a show of pure elation, like a cheerleader in the aftermath of a winning touchdown. "The station's sending me to Mexico to do a story about butterflies!"

CHAPTER 42

The ratings the next morning showed a huge jump. The days of a 40 share were long gone. Even a 30 was unrealistic. But last night—a 28 share—had put Channel 3 farther ahead than we'd been in several sweeps months. Clearly our competitors' audience had switched to us for a chance to look a murder suspect in the eye.

Noreen felt smart.

My parents felt proud.

And I felt trapped.

Besides the ten o'clock news, I was also assigned to read teleprompter for the two early-evening newscasts. My opening line became routine and boring.

((RILEY, CU))
GOOD EVENING, EVERYONE.
I'M RILEY SPARTZ, FILLING
IN FOR SOPHIE PAULSON,

WHO'S ON ASSIGNMENT OUT
OF THE COUNTRY.

That bit about Sophie was to create mystique
for her return and remind viewers that I was just
a temp and could be pulled off the anchor desk at
any moment by the whim of my boss. So if they
wanted to look me in the eye, they better do it
while they could.

Because I was now the lead anchor, the station suddenly cared about me, like they had with
Sophie and all the previous lead anchors. They insisted I park in the basement, where the photographers park to protect their expensive gear and
where the bosses park just to show who's boss.
This way I didn't have to worry about being stalked
arriving and leaving the station. I felt safer on the
job than anywhere else. But the novelty of star
treatment grew monotonous.

I had no time to leave Channel 3 to hunt for
Sam's killer. And there was only so much time I
could devote to perfecting my airbrush makeup
technique. So I continued researching wind turbines and learned they weren't just deadly to bats.

Xiong helped me download government safety
records and I discovered numerous cases world-
wide where wind workers had died on the job.
Unlike black lung, the silent killer in coal mines,
when wind energy kills, death is immediate and
awful.

Some employees fell hundreds of feet because they weren't wearing safety harnesses. Another, with a harness, dangled too long waiting for rescue. His blood drained to the lower part of his body and turned toxic.

Ice can form at the top of the wind turbines—inside and outside—and sometimes chunks break off and kill whoever is standing underneath. I shuddered reading of a wind company employee sliced in half when ice crashed down on him while he was working inside the tower.

The cases got even more grisly. An inside ladder leads to an upstairs chamber, big enough to stand in, at the top of the turbine. Blades are attached to a spinning rotor. One worker's harness got caught, and according to the death certificate, he suffered "multiple amputations."

I was starting to think I had the makings of a major workplace safety investigation. Even transporting the giant turbines can be dangerous. Sometimes, on rural roads, truck drivers are electrocuted when a blade hits a low-hanging power line. Other times, employees get crushed while unloading the windmills, as pieces roll off the truck.

When I learned one casualty died more than a year ago constructing the Wide Open Spaces wind farm, I pressed Noreen to give me a day away from my anchoring duties to interview his widow, who lived in Upper Michigan. But Noreen observed that the overnight demos were still strong and she didn't want to risk moving me from the anchor desk until sweeps were over.

Neither of us mentioned Toby, so I was under the impression he had not said anything to Noreen about his role in the fatal wind bombing. Being an accused murderess myself, I didn't have the influence or evidence to call anyone else a killer.

Meanwhile, in Mexico, the butterflies were running late. And Sophie had been told to just sit back and wait for the monarch migration.

CHAPTER 43

Under the circumstances, I wanted to shut down my Facebook page. But Benny thought that might make me look guilty.

"Just don't discuss the case with anyone—in person or online," he warned me. "The police could be posing as 'friends' just to get you to talk."

Noreen considered my notoriety the opportunity of a lifetime.

I just hoped the whole ordeal didn't hand me a lifetime in prison. An ex-con once told me prison wasn't nearly as bad as the first hours of jail. Especially not women's prisons. But I wasn't buying it. Behind bars is behind bars. I'd always joked that I was just one felony away from thinner thighs, but suddenly I saw the merit in diet and exercise.

Now everybody on Facebook was requesting my cyber friendship. Having a nefarious friend gave them bragging rights. It was like saying Squeaky Fromme went to prom with your uncle.

As a news anchor, I had plenty of time to confirm computer friends. And my number neared three thousand. I wasn't sure how those related to the glory days of 40-share TV ratings, but I knew I had more friends than Clay. And so did he.

When I logged on, I saw one of his Texas gal pals had friended me back after I'd poached her off his list. She'd also sent me a personal message. Puzzling.

"I see you work at the same television station as Clay Burrel. I'm a friend of his wife's and have been trying to get in touch with her. Have you by any chance met?"

Her name was Sally Oaks. According to her profile she was twenty-seven, worked at a small library, and had a pet cat. She posted several pictures of the cat on her Facebook page. It was calico. She also posted covers of the books she was reading. Currently, it was a best-selling tearjerker that showed bare feet on sand.

This was awkward.

Not wanting to get involved in dissecting a shaky marriage for a third party, I sent her a reply suggesting she talk to Clay directly.

Let him explain his own troubles. I had enough of my own.

Meanwhile Xiong was helping me add video to my Facebook page and teaching me how to do it myself so I didn't keep bothering him.

"Go to hell," he said suddenly.

I was surprised to hear such strong language from him. The comment was uncharacteristic. I didn't think I'd done anything to deserve it and told him so.

"Bastard," he replied.

"Knock it off," I said.

"Target dirtbag."

"What's wrong with you, Xiong?"

"Not me," he said. "You." He pointed to my bulletin board, at the surveillance photo of Daisy carrying my flowers, plus the collection of her mysterious messages.

He explained that the first letter of each word spelled out a hidden code. The one by Sam's grave—*"God Overpowers Those Outside His Extended Limitless Love"*—GO TO HELL. The funeral bouquet—*"Be Assured Sam Took A Righteous Direction"*—BASTARD. And the one she sent to me—*"Thanks Alot, Riley, Give Everyone The Disturbing Information Regarding That Bad Ass Gossip"*—TARGET DIRTBAG.

Daisy is such a harmless-sounding name, but names can be deceiving. I didn't know what these messages meant, but I knew I needed to have a talk with her.

I was used to being tired when I got home from work; anchoring the late news made me wired instead. The kind of wired that made me want to play Ping-Pong, except I didn't have a Ping-Pong table, or an opponent. If it wasn't the middle of the night, and I wasn't going through a scared-of-the-dark phase, I'd have gone running outside.

I wished I had a dog to walk. Or a man to walk with.

My cell phone vibrated; Garnett's number came on the screen. I didn't know what to say, so to buy time, I let the call roll to voice mail. Except he didn't leave any message.

That steamed me, so I called him back. And he must have let it roll to voice mail. I didn't leave a message, either. I hung up, set the phone down, and stared at it like it was a test I hadn't studied for.

Thirty seconds later Garnett called back, and I picked up.

He spoke first. "What we've got here is a failure to communicate."

Those were the last words I had said to his face before he turned his back on me down at the wind farm. But instead of responding with *Cool Hand Luke* movie trivia, I replied, "And whose fault is that?"

There was a long pause on the line. "I've been waiting for you to call," he said.

"You've been waiting for me? I've been in jail. I've been in court. I've been through hell. Where have you been?" The fact that I still cared so much surprised me.

"Hey, I thought you wanted me to stay away. You were pretty clear that you didn't want people to see us together. You thought that would make things worse. With all the media swarming, I figured you'd feel even more strongly that way."

He sort of had a point. But he still should have known better.

"I thought if I showed up," he continued, "the police might go even harder on you just to prove they weren't playing favorites."

I informed him that the cops couldn't go any harder on me than they already had.

"I'm so sorry, Riley."

"You should have called."

"I'm calling now."

I was trying to decide whether now was just in time or too late.

"I can be there tomorrow," he said.

I yearned to say yes, but deep down, I suspected that tomorrow was too late. And I told him so. I think I set it up as a test. To see if he loved me enough to come anyway.

CHAPTER 44

If being targeted for ridicule by Sam was bad, it was nothing compared to the national gossip rags. To be fair, as a professional journalist, I could understand how a television anchor accused of murder might be newsworthy. But the coverage went viral overnight, even in the mainstream media.

My anchor efforts were posted on YouTube and scored the number of views usually reserved for controversial reality-show contestants or unusual pets.

And my snickering mug shot was everywhere.

Wall-to-wall satellite trucks were parked outside the station so all the network morning news shows and cable channels could go live with updates about Murder in America's Heartland.

Because I wasn't allowed to talk about the case, Noreen did several live interviews explaining that the station kept me on the air because of a patriotic belief in "innocent until proven guilty."

"What about ratings?" she was asked. "Isn't putting a murder suspect in the anchor chair just an unprincipled stunt to increase your numbers?"

It was for the best that I wasn't doing any interviews, because I would probably have screamed back something like, "Do you idiots think I'd kill a human being to help the station's ratings?" But their answer might have taken the discussion down an uncomfortable path.

Noreen had a much smoother reply. "Channel 3 prides itself on impartial news coverage. Viewers can rely on us for objective reporting. We believe everyone deserves their day in court and are prepared to take whatever action is appropriate at that time."

The media appeal of my case came down to it being a slow week for celebrity dirt (Tiger Woods hadn't had his tree/SUV accident yet), and no famous people died. So the *National Enquirer* put me on the cover, running a handcuff photo they bought from the Minneapolis newspaper. Normally, traditional media organizations shun tabloids and their checkbooks. But during a media meltdown, integrity has a price. I'd heard a rumor that the Minneapolis paper got twenty grand. That was the kind of detail Sam would have nailed in his column had it not involved his own employer.

The scandal sheet's headline read MEDIA MURDERER WINS RATINGS. "*Alleged* Media Murderer," I wanted to shout.

The *Globe* published GOSSIP GRUDGE LEADS TO MURDER.

Again, "*Alleged* Murder." Or "Murder *Charges*." In neither case was I in any position to demand a correction.

I imagined the graphic designers preferred not to clutter up the covers with extra words. I also imagined their media attorneys vetted the copy knowing I'd never actually sue them, because I needed to budget for my criminal defense.

Inside, the *Globe* ran a sidebar interview with the first boy I'd ever kissed. We once climbed to the top of the water tower in town and talked for hours under the moon. I read the item eagerly until I got to the part where he told them he had a hunch way back then that I could be dangerous and that's why he dumped me. I had recalled being the dumper in that relationship. Again, I was in no position to insist on a correction, from either them or him.

People magazine showed better news judgment. Their cover raised the question of whether Kanye West was a jackass and included only a small inset of my mug shot in the cover corner. I considered rewarding their discretion with an exclusive interview, should I ever be able to talk. But by then, the odds of them remaining interested in me were dismal.

My mom and her Red Hat ladies were making a scrapbook of all the coverage to give me for a Christmas present.

What really bothered me was that I was being portrayed as a sociopath . . . psychopath . . . even lunatic. Sam was being painted as a victim. And not just a murder victim, either. A First Amendment martyr.

A pile of flowers, American flags, and photographs of Sam made a giant memorial in front of the Minneapolis newspaper offices. In the middle was an old typewriter. Beside it was a familiar crystal vase full of spectacular wildflowers. The card read *"Those Remaining Are Irate Though Often Regretful."*

I took a picture with my cell phone but didn't need Xiong to tell me the message spelled TRAITOR.

TARGET DIRTBAG. BASTARD. GO TO HELL. TRAITOR.

"I'd like a bouquet of wildflowers," I said, walking into the floral shop before my news shift.

Daisy immediately recognized me and put down an almost-finished Sudoku puzzle. Baby Jimmy watched in a playpen with his thumb in his mouth, holding a stuffed white teddy bear.

"Why don't you tell me about you and Sam?" I didn't offer up that Jeremy had already briefed me.

She started making wedding corsages as we spoke. The story she told was similar to his. After being deceived and dumped, she saw no reason to tell Sam she was pregnant.

"I never wanted to see him again."

I didn't point out that now she didn't have to. But I did ask what prompted her to reach out to me.

"I wish I'd thrown a drink in his face," she said. "So when you did, I wanted to give you an 'atta girl.'"

I told her if I could take back that drink, I would. And if I could raise a baby with his father, I would. And if I could go back and introduce my most recent love to my parents, I would.

"My life is full of regrets," I said.

"You have to also make it full of hope." She picked up Jimmy and hugged him tight. I watched closely, trying to understand what might motivate Daisy, as both a mother and a murderer.

"Raising a child alone is a huge challenge," I said. "Weren't you tempted to make Sam share the cost at least?"

"I didn't want his money."

Just then the phone rang, and it sounded like an order for a green plant to be delivered to a hospital. Daisy handed her little boy to me as she wrote down the details. He and I stared at each other. As far as I could tell, he didn't have Sam's piercing eyes or big mouth.

"I didn't kill your dad," I said as I bounced him in my arms.

His mom hung up the phone fast and took him back from me. But I felt I had scored a victory. She never would have let me hold her baby if she thought I was a cold-blooded murderer.

I handed her pictures of her flower notes with the codes written underneath. TARGET DIRTBAG. BASTARD. GO TO HELL. TRAITOR.

I didn't say anything because I wanted her to speak first. But all she said was that she needed to get back to work and that it was time for me to leave.

Clearly she hadn't wanted Sam's money while he was alive. Perhaps she decided his death would make it bearable.

That night when I drove up to my garage, my headlights shined on a vase of flowers sitting in front of the door. I got out of my car to move them so I could park. The bouquet was Daisy's signature arrangement. The note merely said, *"I hated him, but I didn't kill him."* This time there was no hidden code.

I wasn't sure what to believe.

CHAPTER 45

One of the jobs of Channel 3's phone operators is to keep written logs of viewer complaints. I think it's an FCC rule. Sometimes people complain about explicit violence on a prime-time show. Other times they fuss about talent, hair, or clothing in a newscast.

The main focus of complaints, the last couple days, was me behind the anchor desk. "Trashy." "Insulting." "Offensive." But because the ratings continued upward in our favor, Noreen ignored all the adjectives, figuring our competitors to be the source behind them.

One call it would have been better not to ignore was from a viewer named Lois Tregobov. Rubbish, is how she summed me up. Turned out to be Judge Tregobov, the same one I faced after throwing the drink in Sam's face. The one who, on any ordinary day, hated the media with the same passion as any conservative radio talk-show host.

But her grumbling got buried along with that of folks miffed that our meteorologist didn't predict approaching rain and others mad about some line in a political story they considered too liberal.

So it was a surprise when my attorney, Benny Walsh, stopped by the station to check if I had any boots and work gloves. "Judge Tregobov is insisting you do your community service garbage pickup duty tomorrow."

Noreen was irritated by my sudden unavailability to read the day's news. "That's a Thursday. Don't these sentences usually take place on weekends?"

"Often work schedules are considered," Benny admitted, "but the judge thinks a day off the anchor desk is just the lesson Riley needs."

"You're supposed to be such a hotshot attorney," Noreen said. "Can't you get this changed?"

Benny shook his head. "Judge Tregobov is insistent."

"What about the station? This is only penalizing us. Why should her employer suffer?"

"Normally, that is taken into account, but the judge actually thinks Channel 3 needs to learn a lesson as well. So the less you say, the better."

I could tell Noreen didn't like the sound of that. "So Riley'll miss the early shows but should be back in time for the late newscast, right?" Noreen asked.

The ten o'clock had the most viewers and the highest ad rates. And my boss didn't care that I'd be stiff, sore, and smelly from hauling trash.

"Certainly she'll be done in time for the ten," Benny said. "No way they'll make her pick up garbage past sunset."

I actually didn't mind the idea of a day off the anchor desk, I'd just have rathered any scoops I made be news—not filth. Especially when Benny explained that I was to report for cleanup duty the next morning on Boom Island, along the muddy Mississippi.

I knew the assignment was going to stink.

Liquor bottles, used condoms, hey, once human body parts even washed up on shore after being caught in the St. Anthony Dam.

A city employee handed out orange fluorescent vests, giant garbage bags, and long trash tongs to me and a dozen other minor lawbreakers, then split us up into groups of three.

"Now get busy" was the order.

My garbage team immediately recognized me from the news and felt lucky to be on assignment with me. To them, my presence made the chore more of a perk than a punishment.

"Can I have your autograph afterward?" asked a plus-size woman named Thelma.

"Sure," I replied.

Thelma was there for a drunk-driving offense. Wearing a wide-brimmed hat, she seemed a trifle wobbly but sober enough to spear trash.

Our other colleague, Mitch, had just had his second conviction for shoplifting. He bragged about being a pro at litter cleanup, having done it once before.

"Try to do most of your reaching with the tongs." He demonstrated for us. "Less bending you do, less sore you'll be at the end of the day."

Because the end of the day could have been six hours away, that was useful advice. Our trio developed a system to pick up debris along the river's edge. Occasionally, we'd come across a real mushy item popular with maggots, so we'd do Rock, Paper, Scissors to determine whose turn it was to clutch the junk.

The station sent a photographer to shoot some quick video of me to explain to viewers why I wasn't on the news set.

> ((ANCHOR, CU))
> RILEY SPARTZ IS ON
> ASSIGNMENT TODAY.
>
> ((VID NAT SOT))
> SHE'S OFF HELPING
> CLEAN THE ENVIRONMENT.
> SHE'LL BE COLLECTING

TRASH ALONG THE
MISSISSIPPI RIVER
AS PART OF A COMMUNITY
SERVICE PROJECT . . . BUT
WILL BE BACK IN TIME FOR
THE NEWS AT TEN.

Our rival stations were in a quandary. Normally they'd have liked to remind viewers that I was a criminal scofflaw, but currently that sort of journalism just seemed to backfire against them in the ratings. So the only other camera on the scene was the newspaper's. I could only imagine the cutline under the photo to be something along the lines of "Trashy reporter right where she belongs."

Thelma and Mitch delighted in the prospect that they might end up on television if they stuck close to me. I tried telling them being on TV isn't always a coup.

"How are you going to explain your criminal record to your friends?" I pointed out.

Mitch insisted his buddies had all done worse yet never once landed on TV. Thelma felt the celebrity factor would outweigh any downside of being known as a drunk.

By then the cameras had left, so I gave up trying to convince them of the dark side of notoriety. Now the discussion turned to the cyber world of Facebook. Both my new pals promised to friend each other, and me, the minute they got home.

The day grew hot. And we grew sweaty. No different from the rest of our trash brigade. We were all spreading out farther to finish up faster. The novelty of separating glass, plastic, and aluminum recyclables from just plain ordinary garbage grew dull.

Suddenly Thelma screamed like she was auditioning for a slasher horror film. And had she been, she would have landed the lead.

I rushed to her side. "What is it?"

She covered her face but pointed toward something in a lumpy plastic bag just offshore. Pushing at it with my tongs, I saw hair and teeth. And I screamed, too.

CHAPTER 46

The head was bloated and slimy, the eyes ghoulish. So that grisly find, along with the lights and sirens that followed, put an end to our trash collection. The other miscreants were ordered home, but Thelma and I stayed behind to answer questions.

She didn't have much to say that wasn't a sob. And all her bravado about being a celebrity came to naught because she no longer had any desire to relive her gruesome moment of discovery for the TV cameras. Not even Channel 3's.

I've smelled the odor of rotting flesh before, the real thing as well as a corpse flower. So I managed to take a closer look at the pale face of the detached head than most people would have under the circumstances. While I couldn't tell age or gender, I could have sworn the tangled hair was blond.

Predictably, Burrel thought I was trying to horn in on his story. "I've been on the case from the beginning," he said. "It's mine."

I understood his being irate—good reporters fight for their stories—but heck, I found the head. And when it comes to news, finders keepers.

"We don't know for sure that *my* head is *your* head," I said.

"How many missing heads do you think there are in this metropolitan area?" he asked.

"He's got a point." Noreen sided with Clay, making it seem like I had a conflict of interest—a big journalism no-no. "Riley, you're actually part of this story, too, so I don't think we can have you covering it."

"But who better to cover it than a person with firsthand knowledge of the event?" I asked. "Isn't that why sports reporters go to games, court reporters attend trials, and political reporters watch the legislative debates? My being on the scene makes me the best-qualified person for the story. Especially since the cops aren't talking."

Not all murders are created equal. The amount of media attention often comes down to that early journalism lesson of who, what, where, when, why, and how.

Who might be the most significant. If someone important or interesting is killed, that pushes the crime to the front page and the top of a newscast. If the homicide is just one gang member shooting another, the public won't much care. But if the victim is an innocent bystander, perhaps a child hit by a stray bullet, that's a whole different story.

What is fairly obvious. Murder, what else? Used to be every homicide was assigned a reporter who scrambled to make sure the victim's name and picture made air. Now, run-of-the-mill murders might get a ten-second mention unless they're part of a particular trend.

Where can make a big difference. If someone is killed in a school, church, or courthouse, viewers are curious. If murder happens in an alley in a bad part of town, a blame-the-victim mentality might kick in and affect coverage.

When only really counts if it's a holiday. If someone is slain on Christmas, when news is slow, a camera crew will be knocking on the family's door, wanting to videotape the unopened presents under the tree. Get killed on your birthday or wedding day, and that can be newsworthy, too.

Why might be the least influential when it comes to weighing how much play to give a murder, at least early in the news cycle, because *why* goes to motive, and police don't often discern that until later, when a suspect is in custody. And sometimes not even then. If *why* is obvious, like in a liquor store robbery, that also lessens the mystique.

How is the most morbid of the criteria and perhaps the most riveting. That's why a headless body—or bodiless head—trumps most other news of the day.

Noreen offered a compromise in which I'd anchor the newscast, toss to Clay for the report, then ask him a question in a tag.

"Why should I ask him a question?" I said. "What does he know? I'm the one who was there."

So we struck a deal: Clay would do a live shot from as close to the river scene as the police would allow. He would give the main summary; I would be next to him in the field, where he would interview me as a witness about the gruesome find.

((TWOSHOT/CLAY))
RILEY, DO YOU THINK THE
HEAD FOUND THIS
AFTERNOON MIGHT BE FROM
THE DECAPITATED WOMAN IN
THE WIRTH PARK MURDER?

((TWOSHOT/RILEY))
TOO SOON TO TELL, CLAY.
POLICE WILL HAVE TO WAIT
FOR DNA TESTS. BUT I CAN
TELL YOU THAT TODAY'S
REMAINS DEFINITELY HAD
TEETH. SO THAT MEANS
DENTAL RECORDS WILL BE
AN IMPORTANT CLUE FOR
IDENTIFICATION.

Clay and I went back and forth a few times about missing people in the area and our interview was replayed coast to coast. I found myself hoping a 24/7 cable network might hire him. I wondered if he had any outs in his contract that would allow him to leave Channel 3 without much notice. Maybe if I made him look good during this coverage, I could get him out of this market.

But then I remembered that I had a much more serious problem than scooping competitors.

For the last twenty-four hours, distracted by an unidentified head, I had been able to forget the murder of Sam Pierce.

CHAPTER 47

Another message from my Texas Facebook friend Sally Oaks greeted me at my desk. By her current book cover posted, I could see she was reading an adventure story about an iceberg.

"I have tried contacting Clay, but he has not responded to my messages. I am worried about Jolene. I am their former neighbor and would appreciate any information you could share."

Nosy neighbor. Clearly Clay was humiliated over the whole matter and didn't care to discuss his marriage with her. Clay's wife might even feel some shame over her behavior and not want to defend it to their friends.

Again, I replied that I was uncomfortable discussing Clay's personal life with her.

If she continued to pursue the issue, I would have to take the drastic step of unfriending her from my page. It wouldn't bother me a bit. I now had more than three thousand Facebook friends— plenty to spare.

I scrolled past the latest news my social-network buddies had posted. One had the flu. Another was celebrating an anniversary. Sophie had recently updated her profile picture with a photo of her in the Mexican jungle, sipping what looked like a piña colada. I love piña coladas.

CHAPTER 48

During the afternoon news meeting, Ozzie called over from the assignment desk that Minneapolis police were holding a news conference in an hour about the headless homicide.

"I'll go." Clay and I both spoke up at the same time.

"We'll send Clay," Noreen said. "And cover the news conference live. Riley, you toss to him. Clay, you fill until the police start talking."

I didn't argue, which seemed to relieve Noreen. I actually had a plan to try to shake out some of the death details early and didn't want to waste minutes quibbling.

We speculated about the announcement. Normally it can take weeks, months, even years for a DNA test because of backlogs at state crime labs. But Minnesota has one of the major labs in the country and can push to get faster results in high-profile cases.

"The DNA matches, or it doesn't," I said. "But in an hour we should know whether the head goes with the body."

"Either way, it's a lead story," Noreen said. "If they don't match, we have two murders."

As soon as I got to my desk, I called Della, the medical examiner, who had been handling the case.

"Don't bother pressing me for the DNA results, Riley. The cops are breaking that news and don't want it leaked."

I hid my disappointment but quizzed her on whether she was able to determine the cause of death, now that she had the head. "Remember, I was the first reporter to ask you about that."

"Nothing is ever simple."

I waited for her to continue.

"First, let's get this straight," she said. "I'm not confirming whether the head and body match. I'm merely commenting on cause of death for the head that was discovered by the river."

"Understood," I replied.

Della explained that she was able to rule out traumatic beating or gunshot wounds but couldn't determine if the victim had been strangled or had her throat slashed. "Bones in the neck were damaged, and while that could have happened from choking, it could also have been caused by a tool when the head was removed from the body."

I wrote fast to get all the details.

"Best we can do," she said.

I thanked her for the scoop and rushed back to the newsroom. "Noreen, I just talked to a source and have inside info in the headless homicide."

I proposed we cut into programming early and I fill until the news conference started, then toss directly to the police. I handed her a script.

((RILEY, CU))
CHANNEL 3 HAS LEARNED
EXCLUSIVE DETAILS ABOUT HOW
THE WOMAN WHOSE HEAD
WAS PULLED FROM THE
RIVER DIED . . .
AUTHORITIES HAVE BEEN
ABLE TO RULE OUT
TRAUMATIC INJURY OR
GUNSHOTS . . . AND ARE NOW
CONCENTRATING ON
STRANGULATION OR
INCISION WOUNDS.
WE NOW JOIN A POLICE
NEWS CONFERENCE TO LEARN
MORE . . . PERHAPS WHETHER
THE DNA FOR THE HEAD
MATCHES THE BODY
DISCOVERED IN WIRTH
PARK.

"Clay can recap the highlights after the cops are finished," I suggested. I could tell by the way his eyes narrowed that he didn't like my plan, but I figured there wasn't anything he could do about it. I figured wrong.

"Except I also have an exclusive that I believe trumps yours," he said. "My source tells me that the head and body match."

I was furious that the chief had given Clay that gem. He was taking this make-Riley-look-bad thing a little too far.

Noreen was thrilled with his news. She told me to cut into programming with a "Channel 3 has learned" line and toss to Clay Burrel, promoting him as "standing by live with a big exclusive."

"He'll fill with the DNA match until the news conference starts," she added. "Then you and he can discuss your cause-of-death details and he can package it for the newscasts."

She smiled because she knew we had the competition beat.

Clay smiled because he knew he had me beat.

CHAPTER 49

Please don't hang up," said the voice on the other end of the phone. When she identified herself as Sally Oaks, my Texas Facebook friend, I'd just about had it with manners. Besides, it wasn't like she lived in my viewing area and could threaten to switch channels.

"I'm worried Clay's isolating Jolene from her friends," she said.

I decided to tell Sally the truth and end all this back-and-forth. "I realize you mean well. But you're obviously not as close to Jolene as you think. If she wanted to talk to you, she'd get in touch."

I explained that Clay's wife decided against moving to Minnesota and stayed behind in Corpus Christi, in hopes of one day becoming Mrs. Texas.

"That's not true," she insisted. "Did she tell you that? Or did he?"

"None of us here at the station have ever met her. She never came to Minnesota."

Sally told me how she watched the two drive north together in a moving van. "I haven't heard from her since. Besides, she'd given up that beauty-queen nonsense years ago."

"So she didn't leave him?" If Clay made up the whole story of a marriage in shambles, it was a Texas whopper.

"Believe me, I suggested she leave him more than once, but each time she insisted she loved him and he loved her."

Then Sally described frequent bruises that her friend had always attributed to household accidents. And a black eye she refused to discuss. I knew from covering domestic violence stories that women often love their abusers until the very end. But Sally wasn't hinting at anything that dark. She felt certain Clay was keeping Jolene cooped up at home, under orders not to answer the phone or the door.

"He never wanted her to work. He wanted her totally dependent on him. I think she sits in that house alone until he comes home and snaps his fingers for attention."

She told me she reached Clay at the station once. "I told him I was trying to reach Jolene. He told me she had new friends, then hung up."

I didn't know how to gauge Sally's information. She could have been a kook. Lots of online folks are. So are lots of people who call TV stations.

"Do you have a photo of Jolene Burrel?" I asked. "One that looks like her?"

"I can find one," Sally said.

"Email it to me. I want to be able to recognize her if we meet."

"Good idea."

I didn't ask if she knew where Jolene went to the dentist. That's the kind of remark that can mean only one thing.

So where was Clay's wife?

Reporters like to envision the most newsworthy ending to any story. But Clay could have been telling the truth. If Jolene ever had beauty-queen aspirations, she'd have sported a tiara or two down the line. To check his story, I Googled variations of " 'Jolene Burrel,' 'Texas,' 'beauty.' "

Nothing. But I realized a loophole. Jolene's maiden name.

Xiong had a public-records account that allowed him to search driving, criminal, property, and other public records nationwide, but no way was I going to ask him to find Clay Burrel's marriage certificate for me. So I logged on to an Internet records company, typed in his name, Texas town, and approximate age. Then I paid $29.95, knowing I'd never be able to expense the cost.

Seconds later, I learned he'd married Jolene Bailey two years earlier. She was eighteen; he was twenty-three.

I repeated the Google, this time with her maiden name. She'd appeared in four beauty pageants. The highlight was a win as Miss Teen of Nueces County. The others were runner-up awards. I found a small head-to-toe photo of a pretty girl with a wide smile. She wore a sparkly crown over a big Texas hairdo and a beauty-queen banner over a big bust.

She definitely would have made a beautiful bride. I wondered how the couple met. Once, they must have been happy; but now, regardless of where Jolene Burrel was, the marriage was doomed.

Maybe she did leave him. Maybe out of spite, fear, or anger. She might be starting a new life . . . far from reminders of her old one.

Or maybe he was cutting her off from the world. A prisoner in a controlling relationship.

Or maybe she was dead.

What if he created his own ratings exclusive with the act of murder?

That might explain why the killer went to the trouble of decapitating his victim. Besides stalling identification, a headless homicide certainly becomes a more newsworthy crime to break your first day on the job. And oh, what chutzpah, to keep track of the criminal investigation by covering it. And that would certainly explain all his insider information. He may have been his own best source.

Keep your friends close. Keep your enemies closer.

• • •

I had a whole lot more sleuthing to do before I'd have the nerve to ask Benny to approach the police. Right then, they'd simply have laughed at the thought of two murderers working in the same newsroom.

I decided the best start would be if I could get a second source to confirm marital abuse between the Burrels. I pulled up the State of Texas marriage certificate again and looked at the witness names. Male. Female. Best man. Maid of honor.

The last maid of honor I interviewed knew plenty of secrets about a wedding gone wrong and a missing groom. For this case, I again needed someone close to the bride. And who more likely to be her best friend than the witness to her marriage vows? I found a phone number for Cindy Bellrichard.

She hadn't heard from Jolene Burrel for more than a year. Didn't know about Clay's Minnesota TV job. Didn't feel in a good position to speculate about their marriage.

I sensed Cindy was about to hang up, so quickly, I started talking to her about my own wedding. In Vegas. Spur of the moment. No friends or family. I explained I was now a widow and how I wished I had someone close to me to relive my wedding day now and then.

"I've never met Jolene. But another friend of hers is worried, and I'm not sure how much stock to give her concern and how deep to stick my nose in someone else's business."

I waited, wishing I'd been able to make the pitch in person. Not too many folks slam a door in my face, but I've been hung up on plenty of times. The eye contact certainly makes a difference, but it's the whole package that lands the interview. A sincere smile. A firm handshake. It's harder to communicate trust with just voice inflection.

"I'll keep your name out of it," I promised. "She'll never know we talked."

Either Cindy would hang up. Or she wouldn't. She didn't.

"He made me uneasy," she said. "Jolene could never go anywhere unless he came along. After they got hitched, the whole job of being friends fell on me. I decided to stop calling her, just to see if she missed me. Guess she didn't."

Cindy's voice could have sounded smug; instead it sounded hurt.

"When did you two start being friends?" I wanted to loosen her up but also wanted to learn enough about Jolene that if we ever met, I could loosen *her* up. And if Jolene was the headless homicide victim, the one thing missing from the story was a sense of who she was.

"We grew up on the same block," Cindy said, explaining that Jolene often slept over at her house because her parents were always fighting.

"Fighting yelling?" I asked. "Or fighting hitting?"

"Fighting all kinds," she answered.

Then she told me that Jolene's dad killed her

mom and went to prison. So Jolene moved in with them when she was sixteen.

"I hear she won some beauty titles," I said.

"Not all that many, and the ones she got weren't all that big a deal. At least I didn't think so. She used to say the biggest prize she ever won was Clay."

"What did she mean?"

The way she told it, as a reporter for the local TV station, Clay was asked to judge a beauty pageant. I've judged many contests during my career, but they've all been for journalism awards. Things are different down in Texas.

"Jolene didn't get the crown," Cindy said, "but Clay asked her out after the competition. Told her he voted for her and she should have won."

"How'd she react?"

"Thrilled to pieces. Married him a few months later."

"How'd they get along?"

"Didn't see her much after that." Cindy's voice sounded sniffly, but over the phone it was hard to tell. "Jolene never had time to get together, just her and me. When I'd go over to their house, Clay was always saying mean things to her, like 'You ain't got the brains of a turnip.'"

That sounded like something Clay would say. I had a few other questions, but Cindy had to get to work, or she'd be fired.

"If you see her, tell Jolene I miss her."

• • •

An email with an attachment popped up on my computer screen from Sally Oaks. One click later, I found myself staring at a photo of an attractive blonde.

I wondered what her face would look like decomposed.

CHAPTER 50

My shift didn't actually start until two the next day, but I called Ozzie that morning on the pretense of wanting to check the day's news. I found out Clay was doing a noon live shot on the other side of town about goose overpopulation.

That gave me ample time to head over to his house. I brought along a tuna-noodle hot dish as a prop. No one answered the door when I knocked or appeared to be home when I pressed my face against a window.

An elderly neighbor, watering some mums on his porch, asked if he could help. It was his way of letting me know he had his eye on the place. That's what neighbors do.

"I'm looking for the lady of the house," I said.

"The guy lives alone."

"You're sure?"

"Sure as shootin'. You should know. He works at your station."

That was the problem with being on TV. People recognize you. Usually at inconvenient times. Ordinary folks often wish for star status, but in truth, it's more tiresome than titillating. In retrospect, I should have worn a disguise.

"Have you ever seen this woman?" I showed him the picture of Jolene. If she was around, and if he was as nosy as he acted, I figured they'd have crossed paths.

"Can't say I have."

Just because Clay's wife didn't come to the door or hobnob with the neighbors didn't mean she was dead. Plenty of psychopaths keep victims locked in basements or hidden in backyards—too controlled to attempt escape. Sometimes not found until eighteen years later.

Trouble surrounded me, but I'd always felt safe within the walls of Channel 3. With Clay now working down the hall, I felt vulnerable.

But I had a bigger problem than even I knew. I didn't realize that Clay's neighbor had told him that I'd stopped by his house, flashing a picture of a pretty woman with blond hair.

I was on to Clay, but I didn't know Clay was on to me. Not until I walked into my office and found him sitting in my chair.

"You need to keep your nose out of my hankie," he said.

"I don't know what you're talking about."

He'd obviously rifled through my desk because he held out the picture of his wife. Then his fist crumbled it into a little ball, and when he walked past me, I got chills. The bad kind.

I vowed to keep my distance from Clay. Not talk to him. Or sit by him. If he continued to approach me, I'd accuse him of sexual harassment. Noreen was more likely to believe him a chauvinist pig than a murderer.

Sleep and food should have been higher priorities; instead I started organizing a list of all the scoops Clay had reported in the headless homicide.

He'd been first with the news that the victim had been decapitated. Then blond. Later the manicure and pedicure. And out of thin air, he'd pronounced the head and body a DNA match.

These were things only the killer would know. Unless the police leaked them. Which they'd repeatedly denied. My gut had always doubted Clay could have recruited such a well-connected source so quickly. But seeing him cozy with the police chief, I'd wavered. Now I was back to thinking I was right the first time and that Clay Burrel might give a whole new meaning to the term "dead air."

All I needed was some evidence. Because as far as Noreen, the police, and even my own attorney felt, I was the delusional man of La Mancha obsessed with seeing murderers around every corner.

CHAPTER 51

Some news consultants think reading a tele-prompter comes naturally. Either the camera loves you or it doesn't. Others consider it an acquired skill. I sided with the latter and was getting feedback from the newsroom producers and technicians that my delivery was improving with each show. And my ad libs between weather and sports were more conversational, as well.

I'd gone over that day's scripts earlier and everything seemed straightforward. Now I noticed that instead of being a taped news package, Clay's story about an increase in assaults on city buses had been turned into a set piece. Which meant he and I would sit together at the anchor desk while I debriefed him about the story, violating both vows I had made.

"Don't you think Clay's story might be better as a live shot?" I asked the producer. "He could stand outside next to the bus stop with the highest crime rate." Then, at least, I wouldn't have to sit next to him.

"Too late," she said, "the newscast is already formatted. Plus, we're trying to evolve beyond that live-for-live's-sake mentality."

I wanted to ask, "Since when?" Channel 3 had repeatedly made me stand in pouring rain just to go live outside some dark building where something had happened ten hours earlier.

"How about if Clay did a taped news package instead?" I asked. Then I wouldn't have to talk to him. Or sit by him.

The producer continued to explain that they'd roll some video over part of the interview but basically wanted me to ask Clay questions about bus safety for a couple of minutes.

"Maybe the two of you can even radiate a little on-screen chemistry," she said.

That didn't even deserve an answer.

During the first segment, I told viewers about baseball moving out of the Metrodome, how recent home foreclosures meant an increase in pets being surrendered to animal shelters, and various controversies over whether our mayor should run for governor or our governor should run for president.

During the commercial break, Clay put a cushion on his chair so he could tower over me on the air. If I wasn't giving him the silent treatment, I'd have made an observation about how women may be able to anchor the network news, but if a man and woman appear together on the set, the man has to look taller.

Instead I ignored him, stared straight at the camera, and read the story intro.

> ((RILEY, CU))
> ASSAULTS ON MINNEAPOLIS
> BUSES ARE SURGING THIS
> YEAR, AND RIDERS ARE
> DEMANDING ACTION.
>
> ((TWOSHOT, RILEY/CLAY))
> CLAY BURREL JOINS US NOW
> WITH MORE ON THE
> PROBLEM.
>
> ((CLAY, CU))
> POLICE SAY GANG MEMBERS
> ARE FIGHTING OVER PUBLIC
> TRANSPORTATION AND
> BYSTANDERS ARE GETTING
> CAUGHT IN THE MIDDLE.

He waited for me to throw him a question, but I just nodded and sat there, like he was supposed to do more talking. As he stammered something about the Metropolitan Transit Commission holding a public hearing, the producer yelled in my ear for me to ask him how serious most of the injuries were.

Instead, I asked if anybody had ever been murdered on a city bus.

He stumbled and mentioned certain bus stops being the scene of several shootings.

The floor director signaled for me to turn to Clay while I spoke to him. I realized my camera angle was wrong, but looking at Clay Burrel was the last thing I wanted. Then I considered that maybe my eyes on his was the last thing he wanted. So I turned, stared at his face, and decided to push for answers.

"What motivates killers, Clay?"

His eyes gleamed, and his fingers tapped the news set. I was grateful a vast audience of viewers was watching us and we were not alone in the alley behind the station.

"You've brought us so many exclusives from the crime beat, Clay. You must have a theory about what drives killers."

"Wrap," the producer said in my ear. The floor director frantically gave me a circular hand signal that meant stop talking. I ignored both cues, wondering how far I could push things before news control went black.

I was about to ask what the latest was on the headless homicide, but that wasn't necessary because suddenly Clay was telling viewers that we were taking a break and would be back in just a moment.

"What the hell was that?" the producer said. "That segment was a debacle."

I pretended to be puzzled. "You wanted some on-air chemistry."

We couldn't argue further because I had just received a standby cue to come back and toss to weather. While the seven-day forecast was stretched across the screen, Noreen and Clay were locked in a frantic discussion off to the side. It was hard to tell who was more agitated.

"What was I supposed to do," I heard Clay say, "remind her she was the one accused of murder?"

I bid the viewers good night, then prepared for a major admonishment. I got it from all directions. Noreen yanked me off the late news that night, subbing our weekend anchor. She praised Clay for his handling of a difficult situation and scolded me for going rogue. Then she told me that maybe I wasn't suited to sit in the anchor chair if I couldn't be a team player. As usual, the rest of the newsroom watched the action, mesmerized, through her glass walls.

Clay gave me no chance to be alone with Noreen. Even though my side of the story wasn't terribly persuasive, I still would have liked a chance to tell it. But she dismissed us both.

More interesting yet, I noticed my boss wasn't wearing her wedding ring. And the photo of Toby she kept on her desk was missing. I had a hunch about the problem, but that was the kind of girl talk I didn't dare bring up with Clay in the room.

Even though I ordered him to keep back, Clay followed me down the hall to my office, shaking his head. I raced ahead and locked the door, me on the inside, him on the outside.

I heard a soft tap-tap. "We need to come to an understanding, little lady."

"I understand everything I need to." I spoke with the confidence that comes from having two inches of solid wood between us. My voice was loud enough for him to hear but low enough that nobody else did.

"Don't be too sure. Something tells me you ain't got the sense God gave a turkey. And you know what happens to turkeys."

If he was referring to having their heads chopped off at Thanksgiving ... well, after the headless homicide, I couldn't take that simply as an idle threat.

"You stay away from me, Clay Burrel." At the very least, I feared another blood-splattered nightmare involving poultry.

A fist banged once against my door, then the hallway was silent.

I started locking my office, even if I was just going down the hall. I wouldn't go into the ladies' room alone. And I made the station security guard walk me to my car that night, even though it was parked in the basement. He considered me paranoid.

Things can always get worse, and the next day they did.

Police went through the garbage Dumpsters behind Channel 3 and found a handgun. A Glock. Cops don't need search warrants to root through trash that's been placed outside.

Clay broke the story, because he was just arriving at work while it was unfolding.

> ((CLAY LIVE))
> POLICE SAY AN ANONYMOUS
> TIPSTER CLAIMED TO HAVE
> SEEN CHANNEL 3 REPORTER
> RILEY SPARTZ LEANING
> SUSPICIOUSLY INTO THIS
> DUMPSTER IN THE ALLEY
> BEHIND THE STATION.

Benny later got word that the recovered firearm was the murder weapon that killed the gossip columnist. It had been wiped clean.

"Even if I had shot Sam," I told my lawyer, "you don't think I'd be so stupid as to put the gun in the trash where I work?"

"Let's not make that argument the centerpiece of your defense."

I could tell that Benny was beginning to think he had a guilty client and was just defending me for the money.

"Doesn't anybody wonder why there's so much evidence against me?" I asked him. "At some point, doesn't that become a little suspicious?"

He shook his head. "I've never heard of a prosecutor dropping charges against a perpetrator because their case was too strong."

"Do you think I did it?"

"Never ask your attorney that question. You might not like the answer. We never ask our clients for the same reason."

CHAPTER 52

My boss may have hated me, but the people meters loved me. And our overnight news ratings were tanking since my ouster from the anchor desk. I figured I had at most forty-eight hours before Noreen dragged me back in front of the teleprompter, so I'd better enjoy my reporting time in the field while I could.

My dad called to say that something was happening at the wind farm. Lots of security. Limos. Dark suits. Dark glasses. Even snipers.

I called Wide Open Spaces to see if this was the protection their officials had been alluding to earlier. If so, it seemed a belated gesture of security overkill. The energy company blamed the fuss on the Secret Service. Apparently the king of Saudi Arabia and members of the royal family wanted to tour an American wind farm up close before they flew home.

"A little field trip to check out their energy competition," the manager said. "We're happy to assist."

Visualizing Middle Eastern royalty walking amid giant wind turbines, the station decided that a picture was worth, if not a thousand words, at least thirty seconds of video.

Being out of town would also keep me out of reach of Clay. I'd made knowing where he was part of my routine. And I had nothing to worry about today. The assignment desk told me that my story could run a little longer than usual because Clay had just gone home sick.

The FAA had closed off airspace around the wind farm. So again, no Channel 3 chopper. Malik and I drove fast, not sure if we'd even make it for the money shot.

Predictably, Malik insisted on napping during the drive. So I used the time on the road to call Sally, my Texas Facebook friend, and tell her I could find no trace of Jolene.

She thanked me for staying in touch. "That other reporter promised to call back but never did."

I couldn't believe it. After all I had done for her, she was talking to other media. I was plenty pissed. "What other reporter?" I asked.

She said he was called Sam Pierce.

I wasn't sure I could drive straight the rest of the way, I was so shocked.

Apparently, the gossip columnist had cold-called Sally, looking for scuttle on Clay his first week on the job. So that's how he always got dirt on the new reporters. Probably phoned door-to-door in their old neighborhood until he found something embarrassing.

"What did you tell Sam about Clay's marriage?"

"That I couldn't reach my friend." She paused like she was replaying the conversation in her mind. "That it seemed strange she wouldn't have called me once they got settled."

"Can you remember anything more specific?"

"I might have called him a bully."

"Anything else?"

"I might have called him a bad husband."

I could only imagine Sam's glee at having hit the gossip jackpot with Sally Oaks. "You knew you were talking to a newspaper guy, right?"

"Yes, but I saw him as my only way to get her a message. He seemed so willing to help."

And she might have sensed a chance to retaliate against Clay.

"When did you talk to Sam?"

Their discussion had happened the day before Sam's murder. I reminded myself I had every incentive to try to pin that homicide on someone else. I'd gone through heaps of suspect names that ended up nowhere. This could have been more of the same. But I didn't think so.

I thought Sam had been getting too close to Clay's secret.

● ● ●

I couldn't much blame the cops for having the motive wrong in Sam's homicide.

I had the motive wrong, too.

From the very beginning, the police investigation moved in the direction that the gossip columnist's murder was for revenge.

Now an entirely different purpose emerged: perhaps the killer needed to keep Sam quiet. Maybe the fatal bullet was a preemptive strike to keep word of Clay Burrel's missing wife out of the newspaper.

I should have realized that Sam's death, as a payback crime, would have been unusual because journalists are more at risk *before* a sensitive story airs, not *after*. I should have remembered the best time for a scoundrel to stop the presses is before they roll, not after. Afterward the culprit is generally too busy worrying about going to jail, or losing a business, or holding a marriage together, to focus on the luxury of revenge.

CHAPTER 53

For the last sixty miles of the drive, I played the game of Clue in my mind. Clay in the garage with the gun. Clay in the bedroom with the chainsaw. And every time I glanced in the rearview mirror, I had a smile on my face.

Besides his exclusives in the headless homicide, Clay had been first to report that the newspaper columnist had died from a bullet wound.

And when it came to framing me for murder, well, anyone who worked at Channel 3 had access to my hairbrush to steal a little sample. The minute I got back to the city limits of Minneapolis, I vowed to go straight to the police.

When I saw the tips of wind turbines, I shook Malik awake, and even he could tell I was in an awesome mood.

"I'm just having a really good day," I said. "I'll explain later."

Curious locals had already assembled in a newly harvested cornfield to watch the action from a distance. Some, including my parents, considered it a chance to glimpse an exotic corner of the world without going there. Nearly two dozen Saudi men and women wearing long robes and various head coverings gazed at the rows of turbines and took turns stepping inside.

The only picturesque thing missing was camels. And instead of sand dunes, amber waves of grain made for an all-American background.

Malik shot from a tripod. Even without interviews, the video was certain to make the network news feed. We were the only media, thanks to the buzz direct from my local roots.

"Isn't that your buddy?" Malik asked.

I looked through the camera lens to see the players up close, recognizing one of the Wide Open Spaces owners. Another man, probably an interpreter, stayed close. Then I spotted Nick Garnett and realized that the longer we spent apart, the better he looked. He wasn't dressed like the Secret Service team. I wasn't sure what his role was for the event, but he moved comfortably through the crowd. I wished he had called to tell me he'd be there, but apparently he was still sticking to business.

I tried to phone the station, but the feds must have been blocking cell service again, because my call didn't go through.

The royal entourage spent the next fifteen minutes staring and pointing at the twenty-story metal warriors. I would have liked to have seen the expressions on their faces. I wondered if the woman I'd met shopping the other day was part of the elite group.

Then they filed into an impressive line of limousines, which slowly drove north on a dusty road.

Malik and I grabbed some sound with the wind farm officials, bragging about how well the visit had gone. Then he headed toward the van with the gear while I mingled.

"That sure was interesting," my dad said. "Wish I could have shaken hands with some of those folks." My dad collected handshakes, pressing palms with various presidential candidates whenever they visited the Minnesota State Fair.

"Time for us to run home," Mom answered. "I don't want to miss *Oprah*."

I waved as they drove down a back road, between the fields. I was actually glad to see them off because the person I really wanted to find was Garnett. I was hoping to casually stumble into him and reach an understanding. I could also share what I'd learned about Clay Burrel. There really wasn't anyone else I could trust.

A few bats lay scattered on the ground, and I kicked at one with my foot. Glancing around, I saw that nobody seemed to be paying any attention to me. To appease Noreen on the rabies matter, I wrapped one in some tissue and stuffed it in my jacket pocket for more barotrauma testing later.

I pulled at the door to one of the turbines and was pleased to find it still unlocked. Feeling the interior wall by the door, I found a light switch. Handy because there were no windows. I moved inside for an up-close inspection of the circular structure.

An aluminum ladder stretched far upward, but after my research on workplace dangers, I knew better than to climb those rungs without a safety harness.

I was gazing down into the base of the tower when the door opened behind me. A woman dressed in a Muslim garment and head covering came inside. Surprised to see her alone, I saw an opportunity for information and introduced myself.

Silently, she moved toward me. I thought perhaps she didn't speak English. Her steps made a strange tap-tap sound on the metal floor. I glanced down at her feet and saw cowboy boots.

CHAPTER 54

Through a slit in the black veil, I saw Clay Burrel's eyes.

"Isn't it just a little early for Halloween, Clay?"

I recognized the burka from the green room closet but pretended to be more curious than alarmed by his attire. I had to admire his planning. If any witness noticed him entering or leaving the turbine, the cops would blame the Saudis for my murder.

"You'd make a dashing Lawrence of Arabia," I continued. "But you and I both know you're not hero material."

"I just had one bad weekend," he said.

"I can believe it," I answered, trying to keep him talking until someone came looking for me. "Sometimes our entire life hinges on one bad weekend."

I was pretty sure the weekend he was referring to was the forty-eight hours before he started working for Channel 3. On that first day on the job, he gave me lots of reasons to dislike him, but the best one—that he was a wife killer—had eluded me and everyone else.

"It wasn't all my fault," he said.

He went on to rationalize what happened to Jolene by attributing it to stress over the move and job change. He claimed she went farther than she should have verbally. He conceded he went farther than he should have physically.

"You're right," I agreed, "it wasn't all your fault."

I played along with the image he'd created of his spouse as a self-centered shrew, not letting on that I knew about the bruises.

"I'm glad you didn't kill her just for ratings." I hoped that sounded like praise. "That would have been shallow."

"Well, little lady, I figured something good should come of her death. And if my career got a boost, so be it."

Like most psychopaths, he showed little remorse. I tried not to think about the ghastly disfiguration of her body and couldn't bring myself to ask how anyone could do that to someone they had once wooed and wed.

Killing me would certainly be easier for him.

"By covering the case, you always knew what the police were up to," I said. "That was very shrewd."

"I also kept an eye on you," he said, "always knowing what you were up to." That explained my growing feeling that someone was watching my house.

"You should have just kept your paws off my story," he continued. "Then none of this would have happened."

Actually, Clay had killed Sam *before* I started trying to steal his story, but blame-shifting is a common tendency of narcissistic killers. It helps them justify their motives. Hidden under a flowing robe and veil, Clay's body language was unreadable. His eyes were the only focus of my attention, so I didn't see the gun emerge from a fold in his clothing until he raised it to fire.

The bullet ricocheted off the steel walls and nearly hit both of us. Garnett was right. Texan or not, Clay was a terrible shot.

While he was comprehending the disadvantages of gunfire in such a confined space, I scrambled up the metal ladder—a harness being the least of my worries now. Instantly he was on my heels, literally, grabbing my ankle and trying to pull me down.

One good kick and I heard the gun fall with a clang.

Clay paused to look down, presumably weighing whether to continue to chase after me or go back for the weapon. By the time he decided to move upward and onward, I'd put a few rungs between us. I raced to the top like my life depended on it. And I suspected it might. Somewhere on that twenty-story climb I lost a shoe. That slowed me down. But the Islamic garb slowed Clay down more.

When I reached the ledge at the top, I was panting hard. Burrel was still about fifteen feet below me, lacking my incentive for speed: survival.

I figured I might have time for one phone call.

Even though cell service was blocked, I knew 911 should still work, but my call would be answered nearly twenty miles away in the county sheriff's office. And the dispatcher wouldn't have any idea who I was, what I was talking about, or where to send help.

Then I remembered that law enforcement numbers on the scene were cleared for cell service. So I hit send for Garnett's number. I couldn't tell if I was hearing his voice or his voicemail. I had to scream to be heard over the whirl of the turbine blades.

"Help! I'm in the top of the turbine and Clay Burrel is trying to kill me!"

By then Clay was very close. I tried jabbing my remaining heel in his eye. But I was off balance and he pushed past, and suddenly I was on my butt and he was hovering over me. A swirl of black fabric, laughing.

I threw my phone at him. While he ducked, I scrambled to my feet. The phone lay on the floor; Clay seemed surprised that instead of lunging for it, I kicked it down the ladder shaft. I hoped if Garnett came looking for me, he'd see my phone at the bottom and realize he'd found the right turbine.

There wasn't much room to skirmish but I was surprised Clay and I could both stand. The upper chamber was larger than it looked from the ground. Inside, it felt like a spaceship, but with hardly any view of the outside world. The spinning blades made a loud hum, almost like jet engines.

No room to run. The only way out was the way I had just come. Down the ladder. And I'd have to get past him.

"Give it up, Clay. Help is on the way." I said it with more confidence than I felt. But sometimes, outcome is all in the delivery.

"You're bluffing. I know cell calls can't go through."

For now, I tried keeping the ladder hole between us. Without a gun, he'd have to get his hands on me to kill me. Thinking of the same strategy, Clay grabbed my sleeve and tried dragging me across the floor into the hole. But he didn't quite have the reach to pull it off.

"No thanks," I told him. "Long way down."

"You have as much chance of avoiding that long way down as scratching your ear with your elbow."

As tempted as I was to test his metaphor, I figured it was just a scheme to distract me.

"I'm no threat to you, Clay." Arguing with a psychopath doesn't usually yield results, but I didn't have other options just then. "No one will believe anything I say. Your secret is safe."

"Can't take that chance."

We were both yelling because of the noise from the turbine.

"Killing Jolene was an accident."

Again, I assured him I didn't think he meant to do it. "But if you kill me now, Clay, that's premeditated murder. A whole different sport from simply losing your temper. I don't think you've got that in you."

He laughed at those words. "Killing you will be lots easier. Don't have all that emotional investment complicating matters."

He was probably right. There would be no wasted regret over my death. For Clay, killing me would be as easy as sneezing.

"This ain't my first rodeo, little lady," he said.

He talked like a braggart. And suddenly I realized he wasn't just talking about Jolene, he was also talking about the murder of Sam Pierce. Out of habit, and out of curiosity, I tried getting him to put it on the record.

"Who else have you killed, Clay? Tell me."

"You of all folks should be able to guess."

"But Sam never printed anything bad about you."

"And I wasn't about to let him. He was getting too close. If that damn Yankee had kept his piercing eyes out of my life, he'd be alive today."

"So why frame me? Why not just kill him and move on?"

Clay was the one who'd made it personal. It seemed only fair I get an answer.

"I needed somebody to pin it on, and you had a believable motive," he said. "Besides, it's a better story this way. Isn't that obvious?"

"You framed me to get higher ratings?"

"And job advancement. With you out of the way, I'll rule Channel 3 as their senior investigative reporter."

Even under the burka, his chest seemed to puff with pride.

"You have to admit," he said, "Sam's murder was the perfect crime."

I had to give him credit. It was perfect.

"Yours will be perfect, too," he assured me. "This is better than a bullet. When police examine your broken body at the bottom of the turbine they'll conclude you either committed suicide out of guilt or simply fell to your death trespassing."

Either cause of death would be believable. And from reading the accident reports of all the gruesome wind turbine workplace fatalities, I knew my broken body would be in bad shape. I just hoped my father didn't find it.

"Are you going to break the exclusive of my death?" I asked.

Clay shook his head. "Tempting as it is to land another big scoop, I called in sick today so I could follow you. I thought it best you die in another jurisdiction. Too many murders happening in Minneapolis."

Then, faintly, I thought I heard my name being called but couldn't be sure. Clay didn't react, so it was probably my simple yearning for rescue.

But just in case I wasn't hallucinating, I started screaming, "Up here!"

I saw no downside in making Clay worry that the two of us were not alone. He gave up trying to pull me across the gap; instead he jumped over to my side of the chamber and grabbed me.

"Help!" I kept yelling. "On top!" As he and I struggled, I deliberately kicked off my other shoe, sending it down the ladder hole as a final cry for help. Hoping a Prince Charming might see the slipper and search up high for his Cinderella.

Clay and I struggled. He scratched my hands and arms; I tried gouging his face. He turned my body so my back was facing the ladder hole, and I couldn't gauge my proximity to the edge—and death. But I sensed mortality only inches away. Clay's back faced some revolving gears, so he was in no danger of falling down the abyss.

But I was. The back of my foot could feel the edge along the drop-off.

"You'll be long dead and I'll be at the network," he said, taunting me.

"The Cartoon Network," I managed to retort, pushing at him without much luck.

This could have been the moment when my life passed before my eyes and I bade farewell to our world. Instead, I found myself grappling with the central theme of *Don Quixote:* is it better to die delusional and happy, or live miserably but sane?

Perhaps if I imagined I was flying, the downward spiral in the wind turbine would be less horrific. Maybe heaven was like an eternal 40 share. I tried telling myself Hugh was waiting to catch me at the bottom and carry me over a cloudy threshold to an everlasting life together.

I had to think fast, before the abyss won. I opted to fight for life, even if my last minutes were anguished, rather than succumb to the comfort of delusion.

Even though Clay wasn't more than a few inches taller than me, he was much stronger. To change circumstances, I reached into my pocket, feeling for some kind of weapon to wield, even just a pen. My fingers touched leather and fur. Figuring rabies was the least of my troubles, I pulled out the dead bat and pressed it against Clay's eyes.

He made a gagging sound and stepped back, dragging me with him, away from the drop-off. Not wanting to release his hold on me, he shook his head sideways to avoid the lifeless creature. I tried squishing the animal up Clay's nose, so he couldn't breathe, but his head covering was in the way.

I blinked when his veil flicked in my face, so I didn't see the flowing fabric sweep backward, catching in the spinning mass of the turbine's rotor and pulling him inside the sharp gears.

Clay dropped me to free his hands in an attempt to escape the mechanical monster.

His death was silent, it came so quickly and horribly. There was no time for either of us to scream.

Unlike his dead wife—who probably didn't bleed much when he cut off her head—Clay bled plenty.

His heart must have continued to beat as his limbs and head were ripped from his body by the twisty machine. I dropped to the floor, trying to shield my face from the red spray. My entire body was warm and sticky. My hair felt like it had too much mousse. Most of the floor, the walls, and the top rungs of the ladder were slippery from Clay's blood and my vomit. My gut was telling me future nightmares would be much worse than butchered chickens.

I didn't want to stay up high with what was left of Clay. But I was too shaken to climb down. And even though I was barely a mile from the farmhouse where I grew up, I had never felt so far from home.

CHAPTER 55

Clay died with his cowboy boots on.

The first rescuer to arrive tripped over one of his legs.

The wind team decided to lower me from the turbine to the ground rather than take me down the tower ladder.

They opened a small trapdoor on the chamber bottom and assured me they'd practiced this once before. Fastening a harness around my chest, they clipped a cable to the front. Slowly, they lowered me down to a crew on the ground. I closed my eyes tight until my feet hit dirt. Even then, I was too shaken to stand.

Word had spread from farm to farm that I was trapped on top of a turbine, so a crowd waited. So did Channel 3's camera. When Malik dropped the lens from his shoulder, his face looked pale. The close-up video of me ended up being too grisly to broadcast.

But repulsion didn't stop my parents from rushing to my side. Mom got there first, because of Dad's bad knees. She was crying. He was crying. I think I was crying, too. I didn't care anymore whether or not adult children should cry in front of their parents.

Vibrant splotches of red now decorated my mom's blouse from holding me, and I thought of Edgar Allan Poe, whose mother, dying of tuberculosis, continually coughed up blood when she held him as a child. Maybe that parental horror inspired his literary genius. I prayed that something good would happen to me. Was there anything I could take from this bloody experience that could strengthen instead of shatter me?

Out of the corner of my eye, a shadow moved. I jerked back, bracing myself for one more terror, but a closer look revealed Nick Garnett, holding one of my shoes. My throat got all choky. And I knew he had answered my call for help.

At that moment, I was stalwart enough to tell him I loved him, out loud, in front of a throng of people. But I also knew that wasn't what he needed to hear just then.

"Mom, Dad, there's someone I want you to meet."

Garnett swooped me up and it was like that final scene from *An Officer and a Gentleman* with Richard Gere and Debra Winger, only instead of Debra Winger, picture Sissy Spacek as Carrie, covered in pig's blood.

The farm crowd even cheered, like the sweatshop workers in the movie. I thought if the director could just roll the credits then, happily-ever-after would be mine.

EPILOGUE

Certainly, it could have been worse.

The cops considered charging me with killing Clay Burrel, too. But when the headless woman was identified through dental records as his wife, and when my Texas Facebook friend verified that one of Sam Pierce's last acts as a newsman was to nose around in Clay's private life, they dropped the murder charges against me.

Benny negotiated a plea bargain in which Toby surrendered to authorities for his part in the wind farm fatality. He was sentenced to five years for manslaughter at the federal prison camp in Duluth, where minimum-security male inmates are housed. He joined a prison program to train dogs for disabled people. Noreen divorced him.

After being sued under the Endangered Species Act, wind farms agreed to curtail turbines on slow wind nights during bat migration season after experiments showed bats were more likely to be on the move then.

DNA tests proved that baby Jimmy was Sam's child. He inherited two million dollars from his father's estate. His mother and grandparents are still locked in an ugly court fight for visitation.

The Minneapolis newspaper advertised for a new gossip columnist and received nearly five hundred applications, mostly from unqualified candidates. Then the paper went into bankruptcy and eliminated the position.

Buzz Stolee was traded to the L.A. Lakers.

The Saudis brought a second 747 to Rochester to carry all their spoils back home.

Father Mountain gave a sermon about how, while we all want terrorists and killers to be distant strangers, often the greatest danger comes from those closest to us, whom we would not suspect.

Judge Tregobov sentenced the dine-and-dash thief to pay restitution for his mooched meals and work eighty hours of community service in a kitchen for the homeless.

• • •

Channel 3 changed its social networking emphasis from Facebook to Twitter. Employees were ordered to recruit followers and break news by constantly tweeting 140-character messages.

Channel 3's story about the monarch migration was the highest-rated night of the sweeps month, higher even than the nights viewers were invited to tune in and look an accused murderer in the eye.

The numbers were helped by heavy promotion of Sophie completely covered in orange and black butterflies. A noise startled them and they scattered, leaving her standing in a Mexican jungle, wearing a string bikini.

I was so depressed Garnett promised to take me to see the butterflies for our honeymoon if I married him.

I told him I'd think about it.

ACKNOWLEDGMENTS

My editor, Emily Bestler, tops the list of people I owe special thanks to for *Silencing Sam*. She made me feel welcome at Atria Books, and her words—after I handed in my manuscript—about enjoying the read so much, meant a great deal to me.

It hurts to write a book. My gal pals Kevyn Burger, Caroline Lowe, Trish Van Pilsum, and Michele Cook offered comfort and humor along the way.

The following folks earned my gratitude by sharing their special knowledge: Doug Jones and the Pioneer Prairie Wind Farm folks for bringing me into the world of wind turbines, and especially to Brodie Dockendors for giving me an up close look at the mechanical giants; Linda Anderson Carnahan for suggesting the wind turbine/bat connection; Sgt. Kathy Hughes for allowing me to tour the Hennepin County Jail with the Citizens' Academy and Hennepin County Sheriff Deputy Andy

Peterson and his explosives detection dog, Bunny; St. Paul K-9 officer Mark Ficcadenti for his training talent; Judy Baccas for telling me about a special night in her life; Liz Zilka for her knowledge of airbrush makeup; Joe Kimball for his word puzzle expertise; Scott Libin for discussing how television stations deal with dirty words on the air; Vernon Geberth, author of *Practical Homicide Investigation*; Dr. D. P. Lyle, author of *Forensics*; and especially to Dakota County Medical Examiner Dr. Lindsay Thomas, who looks death in the eye each day with class.

The rest of the gang at Atria for all they did for *Silencing Sam*: assistant editor Laura Stern for handling numerous details; Jeanne Lee for cover design; Isolde Sauer for production and copyediting; Mellony Torres for publicity; Rachel Bostic for marketing; and my publisher, Judith Curr, and associate publisher, Chris Lloreda.

Agent Elaine Koster and her associate Stephanie Lehmann did more for me this past year than there is room to tell.

Kinfolk merit mention for their work in building buzz about my series (although I suspect their help stems from their joy in seeing their names in the back of a book): Ruth Kramer and her Red Hat ladies; George and Shirley Kimball and their church gang; Rosemary and Don Spartz and their Lake Summerset neighbors; Mae Klug and my entourage of cousins, especially Beth Klug and

Rosemary Jacobs; all my far-flung Spartz- and Kramer-rooted cousins, many of whom I've become reacquainted with through Facebook; Jerry and Elaine Kramer; Joe and Delores Spartz; Tom and Rena Fitzpatrick; Jerry and June Kimball; and Lorraine Kehl. My siblings and their families: Teresa and Galen Neuzil with Rachel; Bonnie and Roy Brang; Mary Agnes Kramer; Steve and Mary Kramer with Matthew and Elizabeth; Kathy and Jim Loecher with Adriana and Zach; Mike Kramer; Christina Kramer; Richard and Oti Kramer; Jenny and Kile Nadeau with Rebecca, David, and Daniel; Jessica and Richie Miehe with Lucy; George Kimball and Shen Fei with Shi Shenyu (Huan); Nick Kimball and Gannet Tseggai; Mary and David Benson with Davin; Steve Kimball with Craig; Paul Kimball; James Kimball; Vicki and Paul Blum; and four generations of friends and relatives in the Adams, MN, area, including my school teachers and 4-H leaders.

My children have all grown up loving to read, and their pride in having an author for a mom keeps me writing through the rough patches. My thanks to Alex and Andrew—the best kids anywhere; Katie and Jake Kimball—Minnesotans in their hearts always; and Joey and David Kimdon— with dear Aria and Arbor.

And always, to my darling, Joe.

Atria Books
Proudly Presents

KILLING KATE

Julie Kramer

Available in hardcover from Atria Books
in July 2011

Turn the page for a preview of
Killing Kate . . .

PROLOGUE

The night began with a teenage dare. She followed reluctantly as he led her by the hand to the shadow of the Black Angel.

A full moon gave them less privacy than she would have liked. Her back now against the horizontal concrete slab, she waited for him to lay his body across hers. Her lips prayed for the encounter to be quick because out of the corner of her eye a raven watched them intently from atop a gravestone.

Unlike most cemetery angels, whose heads and wings lift upward toward heaven, this statue's face and wings bent downward over the grave it guarded—as if pointing straight to hell. And while angel sculptures are traditionally a golden bronze or white marble, this one's hue was black. Besides the figure's sinister posture and color, its stony eyes seemed to stare into hers as if issuing a personal condemnation.

Her feeling of doom was so strong, the girl struggled to move away. But he held her down, pushed her dress up to her waist, and there, at the hem of the Black Angel, they sinned.

The writer paused over the keyboard and re-read the scene. Then with a smile, added sensory and sensual details about places the boy was hard and the girl was soft, and how their throaty moans were the only sound of life amid the dark tombstones. A final tweak when the female character closed her eyes tight to shut out the angel's glare completed the carnal passage.

CHAPTER 1

Waitresses were easy to research. For the price of lunch or coffee he gathered most of the information he needed.

First, he'd stall in the doorway of the restaurant skimming the menu. Then he might walk past the tables to the bathroom. Or maybe even pretend he recognized someone sitting on the other side of the room. All were opportunities to scan for a promising target—preferably a blonde—and note which section of the room she was serving.

Once he was seated, the rest came effortlessly. Often she wore a name tag. And if not, her name usually appeared on the bill. So no introduction was necessary. Her job was to be nice to customers. Even those she might give a cold shoulder to under different circumstances. Flirty charm meant the difference between twenty percent of the tab or being stiffed.

He could pretend they were new friends and practice making sociable conversation. Sometimes he even imagined they were married and she was preparing a home-cooked dinner for him after a long day at work. And he always paid in cash, so there was no check or credit card to trace back to him.

While she fetched water or restocked the bread basket, he recorded details in a small notebook to further the illusion his meal was business-related. Name. Physical description. And most important, how he was treated. If he detected scorn, he circled that entry with a red pen. That was his code for which ones needed to learn respect. He chose the color red deliberately.

Once, he stared so intensely at his server that she dropped silverware and backed away clumsily into another diner. He had meant his attention as a compliment. But instead of being flattered, she pointed him out to a coworker and even from across the room he could see her lips mutter "pervert."

He wrote down the affront. Then circled her name in red.

When she finished her shift, he was waiting in the parking lot to see which vehicle she drove. Women were always cautious going to their cars, and security cameras were mounted everywhere. He knew better than to approach her during that short trek. Home was where they felt safest, and there, it was simple to catch them off guard and out of sight of witnesses.

Patience was paramount.

He knew better than to follow her directly home, because the last thing he needed was a suspicious cop and a police report with his name and vehicle information on file. He stayed on her bumper only long enough to get her license plate number. Later, he popped her address from public records and watched to become familiar with her work schedule. It was important that she be dressed in the role.

To be assured of privacy, he also needed to learn the routine of her household. Whether she lived alone, with a roommate, or had a family. The journey to the end took weeks.

He also hungered for permission. But that blessing now came easily.

So one day when the garage door opened for her car, he followed inside . . . crouching low and close to the side of the building. When he cornered her, he was disappointed that she had no idea who he was, how he had picked her, or why he was wearing gloves and a hairnet.

"Say it," he told her.

But she was confused and didn't know what he was talking about. All she could mumble were a few shaky words that sounded like "please" and "don't hurt me."

But he'd heard similar stammers before. "Say it," he threatened her with a club held high.

She covered her head and sobbed, her shoulders quivering. She couldn't seem to hold eye contact with him. That wouldn't have changed anything, but he relished the fog in their eyes.

"Say it," he insisted, "say 'pervert.'" He smashed his weapon against the garbage can, denting the lid.

Finally, she raised her face and repeated the word.

Then he brought the club down. And when she was dead, he arranged her body just perfect and added his special touch. Turning her from devil to angel.

He was their salvation.

He never visited the same restaurant twice. He never cruised places in the town where he lived. He didn't mind driving long distances because he enjoyed the feeling of control behind the wheel. And on the special nights, he parked about a half mile away, carrying his tools in a backpack. After all, he had plenty of time.

He also had a formula that worked. But it soon grew unsatisfying.

So he broke the pattern. Ditched his distant waitress mania, instead focusing on a closer, more deserving target: Kate.

It was hard to admit to himself, because it meant acknowledging he'd made mistakes, but he'd come to realize he hadn't played fair with the first ones. Those women had deserved to know why he had come. Initially, he had worried that such a warning might alter the outcome, but he also savored the idea of them brooding over who or what or when or where.

Kate's transgression was plotted, not fleeting; so she had plenty of warning about his displeasure.

But the risk of discovery was worth the expression in her eyes as the club came down.

He would kill to see that look again.

CHAPTER 2

Until Kate Warner's homicide, it had been a slow news day in Minneapolis.

In the first hours after her body was discovered, media coverage was fairly predictable. Television live trucks and camera crews with tripods camped out along the street because the neighborhood where Kate had lived and died was previously regarded as safe and quiet—the Minnesota ideal of above-average income and below-average crime.

So when her neighbors learned she had been murdered in her own home, Kate's death became more interesting to them than her life had ever been.

My name is Riley Spartz. I'm a television reporter for Channel 3. Normally I'd describe myself as an investigative reporter, but those glorious days of long-term special projects are diminishing in the news business. While the word "investigation" still has promotional value, newsrooms simply don't have the budget for the real thing anymore. Now journalists are under orders to turn breaking news into "instant" investigations, hoping the public won't discern any real difference.

"Keep back, everyone."

A uniformed officer motioned to the curious to stay some distance from the crime scene tape. The yellow-and-black plastic ribbon was the only splash of color across the dried-up yard. If there were any spatters of blood, they blended invisibly into the grass—brown due to the summer watering ban.

A terse "No comment," directed at me and the rest of the media, were the only other words the policeman uttered. I made a note of his ID pin, "Stanley," but didn't press him further, because as a street cop, rather than a homicide detective, I doubted he actually understood much about what had happened inside the brick-and-stucco rambler. He might have secured the scene, but the homicide team would have quickly shunted him aside with the busy work of crowd control.

A large crowd hadn't gathered—that typically happens only with brutal crime in public places like parks or malls. Most of these onlookers were pretending not to look.

One man walked his dog up and down the block. A woman kept checking her mailbox. Another pushed a young child on a swing in her front yard even though the toddler made noises about wanting to go inside. And more folks than usual strolled past, feigning appreciation for the hot August weather.

But their eyes were all riveted on the homicide house.

I whispered to my cameraman to casually shoot video of all spectators, because sometimes the killer likes to watch the ensuing commotion. Occasionally the killer even volunteers to be interviewed for television newscasts. Researchers have no solid explanation, but know that for some psychopaths, the aftermath is even more rewarding than the actual deed.

"Why Kate?" one woman asked, looking with anguish into my photographer's camera. Her delivery smooth, as if she'd practiced in a mirror. "Who would want to kill her?"

Both legitimate questions—posed as a perfect sound bite that would definitely make air—but two separate queries that might never be fully answered. Such is the reality of violent death. "How" is much easier to explain than "why" or "who," and the medical examiner would likely release the "how" answer within a day or two.

Often, but not always, when a woman is slain in her own home, the murderer is someone she knows. From a career of covering crime, I knew the police would be looking for signs of forced entry, robbery, and sexual assault as a means of determining motive and focusing their investigation.

Two men were nailing a piece of fresh plywood over the front picture window when we arrived; while their actions resembled hurricane preparation often seen along the coasts, here in the Midwest they suggested a break-in. Though why an intruder wouldn't opt for a backyard entry seemed puzzling.

I knocked at the door of the two-story stucco directly across the street from Kate's place. No one answered, and I was about to shrug off the house as empty when I caught a glimpse of someone at an upstairs window. Most of the neighbors had been neighborly, likely hoping to hear whatever information I had without waiting to watch it on TV. This inhabitant was coy.

A woman a few doors down thought Kate had a boyfriend, but didn't think the relationship was particularly serious because she'd never introduced them. Once the police got wind of him, I knew they'd be pursuing the idea of a domestic squabble turned savage.

I glanced at a snapshot of Kate that a friend of hers had given me with the promise I'd return it later. I could have simply had my cameraman videotape the photo on her doorstep, but then other media might have landed the same shot. This way, I'd be the only reporter with this particular picture.

Kate's appearance was ordinary. Her hair brown. Her smile pleasant. No clues there. I weighed what details I had learned about the victim during the last couple of hours and saw no overt reason for anyone to want her dead. The script was practically writing itself. I made notes.

Kate didn't dress to attract trouble.

"Very modestly attired," said an elderly woman who cherished the deceased because she drove her to doctor appointments.

Kate sang lead in the church choir.

"A voice like an angel," said a man who regularly attended the same Sunday service.

If Kate had money, she didn't flaunt it.

"Frugal," said a woman in Kate's book club. "She preferred waiting for the paperback."

They confirmed that Kate worked at home as a medical transcriptionist, so it wasn't as if she upset retail customers or annoyed office colleagues. She didn't even have a dangerous commute.

Hers was a common case of Girl Next Door Gets Murdered. We all want to believe if someone dies violently, they must have done something to deserve it. That makes the rest of us feel safer. But a career of watching body bags being loaded in the back of medical examiner vans has taught me that nice people are sometimes killed for no good reason.

While it's not something we tout, the media appreciates a good murder, particularly if the motive contains some mystery—a disputed inheritance or a covert celebrity lover can bring an audience to a broadcast in numbers that robbery or rape can't.

If a case isn't solved right away, that can be okay as long as there are fascinating follow-ups and indications it will eventually end in an arrest. Cold cases frustrate families, police, and the public.

And, to be honest, we newshounds also want endings to our stories. You can argue that we don't care whether it's a happy ending or a sad ending, just as long as it ends. And that might be a fair assessment; we can't cover the same victims year after year without craving closure ourselves.

Our interest isn't just professional. Even we have a personal need to know what happened to the missing, whether it be eleven-year-old Jacob Wetterling, abducted two decades ago on a rural Minnesota road, or Iowa TV anchor Jodi Huisentruit, vanishing fifteen years ago on her way to work. Instead we settle for anniversary stories reliving the crimes.

So that night on Channel 3, I told viewers everything I could substantiate about Kate Warner's death. No sense in holding back a juicy fact for later, because you're only likely to get beat by your competition and reamed by your boss.

Right then, none of the other newsies in town seemed to have an inside track on the murder investigation, so I was sitting fine journalistically because it wasn't clear yet whether this homicide would have staying power with the media and the public. That status of a victim becoming a household name is awarded to only a handful of the more than ten thousand Americans murdered each year.

I didn't know yet that Kate had led a secret life, and that her secret did not die with her.